W...

Not the Same Sky

Evelyn Conlon is a novelist, short-story writer and radio essayist. Born in Ireland, she lived in Australia for a number of years. Her last novel *Skin of Dreams* was shortlisted for Irish Novel of the Year. The title story of her collection *Taking Scarlet as a Real Colour* was performed at the Edinburgh Theatre Festival. She is a member of Aosdána, the fellowship of honoured artists in Ireland, and lives in Dublin.

Also by Evelyn Conlon

Novels
Stars in the Daytime
A Glassful of Letters
Skin of Dreams

Short stories
My Head is Opening
Taking Scarlet as a Real Colour
Telling – New and Selected Stories

Edited
An Cloigeann is a Luach
Cutting the Night in Two
Later On
Annaghmakerrig (associate editor)

Not the Same Sky

A NOVEL

Evelyn Conlon

Wakefield
Press

Wakefield Press
16 Rose Street
Mile End
South Australia 5031
www.wakefieldpress.com.au

First published 2013
Reprinted 2014, 2015, 2016

Cover designed by Stacey Zass
Edited by Laura Andary
Typeset by Wakefield Press
Printed in Australia by Griffin Digital, Adelaide

National Library of Australia Cataloguing-in-Publication entry

Author: Conlon, Evelyn, author.
Title: Not the same sky: a novel / Evelyn Conlon.
ISBN: 978 1 74305 242 6 (paperback).
Subjects: Irish – Australia – Fiction.
Dewey Number: 823.91

CORIOLE
McLAREN VALE

Wakefield Press thanks
Coriole Vineyards for their
continued support.

Dedicated to
Leon, Juliette and Lorcan

PROLOGUE

2008

Joy Kennedy was standing in her pine kitchen, looking out at the surprised spring morning wondering if she wanted her life to change. This was something she did quite often. She knew she should stop, and she did try, because waiting for things to change eats up the bit of time we've got. Always wanting to be someplace else makes nonsense of being here. She wanted to stop whizzing about so much and planning ahead. She wanted to keep her hand on the earth.

It may have been her job that drove her to rearrange the truth of her life continuously, all that dealing with death. Although it was not really direct dealing, just the words of it. But words can be tricky things. Take *contúirteach*, meaning dangerous, which she'd just heard on the radio. There's a ring of foreboding about it, or so we think, but maybe that's only because we know what it means. Maybe if one went up to an Inuit or a Senegalese and said the word they'd take their own meaning from the sound, and instead of saying, ah yes, very, they would laugh uproariously, gurgle like a drain, throw their arms out and say the equivalent of thank you, thank you, that was unexpected. The other might glare, step back, and make warily for the door, like one would at an alcoholic's party when the sound of dissent and dramatic outburst suddenly turns itself up for no apparent reason.

Joy was preparing to leave for work. She was proud of her job – it certainly gave her an initial edge on the competition for conversations at parties. While people introduced her by name, she knew for a fact that as soon as she turned her back to throw her coat upstairs on the bed they'd say, 'She's the stonemason who does the gravestones.' She'd heard the hiss of the words wafting up after her.

Joy wondered if the air outside was as pleasant as it looked from the warmth of the room, or if maybe it was sharp and bitter. That's all she had to worry about really, small things, not much. Her life was settling into itself. She did not need the letter that was dropping through her letterbox.

'There's a letter for you,' Oscar said. 'It's from Australia.'

'Australia! I don't know anyone there. Do you?'

Oscar and Joy had just moved in together and were delighted by the new intimacy, made even more interesting by the fact they still didn't know everything about each other.

The letter had an embossed logo at the top, directly in the middle of the page, drawing the reader's attention. She read it, becoming more puzzled with each sentence.

Dear Joy Kennedy,

We, the friends of the Memorial Committee, are well progressed in our initial stages of having a memorial built to the 4414 Famine Orphan Girls who were shipped here to Australia between 1848 and 1850. There can be disagreement about the precise number but not by much. I'm sure you know all about them, but we've included some reading material and some short statements from descendants of theirs just to update you. We will be making an estimate soon of the number of descendants, in the region of a million as you can imagine. Our committee is contacting you because one of our members suggested that it might be both interesting and appropriate to have a mason from Ireland working on the piece if and when we get the go ahead. On searching through a list of masons, I hope you don't mind me remarking that your name came as a surprise. It seemed doubly appropriate to approach you to see if you would have any interest in doing some work for us when the time comes. We'd be delighted if you would at least consider getting in touch so perhaps we can discuss the issue further.

Signed on behalf of the committee,
Simon Kennedy.

PS. And maybe we are related?

Joy read the letter again, her eyes wandering to the embossed logo as they were meant to. She then read it out loud to Oscar. 'I've never heard of them, have you?'

'Don't think so. No. No, of course if I'd heard of them I'd remember.'

'Gosh, what a strange letter. Australia. Funny I've never had any desire to go there. Have you?'

'No. Not really. Well at least not that I've thought about.'

'Well, that means that you haven't.'

She took the atlas down from the shelf. 'Look at that. Would you look at that, it's far.' She ran her finger down the page. 'I mean I knew it was far, but ...'

If you wanted change, wanted to be someplace else, this was it.

CHAPTER 1

1848

If Matt Dwyer thought about himself at all it was not in terms of being either a good or a bad man – he simply tried to be just and fair in the dealings he had to negotiate as an Irish servant of an English Crown. This was not always easy. He went to his cabinet and took out the sheets of paper that had arrived yesterday. Lists. He peered at them. It would be nice to be able to afford spectacles. Still, the handwriting was distinct enough and clear enough in its orders. The potato failure of 1848, following on from 1846, flowing on from 1845, with the nervousness of 1847 in between, would be known to every school child eventually. Matt thought about these things in the future tense, it made the present more bearable. Facts, dates, numbers dead, numbers emigrated. There would be children who would want to be boatbuilders when they heard the news, who would know they could make better ships than those that were at this minute struggling out at sea. There would also be children who would want to be statisticians, politicians, revisionists, farmers, or rebels. Or perhaps singers, as if making music out of the facts could undo some of the damage.

In other places 1847 was much as expected – crops grew quickly, people were fed, commerce continued apace, astronomers found new galaxies, and operas were performed. In America a newspaper rolled off a rotary press, but what had that to do with the price of bread? In Edinburgh a new baby boy was born and named Alexander Graham Bell, and if Matt had known that, he would have wondered what that had to do with the price of bread. And a man called Charles Strutt translated a book, but what had that to do with the price of bread, and who was he?

The potato famine caused hunger before it caused starvation. Hunger: a desire for, or lack of food. Any strong desire. But this hunger was not a desire for, let's say, Pernod with ice, olives, lobster bisque soup for starters, a taste of dry wine, duck à la plum for main course, a good strong purple burgundy, glazed custard, a plate of three cheeses, a port, a brandy, a liqueur, or a coffee. This was a slow gnawing feeling, one that centred first in the stomach, stayed there for days, weeks even, and then grew bigger, even when appeased with a little food.

It radiated to the senses. All one could hear was the clanging of saucepans, the washing of pans, the kicking over of buckets in haste to get the cooking started. All one could see was field upon field of profuse food and tables buckling in the middle with the weight of all that was cooked. All one could touch, especially at night in dreams, was food on a plate – touch it to make sure it was there, touch the potato so it mushroomed out into dry, sweet, beautiful froth. All one could smell, everywhere, outside, inside, was the overwhelming odour of food cooking, the odour of raw food about to be cooked, the odour of neighbours' food, the odour of food on the road, the odour of food eaten. And finally taste. A little flick of the taste spots on the tongue, salt, sweet, hot, cold, savoury; a mouthful, a mouth full, and all taste blossoming into one satisfied swallow, a rainbow in the mouth, disappearing slowly down to the stomach, where the whole dream had started.

When hunger had filled all the senses and dried them brittle, the imagination left – it could not bear itself and was now as good as dead without nourishment. Nourishment: the giving of food so that hunger does not assault the stomach and senses, thus killing imagination with a final hammer blow.

After hunger comes starvation, being in continuous want, the suffering greatly from hunger.

And after starvation comes death, which precedes being dead by a few seconds.

Hunger and starvation might be a solitary matter, a thing known to one person, not a disaster. But when hunger is happening all over a place, when people look at each other and know that the other person is also hungry, then it's a state of famine. What we do not want to know is that while famine infers extreme scarcity of food, this may not always be the truth. Famine could be extreme scarcity of food getting into mouths, not extreme scarcity of food in fields; in other words, food being taken away, stolen, used to pay debt, in the middle of the night, used to feed faraway armies, causing extreme scarcity of food going into mouths and leading to a person being able to read his neighbours' eyes.

The resulting slow chaos grew worse until this hunger could no longer be ignored. In London many people spent time thinking about what to do. This may have included deciding to do nothing, or deciding what not to do, or deciding to put these thoughts to the back of minds, where they could not interfere with London life. It may have included the promise to re-visit the facts a year on, to check the progress of death and hunger, checking also the strain on public funds. It may have included a continuous desire that when the facts were re-visited, all would have sorted itself out. It may have included a lot of worry. Or it may not. The response did include the making of these lists, which were now in Matt's hands. He would have to think about the journey he was to make and how best to deliver these papers. The background provided to him, in the elegantly slanted black ink, had been sent to help him explain at a local level how this scheme was perceived. It was time he made arrangements.

CHAPTER 2

In the previous year, Caroline Chisholm had come to London from New South Wales, where she had chosen to put her blessed life down among the people who had tripped and fallen into one of the holes littering the setting up of a faraway colony. She had seen many things, far more than her outward appearance would suggest.

When Caroline James from Northampton accepted the proposal of marriage from Lieutenant Archibald Chisholm she did so with the stipulation that she be able to continue her philanthropic work, rather than sew and narrow her eyes. She had already spent six years in India doing such work before she and her husband went to Australia, no doubt a bright posting. But she was soon horrified by the condition of the young migrant women unable to get jobs. She saw them skulking on the streets, trying to pretend they were not, and if a woman could not get a job, there was only one other way to get food.

Caroline wore a blue dress with a high-necked collar the day she went to see the Governor of New South Wales. He did not want to meet her, but was doing so in the hope it would stop her intrusive insistence. Good Lord, the woman had even written to his wife. Sir George Gipps was surprised by the blue dress and Caroline's clear eyes, not to mention her handsomeness, which he tried to not let distract him. She drew a picture of the streets for him: migrants arriving off boats into a city with no work and no help being given to them by the people who had allowed them to come. She spoke of dusk horrors, sparing no sensitivities. If at moments he felt annoyed – it was because he too took a carriage home – he knew something of the city. But Caroline's facts and figures finally swayed him. She wanted a home for girls who were forced to live on the street, and she wanted a registry where workers and employers could meet. She was a practical woman.

George Gipps thought about this practicality and about how much it was needed in this place. It was true that small changes could help move things along more smoothly. While he was thinking of this, although still distracted by the neck of her dress – I suppose you'd call that a silk bow – he said yes. So Caroline got both her wishes. And even if on her first nights in the quarters provided she had to lure and poison rats, shaking as anybody would, they would not run her out of these rooms, because if they did, her project would fall into a hole. She was convinced they thought the rats would change her mind, but she had no intention of falling for that one.

She wore a dark dress the second time she met Sir George Gipps, yet somehow the staidness of the colour managed to burst into a red collar. Sir George couldn't see how it did, but he noticed it nevertheless.

Caroline Chisholm was good at overall pictures; she too could think into the future. She became concerned about attracting suitable female emigrants, female domestics, to come to a place where they were truly needed. Scottish, Welsh and English girls did not appear to want to come in the numbers required, and if they weren't being caught committing crimes, they could not be forced. Yet there was such a scarcity of these domestics, a famine you might say, that Caroline could see trouble ahead, and she was dedicated to notions that would erase trouble for this colony, which she was determined was going to offer a better home to so many.

Earl Grey had not *made* tea nor had his father, but he had imported tea from India. He had sat in an office and organised ships that sailed the seas with cargo upon cargo of tea. He had moved ships on maps. He had made sure there was another ship to follow as soon as the wake of the last one had spread back into the ocean and swallowed into the flatness of the sea. He was good at getting ships back onto the ocean fast, at solving the everyday problems of dozens of decks at the beginning, middle, and end of sea journeys. If he wasn't, he was good at getting men who were. He too was dedicated to the notion of the colony.

Earl Grey's and Caroline Chisholm's thoughts collided, making one thought. And that thought collided with what had come to the surface of a government's worry: what to do about the Irish workhouses filling up with female orphans, or girls unable to be cared for at home. They were flocking into workhouses at an alarming rate. They were young, scared and hardened with fright, and they sat there becoming a burden.

In London a second collision of thought occurred, making a ripple that could be heard growing into a solid idea. The futures of the girls in workhouses around Ireland were taking a possible shape. They knew nothing of this.

Caroline Chisholm came to London to talk to Earl Grey. Outside the House of Commons two members of parliament debated the ideas that were being bandied about. They spoke quietly. One of them approached the topic with an academic gesture, smiling slightly, as a boy might who was playing with a ball where he shouldn't. The second showed signs of agitation, further aggravated by the waving hand and the smile.

'But if they are sitting idle in workhouses and we are paying for that, surely it behoves us to think of a better solution than their continued useless sitting there. Even you must see that.'

'Is it not a dangerous precedent to pick up orphan girls in their vulnerable state, unable to put up a fight, and ship them to our colony simply because we need domestic servants?'

'Females to bear children, don't forget that. And wouldn't it be a better place for them to do that, better than where they are now, where the likelihood of a happy outcome is limited. At this present time I mean of course,' he added hastily, as he saw the frowns gathering before him.

'But I am concerned about the moral implications of such a plan.'

'And what would you have us do, my good fellow. Do you have a better solution in that worried mind of yours? We are, after all, assisting them to stay alive.'

'We could try feeding them in their own homes.'

'Balderdash. The crop has failed, again. Haven't you heard the news? Failed repeatedly.'

'But there is other food being grown there, shipped out to pay rents and such like.'

'What do you suggest we do about that? Allow an entire region to renege on its rent? Do you suggest that we no longer feed our armies in India and other places?'

'For the time being perhaps. Yes. About the rent I mean. Surely we can get food for the army elsewhere.'

'But if you allow one or more who have not paid their rent to stay in their houses what would you say to the person who has paid? Should you tell him that he must continue while his neighbour doesn't bother?'

'I think that most people will want to pay their rents, for their own security and peace of mind, if not from good will.'

'Enough. This discussion is for the history books, waste of time having it today. It will solve nothing. No more than your knotted brows will. I believe my man is waiting for me. Good day.'

There was work to be done. A plan had to be agreed. An argument had to be made foolproof, so that the doubters, the downright against and the lazy or unconcerned, could all be brought into line. Ships had to be made available, perhaps pulled off more lucrative routes, but it would pay in the end. Ships had to made seaworthy, new ones might have to be built, but they could later be diverted to more immediately profitable use. Public servants had to get excited, go to their clubs and then home, not telling their wives in case the spilling of the half-made plan might scupper the whole. Wives would have to feed their husbands, so that each day the imaginations of these men could stretch a little more to allow the plan to grow. Non-scrupulous men had to be contacted, and scrupulous men had to be talked to. And surgeon-superintendents had to be found so that the cargo would arrive alive.

And so the plan was made. God made the world and the public servants made the plan and it was agreed upon down to the last nut and bolt, so the lives of girls in workhouses made a leap forward into what they would be.

The plan was put into action. It looked well thought out, neatly written on the papers that were passed around. These contained the ships and their dates, with four of the embarkation dates not yet agreed. This was a pity because it gave the sheet a lack of symmetry, but surely that would not destroy the appeal of this worthy scheme. Even the numbers were already meticulously decided.

Ship	Embarkation date	Port of Arrival	Date of arrival
Earl Grey	June 1848	Sydney	6th October 1848
Roman Emperor	July 1848	Adelaide	23rd October 1848
Lady Kennaway	September 1848	Port Phillip	6th December 1848
Inchinnan	November 1848	Sydney	20th February 1849
Ramilies		Adelaide	24th March 1849
Digby	December 1848	Sydney	4th April 1849
Pemberton	January 1849	Port Phillip	14th May 1849
Inconstant	February 1849	Adelaide	7th June 1849
Lady Peel	March 1849	Sydney	3rd July 1849
New Liverpool	April 1849	Port Phillip	9th August 1849
Elgin		Adelaide	12th September 1849
William & Mary	July 1849	Sydney	21st November 1849
Lismoyne	August 1849	Sydney	29th November 1849
Diadem		Port Phillip	10th January 1850
Panama	October 1849	Sydney	12th January 1850
Thomas Arbuthnot	October 1849	Sydney	3rd February 1850
Derwent	November 1849	Port Phillip	25th February 1850
Eliza Caroline		Port Phillip/ Geelong	31st March 1850
John Knox	December 1850	Sydney	29th April 1850
Tippoo Sail Saib	April 1850	Sydney	29th July 1850
Maria	March 1850	Sydney	1st August 1850

County	Number to be sent	% of total number
Tipperary	519	12.43
Cork	381	9.13
Galway	246	5.90
Down	173	4.14
Limerick	164	3.93
Dublin	160	3.83
Wexford	157	3.76
Antrim	151	3.62
Fermanagh	151	3.62
Waterford	148	3.54
Londonderry	135	3.23
Westmeath	123	2.94
Mayo	122	2.90
Kerry	117	2.80
Clare	113	2.71
Leitrim	111	2.66
Tyrone	106	2.54
Longford	101	2.41
Meath	101	2.41
Monaghan	97	2.32
Donegal	96	2.30
Kilkenny	87	2.09
Sligo	83	1.99
Cavan	75	1.80
Offaly	71	1.70
Roscommon	71	1.70
Laois	65	1.60
Kildare	60	1.40
Armagh	57	1.40
Wicklow	53	1.30
Carlow	52	1.20
Louth	29	0.70

The speaker who introduced the tables read them out. The numbers sounded arbitrary, this very reason making them indisputable. The member of parliament who had frowned so much on the steps was silent. In the face of such organisation, what could he say? Another member of parliament two seats behind him had digested the numbers quickly, and in order to stop any accompanying images that might have come into his head, whispered, 'I don't think I'd fancy sailing on the *Inconstant*.' Everyone around him laughed, except the member who maintained his frown.

In total there would be over 4000 girls aged between fourteen and twenty – seventy-two per cent aged between sixteen and eighteen – dispatched within two years. There would be a Government Dispatch Reel number for each ship.

There was no more time for debate. There had been debates on what to do about this problem before, and these had an infuriating habit of coming up repeatedly in the London *News*. There were two strongly opposing views as to what should be done – that which said we cannot interfere with the market, and that which said we must.

People on both sides aired their positions loudly because they meant them, while others gave spirited addresses because they loved the polish and history of this oratory, this fine form of speaking practised in Ancient Greece.

'Surely you don't believe that?'

'Perhaps not in its entirety, but how did I put it forward do you think?'

There were others in between these opposing views who looked to the proponents of either to convince them. Debates also took place closer to the actual disaster. In halls in Ireland, men turned up to shout their anger while they still had it, to whisper their despair when that was all they had left, and later to stay silent and merely observe.

But now there was an actual plan worked out on paper.

That was how Matt was reading this list, with the beautifully slanted hand. Some of the ships had already gone, but more girls were still needed, and it was his job to find the cargo for the *Thomas Arbuthnot*. It was suggested that he make his first visit to County Clare – there were plenty of girls there.

CHAPTER 3

Matt arrived by coach and put up in Ennis town for the night. He did not relish this part of the task. As he travelled down through the Midlands, past silent houses, over the Shannon River, he began to have doubts about the morality of the plan. But who was he to argue? And what difference would it make if he did? Matt knew that the sooner he met the matron of the Ennis workhouse and passed on the instructions, the sooner he could return to Dublin and on to other things. He found it best not to dwell too minutely on the present.

He slept passably well, and in the morning rode out to the workhouse carrying the list in a leather bag.

Matron welcomed him but seemed to have no time for small talk, so he got down to business immediately. She looked a little taken aback by what she read and by what he pointed out to her.

'Well, it's something. I'm not sure if it's right, but it's certainly something.'

Matron got up and moved towards a room that seemed to shrink into darkness. Matt didn't follow, opting to stand just outside, where Matron's voice sounded muffled until she began to name names.

'Mary Traynor, Anne Sherry, it's Australia for you. Honora Raftery, you too I think. And Julia Cuffe, maybe.'

'What do you mean Australia?' a small pale girl asked.

'Not you. It doesn't apply to you,' Matron said. 'No it wouldn't apply to you. You're too young.'

'I'm old enough,' the girl said, but Matron said, 'No,' again.

'And you, Bridget Joyce, it's Australia now for you.'

'When?' a voice dared.

'Next month, yes, the sooner now the better,' Matron added.

'Can I go too?' another voice asked tentatively.

'No, Betsy Shannon, you're too old.'

'I'm young enough,' she said. 'Twenty-four.'

'Duffy, you're young enough, you'll do. What's your first name again?'

Matron continued to call out names and Matt strayed out of hearing.

'And Anastasia Curran. That will be all, for now anyway. I'll speak to those I've called out later today to see if they want to go.'

Matron left the room, the girls looking after her. Honora Raftery sneaked a look at Anne Sherry and Julia Cuffe. Others looked at the ground. It was a lot to take in. Staying alive was the job they were all involved in now.

Matron rubbed her hands down her front, as if wiping off the part she had just played in this scheme. She wasn't sure what she thought of it. She did know that around the towns more and more people were flocking into workhouses – the state of living worse than the previous year. Disease was stalking now too, as if it was indeed a monster grown from hunger, wandering the roads looking for likely prey to overcome. People were beginning to take on a listless bewildered persona, unable to remember the neatness of their previous lives. They could not remember the rhythm of their past days. Nor could they remember that this life had not always been so. In places less terribly marked, people talked of the dying in whispers as if the act of raising their voices might bring them woe. People working in poorhouses or soup kitchens battled despair, urging officials to listen to them. Children looked at adults but didn't know what questions to ask. The news of discussion for this or that plan provided a momentary answer for some. Any kind of half answer was better than none.

Anastasia Curran claimed to have learned of a letter sent by a girl already gone to Australia. Matron had heard her talk about it last week, which is why she added her to the list. But the story of the letter seemed ridiculously farfetched, especially in these rooms where girls thought of food and tried not to think of being sick or about the fright of the future. They wanted to live on a patch of land nearby, to grow potatoes, or turnips even, and other produce to pay the rent. They didn't want to be talking about places with names like America, where aunts and uncles and cousins had gone, and now Australia, which some said was in the opposite direction, and further away. So far away that you needed several changes of clothes to go, more changes than for America.

Whispers had come about this plan and that plan, so this list, Matron thought, was proof that some of those whispers had teeth. Of course she did not know how the discussions that led to these whispers were actually conducted. Did a London man talk first to a Dublin man, like that Matt Dwyer, then to a regional man, maybe last night, and finally to her this morning? She now knew the specifications as to age, young enough to be able to fit into the scheme of things – under twenty – and old enough to be able to fit into the scheme of things – over fourteen. And orphaned in the main. The specifications about suitability were more difficult. Did it mean there would be no place for spirited girls, if such a thing still survived in these workhouses? Or did it mean previously spirited girls should be chosen, ones who had shown the capacity to withstand a journey too long to be imagined and a removal from all things familiar? If they had shown it once before maybe they could be depended upon to show it again? Matron did not know if there were small notes containing answers to such questions, and if there were, who had them.

Matron had seen no note, nor had she been given advice as to how to pick out the suitable ones other than the vague specifications she still held in her hand: suitable orphans with good English. They had not told her how this was to be put to the girls. They did not tell her how to point at girls and say their names out loud. What was she to say to them this afternoon? No one had told her how to do these things. She would have to see Matt Dwyer on his way back to Dublin. Perhaps he might have some ideas.

In the afternoon Matron called the named girls to the doorway and stood before them. 'As you can see, things are not good here, look around you.'

Some did take a quick look around, trying not to see into the darker corners of the room.

'Things will be better for you in Australia, there is plenty of food there.'

Honora Raftery's sister, who had not been mentioned, stood behind Honora in the shadows and whispered, 'You should go,' implying they had a choice in the matter.

Matron continued, 'And you'll be able to get work. It will be for the best. But only if you're fit and can get a reference.'

She had just remembered about the references. Would she

have to write them? If not she would certainly have to go out to the places they came from and find suitable people to vouch for their character. Who would read the references? 'Australia, away out of that with you!' Julia Cuffe said. Matron left the room. Was that laughing she heard behind her? Was there ever laughing in the room when she was not there? She did not know. Now she would have to prepare the girls for departure, and find out who had relatives fit to come visit. There was much work to be done.

Matt Dwyer said his goodbyes. He was glad to leave, to return to the order of his office. Matron would be able to handle the arrangements without him being there.

CHAPTER 4

Matron called Honora Raftery aside and designated her to help with departure preparations. There were trunks already arrived into the back hallway that needed to be cleaned and filled. When Honora's sister saw them she looked to the top of the opposite wall and walked past. The instructions clearly stated that each trunk, measuring two feet long and fourteen inches high and wide, was to contain new clothes provided by the workhouse. There was to be a gown, a cloak, a shawl, handkerchiefs, collars, an apron, stays, a comb, hairbrush, prayer book, needle, thread, tape and scissors. The trunks were to be clearly marked, the name of each girl painted on the front, and the list of contents written on the inside of the lid. How could these things be afforded when other things could not? The instructions did not state whether any of the girls' own familiar smelling clothes were to be folded in with the new. Matron thought this might give some small comfort, but wasn't sure how to get old garments up to standard. And perhaps that was too trivial in the face of all that had to be done in the next few days. The filling would be done by local endeavour but Matron would need Honora's assistance to ready the trunks.

They did not speak much as they cleaned them and covered the insides with paper donated by the local minister. Matron did not know what to say. The silence grew uncomfortable.

'Do you know any of the other girls?' she finally asked.

'Not before here,' Honora said.

'You'll get to know them now. You will all have this in common.'

This last sentence sounded unfinished, but what could she say?

'There will be girls from other places too. Near two hundred of you.'

'That many,' Honora said, because she had to say something. In truth she couldn't really imagine what that would look like.

'How will we go?'

'You will be brought to the ship, Dublin for you, and then to Plymouth I think, yes that appears to be the assembly point, that's in England.'

'Yes I know that. My father said I was good at knowing other places.'

Matron stayed silent for a moment. 'Have you ever seen a ship?' she then asked.

'No,' Honora said. 'What will it be like?'

Matron hesitated. 'I don't know myself.'

'Oh,' Honora said, and leaned in to another trunk to brush the corners clean of dust.

'But you will meet the others at the ship, I should think.'

'Will we go together from here?' Honora asked.

'No, that won't be possible. Some have relatives to go to for a day, and some will be put on the first carriage available and it will depend … I'm not really sure yet,' Matron said, realising that she was not sure of a lot of things.

'But we will see each other at the ship?'

'Well certainly in Plymouth. That will do for now.'

Honora went to the edge of the room where some gathered around her. Others were too sick today to move or were uninterested. Betsy Shannon was heard to say, 'I'm glad it's not me that's going.' No one knew if she meant it or if she was making do with the fact that she was too old to get the chance.

'Australia – mad, mad, bloody mad,' Julia Cuffe said. She was good at English, could already swear in it.

The night before Honora's leaving, her sister Florrie whispered to her for many hours. There were other whisperings in the room, but Florrie's was the clearest in Honora's ears. 'It is best you go,' she said again and again, trying to give her sister the backbone that would be required of her.

'But what will I do without ...'

'Shh, shh,' Florrie said, not allowing some things to be said. 'Now go to sleep, you will need strength for tomorrow's journey.'

Was that a sigh of relief that Florrie heard, rustling before sleep? Could she hear a sigh, *I will live*? Could she hear that from above some other straw bed in the corner, or could she hear, *I don't want to go, it's better to stay* – because that was what the leaving had to say to those who were remaining here? 'Shh,' she said again, and a kind of sleep did descend.

Dawn came and the sleep was still around enough to dull the ache of girls getting into carriages. The sound of horses' hooves moved out to the end of the town. The sound drowned out the noise of weeping. The journey was begun.

CHAPTER 5

Charles Edward Strutt didn't think of himself as born for bravery or even excitement. He would have been happy to get lost in a village in Somerset, avoid war and get a desk job. If he had found himself in a place like that he would have been content. True, he might not have been interested in the tittle-tattle of such a place, the minutiae that makes an 'our' for the front of 'town'. He might have grown impatient with the re-telling and embellishment of every single private thing. But he could have absented himself from the gossip, read in the evenings, and repaired his mind each night so that it could freshly, each morning, dwell on topics of more importance than gabble. Minor importance, perhaps, but the sort that keeps things ticking over on a daily basis, gives a rhythm to the hours and thereby provides comfort. He wouldn't have dwelled on major questions – questions like why some are born to hunger and some to comfort. Presumably he would have found a wife. He looked like someone who would be made happy easily enough. Hopefully they would have healthy children and be kept busy by the minding of that health. He would never have suffered from pompous self-righteous zeal.

Yet this decent-enough plan eluded him. Perhaps it was his mother, perhaps his father. On the first days after he was born his father had looked at his son, given up the practice of medicine and started to paint. It may have been that the shock of watching the opening of his child's eyes awakened a sensitive seam in him and he was simply unable to stop the expression of it. His mother, on the other hand, had always regarded her contributions to the world of books as the essential work of her life, as well, of course, as being a wife and mother. So she understood this rash departure from the world of realism. Now, with her husband's decision, she would be better supported mentally, if not financially, in her endeavours. They would be able to say to each other at night, 'And were you happy today?' and it would mean did you scale an inch today, and can you see the mountain ahead? It would not mean happy as in some vague non-esoteric sensation.

His mother then lost a daughter. People said this as if she'd mislaid her. It was a better word than dead, it gave some possibility for hope. They did not say that both the mother and father had a dead daughter, no, simply that the mother had lost one, as if her battle to keep her daughter by her side had been fruitless. His mother then wandered into Swedenborg's New Church, where she found comfort in a sermon about the state of new infants in heaven. She was thus able to continue writing, as opposed to spending her days in hopeless mourning.

Charles grew up affected by these events. When he had learned his languages well, he translated two works of Swedenborg's into English, perhaps to know better what gave his mother hope. He trained as a surgeon, perhaps to finish his father's work. He took a once-off job, or so he assumed, as surgeon-superintendent of the *St Vincent*, a ship that was to take two hundred and fifty-one emigrants to New South Wales, nine of whom were Irish.

This job could be his adventure before life. It was the first time he had met an Irishman. He did not have to necessarily know these Irish – they made up a small number of his passengers and looked the same as his others, in skin at least, if not in eyes. He enjoyed the job. It created in him somewhere a dangerous straying from the steady tread towards that Somerset village. But this would be his one adventure before steering himself back towards that desk. It might make him more attractive to the wife he wasn't yet searching for.

His successful superintendship was talked about, and the talk made the rounds, becoming part of the plan, which was now well made by the public servants who were no longer going to their clubs and home to their wives and remaining *shtum*. The plan could no longer be upset by loose talk. Already ships had gone and there was a list of further possible surgeon-superintendents to be approached.

So Charles found himself here, at Plymouth, with a job to do and around two hundred Irish girls to meet. He wondered what condition they would be in. He had been filled in on the state of things so far – a local shipping officer had met him in his office, and further instructions had come by post. He was told that ships had gone and arrived, and while the reaction to the girls was anything but desirable, this was a minor thing to be borne in whatever way it could. It didn't matter much. It didn't matter at all in Ireland.

By now it was known that one year's potato crop had not died and so hope should have been tentatively possible. But so many were gone, and dead, some never even buried. Their voices warned against hope. It is now known that never again was there a single day in which all the potatoes, those dug and those still in the ground, absorbed a silent disease and burst forth quietly into rot. But that is hindsight. The gathering up of girls from every county had begun and would continue.

Charles had been given a map of where all these girls

came from, the ones on his ship and the ones already gone. But he was not told what the girls in Ennis, in Listowel, Dingle, Ennistymon, Scarriff, Loughrea, Gort, Portumna or Tuam said the day they were told. Nor was he told if they differed in what they thought and felt. That perhaps was the worst thing. He had seen names, dates of births – some of them only probable dates of births – addresses of workhouses at the time of departure, but there was no mention of their reactions in the notes sent to him.

Nor did Charles know how much warning the girls were given and if they had gone home to bid their farewells. He did not know how they left. Was there for instance a walking out the roads from towns, to Clarecastle from Ennis, let's say, on the way to Limerick, or on previous boats was there a walking to Ballybay from Aghabog, let's say, on the way to Castleblayney? And were there relatives walking with them? And could cries be heard far? He did not know and thought maybe that was just as well.

What Charles did know, was that this day in October 1849, around two hundred girls, by whatever road, had assembled here in Plymouth, England, and that he had better get on with his job.

CHAPTER 6

Charles Strutt looked towards the quay and saw what must be them, a bunch of girls. He walked towards them. Dots of things really, when looking at them from afar. Some of their clothes were too light, some just right. Some wore hats, well made. Even in hungry times things can be sewn. A couple of them had lace on their collars. He wondered about the provenance of this lace. It took his mind off the look of them.

Some had boots, some shoes. It was hard, looking from the end of the pier, to make out what kind of girls they were: sad, surly, hopeful, rough, gentle, tidy – all of that presumably, and variations. Nervous certainly, having first seen the sight of a ship only a few days before. And confused. Some gave small shouts as they moved about trying to keep warm. Some shuffled quietly, swallowing tears they had already swallowed hundreds of times since leaving Ireland. Some, dry-eyed, tucked at their belts and took up a new profession, that of making the best of it. They would polish this profession, and its gleam would crystallise to form part of the national character of where they were heading.

There were sounds of whispering. Some girls tucked in close to each other, and spoke about their leavings. They made them into tales that seemed to be from a distant past belonging to someone else, still in awe of what had happened. Anne Sherry told Honora Raftery that her aunt had seen her off. She said it was a clear day. Her voice didn't waver as she spoke of this. 'Wasn't the boat from Dublin terrible,' she said. She shivered. She could still feel the fright of it in her bones. She put her arms around herself, it helped to pat down the misery. Anne also said that her brother had danced a jig for them when they were leaving.

'On the pier, did you see him? He's all right, not sick.'

There had been a man drawing a picture of it.

'Did you not see him?' Anne asked again.

'No, I didn't,' said Honora, afraid to lie.

'Are both your parents dead?' Anne asked.

'Yes, both dead.'

'I think that's the same with everyone here.'

'When did yours die?' Honora asked.

'Last year.'

'Mine too.'

'I heard that that girl,' Anne pointed, 'has a mother alive.'

Honora looked at the girl and wondered if you could tell by looking at someone that they had a mother alive.

'Who told you?'

'That girl there, you know, the Julia one.'

Honora Raftery told Anne Sherry that her sister had seen her off, and one brother too. She said it was sad but for the best. She said her sister Florrie had told her not to cry but that she herself had cried. She said her brother had told the two of them it would be all right.

There was more to Honora's leaving than that, but already she was choosing what to say. She would have chosen what to remember if she could. There had been four girls and three boys in her family. They had been poor yes, but so were their neighbours. And they had had enough to eat. Her mother made their clothes, favouring red as a colour if she could get it. She could sew beautifully. She also knew about the Brehon Laws, which made her a bit of a novelty. Honora's father had a sense of humour, and boasted about his wife knowing about the Brehon Laws, 'Even though a man could be done by them,' he'd laugh. Honora's mother knew all sorts about the Brehon Laws, the importance of bees, for example.

The children helped with work but still played, not yet knowing the seriousness of matters. Though they did not play too loudly, sensing somehow that an ostentatious display of wellbeing might be misconstrued. Neither of their parents had ever said, 'Shush, that's too much noise,' or 'Play away from the house would you.' Her mother had never said, 'Can you keep that down, I'm not well.' In fact, their house had a type of merriment about it once everyone had scratched and yawned themselves into daylight. Merriment is given, a gift from nowhere, in the same way disease is bestowed upon a house.

An outsider could not say why in their house, at their table, a light seemed to be handed around with the plate. And neighbours came to visit. Advice might be sought without being blatantly stated. A neighbour might bring the conversation around to a problem that someone, not them, was having with the landlord. And maybe one of Honora's parents would say something that could be done, or that, 'Nothing can be done about that.' Honora's father laughed with his talking.

When they were four years of age they were taught the alphabet. Honora's grandfather had said it was a good plan to be able to read and write, even for girls, and maybe more so because so often they had to go away. So Honora's mother could read and she taught her children. They were told that every letter has a sign and it's up to us to put the signs together to make a word. There are seventeen signs – that's what's called an alphabet. In English there are more, twenty-six, but that will be for later. They would go to school where they would have to learn English, so she would do some of that when they had mastered the notion of reading.

Honora had shared one side of the bedroom with her sisters, her brothers were at the other side. She had found a way to turn her neck so she could see the kitchen window through the crack in the door if she woke before everyone else. There was only one window – her father told her that you had to pay if you wanted more. But you can get plenty of light outside, no one can charge for that, he would say. If Honora was woken by the birds, she would check the window to see if it was bright and blue outside. And if it was then it might be breezy or it might be calm with noises carrying across the fields. It might even be a little hot, warm enough to feel the sunrays through your dress, a sudden heat like standing before the fire, but clearer and brighter. If there were no birds and it was a dark winter morning, she would know and would move closer to her sister before she had a chance to get cold. Her oldest sister Florrie had enough heat for all of them. It even seemed to go through the one beside her, straight through to the next one. 'Florrie's a godsend,' her father said – maybe that's what he meant. If Honora could see rain streaming down the window she might watch it for a while, slip sliding down around the hump in the middle. But sometimes she wouldn't watch it. The sky was crying, her father would say, before being silent for a moment, and wondering how he could talk himself away from what he had just said. If there was frost on the window, Honora would try not to waken her sisters because, although it was beautiful, it was cold too. Maybe even Florrie would not be able to warm them if they all sat up to look, letting the heat escape out from under the quilt where it would just disappear into the air. And then it would take all of them and Florrie ages to make it again. Also there was no need because

33

frost always stayed until she got up, the best thing about frost was that you could touch it. Frost was so beautiful – twinkling cracks drawing wild pictures and then perhaps a plain patch in the middle. You could look at frost forever and never tire of it. If there was snow in the window, Honora would have to wake her sisters.

The quilt had been made by Honora's mother and sisters, every stitch put in by them. They had preferred some patches to others. It had been made in preparation for all of them to be lying under, as they were now. Already there was talk of Florrie's quilt and who might help. Honora would like doing that. For all the heat that Florrie gave.

Honora remembered the evening the O'Brien men had come. They brought in with them a cold that came from far outside. The children were sent to bed, the boys at the same time. Instead of making their customary noise they had all stayed quiet, even the boys, because although children do not wholly know the seriousness of particular events, they can sense danger. The mumbles from the kitchen sometimes cleared out and a voice could be heard speaking.

'We're going to America. The Shannons are going to Australia. We're going to America. The landlord said that he'll give us the fare, we'll give him all the corn and whatever else is there before next week. And the week after we're going.'

'All of you?'

There was a long silence from the kitchen.

'Where's Australia?' Honora asked.

'Shssh.'

'You can't all go.'

'It's a famine. Can't you see that?'

'What's a famine?' Honora asked.

'Shssh.'

There were more mumbles.

'No, but Florrie what's a famine?'

A boy's voice answered. Honora couldn't tell in the dark which of her brothers it was. 'It's hunger, I think.'

'We'll be over before you go,' they heard from the kitchen.

'Yes, people are coming.'

That was a long time ago. And then two of Honora's brothers had gone to America. Then Honora's parents had died – her mother first, her father soon afterwards. And then two sisters went to join the brothers. The last brother got work on the road that started away from the town and went to the bog, but he had food, until that money dried up too. Florrie and Honora had gone to the workhouse together. The day Matron called Honora's name, Florrie sighed another sigh, but, now used to partings, bent her head and did not weep.

'I will stay with Dan. But you must go. We cannot all stay here, we could get sick. You must go,' she said.

Florrie found the required references for Honora – she had gone to Matron and said she'd like to do it as a kind of parting gift. She had not talked much on the day before the leaving, instead busying herself with anything she could find to do.

Honora looked at the crowd of girls at the quay. She knew there was a house and a mother and a father and maybe sisters and brothers behind all of them. But in the past only. Standing here, everything was past. So that meant it was gone. There's a past, a present and a future tense, her mother had said. So this must be the present. Peculiar thing the present tense, it didn't feel like anything. The past felt, it had sounds, smells and colours, it even had feelings – touches running up your arms and into your chest and head. Presumably the future would also have colour and sound and smell at least. Where was this Australia? She would measure it in time, that might tell her. Or it might not, because Honora was losing track of time. But this present, what did it have? There was a smell of fear in it. Perhaps if she could concentrate on the signs in it, like letters in a word, she would understand it. So she stood, oblivious now of Anne Sherry and those around her in the line.

First there were the noises. It was hard to separate them. There was a lot of shouting, although Honora couldn't be sure if it was all in English – it could have been, but shouted in a different accent. Her teacher had explained all that when he had taught them English. He had even told them their own language had different accents depending on what part of the country it was spoken.

'But it would still be the same language?'

There were a lot of questions at school.

'Yes, yes of course, but one might have to listen more carefully to hear the exact sounds of the words.'

'Do you know everything in English?'

'Can we get back to our letters now.'

'I mean everything you know in Irish, do you also know it in English?'

'The letters and the sounds, let's get back to those.'

So Honora listened, gathered the sounds from the wind, hoping to recognise something. But nothing was familiar. But it didn't matter. Everything did not have to be familiar, she had learned that since leaving Dublin, thirty-six hours ago, or was it longer? That was of little consequence either way, because no matter how she looked at it, she was caught here between time and language. There was nothing to do but wait, and step forward as the line moved closer to yet another door, yet another taking of names. And then there were the colours – not much difference there. The men who were running around the ship shouting all wore grey and black. Her father had worn a red waistcoat. She could have looked at it the way she looked at frost. The men who were taking their names also wore grey and black. Cleaner, but still grey and black.

Honora had glimpsed a few women who came to the room beside where she and the others were lined up. They appeared to be delivering boxes. They had colours in their clothes, their hats and their collars, but nothing spectacularly different to black and grey. Yet her eyes lingered on them as they walked briskly away. They had brought with them a dash of a different settled place. A place of streets without aimless wanderers, of tables set for tea. A town ticking over day by day. Curiosity fluttered in Honora, perhaps for the first time in weeks, but she had learned that it was best to keep curiosity in check these days. All her energy was needed for the one task of standing, still cold, or edging up the line – the end of which would surely bring better things – being present to follow the next order, or staying awake when required and sleeping when told, if possible. This tending to the present required curiosity be kept in check – unbridled imagination could lead to panic.

The smells allowed her tolerable enquiry. There was food among them, raw fish, she thought. She had also smelt other food being carried by the shouting men, she was sure of it. Her nose had become sharp to these things. She wasn't hungry yet. Those in the line had been given porridge this morning and it was still warming her inside. They had eaten silently, every girl concentrating on her own bowl. They had been told there would be a meal here while they got ready for the next boat, a better meal than the last one. Honora believed that. She had to.

More boxes were brought through, closer to them now. The large crates were dragged and pushed and wheeled noisily by. When the men were close like that she could pick out some of the words.

The line moved another bit. Anne Sherry spoke again.

'I wonder, will it be like America? We've had letters from America.'

'My uncle said it would be more like England.'

'Will that be good or bad for us?'

No one knew.

Anne was suddenly irritated by the chatter of the other girls. She wanted to concentrate only on the next hours. She had heard one of them shout three months, she was sure of it, three months, and this had her rattled. She should be more tolerant of the wonderings. Just because they were all together in a line did not guarantee there would be a uniformity of feeling, that they would be thinking the same. They voiced their thoughts to see if they found consolation, any consolation, even if it was wrong. But surely they couldn't be on the ship for three months. Surely that was wrong.

'We'll be all right,' Honora said, as if she believed it, in that moment pretending to be older than she was, pretending she was not afraid. Becoming someone she was not.

Anne looked at her gratefully. Maybe she'd stay near her on the boat.

The feet of the girls shuffled forward a few more steps. Names were spelled and checked again. There was more confusion. An official in a black suit, his eyes glued to the papers before him, lost his temper and roared, 'Get into a straight line. I said a straight line.' There was a movement, almost imperceptible, the slightest rustling of dresses. He looked up, surprised at the echo of his own voice. The line was perfectly straight. Honora heard a voice making a noise, more a growl than a whisper. Honora thought it was that Julia girl, the noisy one. Honora wouldn't like to be like that, it could be dangerous. She now knew the names of two other girls – that was enough for the moment. The man in the suit seemed confused by the acquiescence. He would take a deep breath and pray for reasonableness, allowing for a certain leniency in spelling.

'I can spell in my own tongue.' That was definitely Julia.

A new man joined the desk, his job to peruse the health certificates each girl held in her hand. He also glanced over the references – these were not needed yet, they were for the journey's end. Although this had nothing to do with him, it was easier for him to imagine that time than it was for anyone in the line before him. This ease came because he knew that ships left and arrived, he had seen the certainty of it. He did not have to do the journey to know that. These were the advantages of this sort of job, at this time, at this port, where ships came and went in dizzying patterns, to and from places you might never have heard of. And couldn't remember even if you did.

Eventually all were accounted for, so the girls and the few others were ushered into a depot, a kind of shed. The other passengers, who were not like them, boarded the ship. Mr Charles Strutt came into the room. The girls looked at him, but didn't register him particularly – he was just another English man.

Charles was not in top form, shaky after a bout of influenza. He was also rather apprehensive about taking charge of so many girls for such a voyage, and displeased because he had just been informed that his fare back was not guaranteed. Still, when the dregs of the influenza passed, he was sure he would be fit for the task. He had, in fact, felt moments of almost cheer on the train from Paddington despite his original plan of only one trip.

The memories of his previous journey had created a life of their own, rendering his desk job less attractive. To his amazement he had found himself spending an inordinate amount of time thinking about the achievements of sea travel: the satisfaction of filling in the log before sleep, the thrill of overcoming a few days rough weather. He found that he couldn't exactly remember the sensation of battling a full-blown storm: the brawl of the wind, the bashing of the waves, the rolling from sky to water. He had started to buy papers that gave good reports about developments in boat travel. He now checked the shipping news as often as he could. His ears were tuned to the ramifications of the weather at sea, not on land where he lived. He found himself thinking of easing into Sydney at dawn, even while undertaking the most menial of tasks. He found himself wondering what the quay was going to be like when it was completed. Semi-Circular Quay, though it would be shortened to Circular Quay. Had the men's work noises already started to fill the air? Did evening passers-by not remember when there had been only muted sounds? Had the clash of the sounds of men and tools overcome the cries of the birds and the creaking of the boats? Surely not.

Charles had often let himself dream of his previous journey, so in truth it had been a pleasant surprise when he had been summoned to discuss the possibility of being a surgeon-superintendent again. There was no reason why he shouldn't do it. So here he was. Although the irritating symptoms of his illness cast a shadow over the proceedings, the closer he came to the smell of the port, the more his happiness increased. He walked towards the ship full of controlled excitement.

Charles's first task was to find Mr Foulds, the Depot Superintendent, in whose overall care the girls had been since arriving from Ireland. He had been overcome with a moment of despair when he looked at them, now almost ready to board. They looked so wet, he thought. Or cold, maybe cold. And famished. He would have to start without Mr Foulds. Then, under supervision, he commenced his next task – the examination of each girl. This he proceeded to do in a small room to the side of the depot. He became shocked at the temperature of some of them. With a touch of his hand to their forehead he could ascertain that they were both hot and cold, clearly roughed by the boat journey. And he was not too happy with the hair of some. He took meticulous notes, coming to his conclusions silently. He called to Mr Foulds then and told him that no way could some of these dirty and cold girls continue aboard without baths. They were dirty he said because of the conditions of their travel, and cold for the same. He wrote bath prescriptions for most of them – hot baths, be sure – and also ordered a number of haircuts.

'Just haircuts,' he said. 'Not scalping.'

The girls had now noticed him but deferred judgment.

The baths were readied in a designated room, and their hair was cut. A new heat came into the shed. Charles examined them again, not individually, but as a group. He looked carefully.

'They appear a decent enough set of girls,' he said, to anyone who was listening.

CHAPTER 7

The afternoon and evening crept on, the minutes ticking by towards embarkation. There was the occasional flurry of what could be called gusts of hysteria, but they faded quickly and inexplicably, just as fast as they had erupted. These flurries of high-pitched noise sounded as if a flock of birds, noticing autumn, had swooped down and made sharp sudden complaints, then flown away again unexpectedly. Charles went on board first and set about the job of organising sleeping places. In this he knew he would make some mistakes, but altering places would be a last resort. The girls would know that order and certainty were to be the rules here. The inhabitants of each bunk would now know each other, for good or for bad.

He consulted the list he had made, some of it tentative, allowing him to make occasional snap decisions. He was now as ready as he could be for this voyage. He knew the girls were not, but there was no turning back now, the trajectory of their futures, of their lives, was about to take off. He could hear the voice of a girl carried on the wind. 'We're not going in that thing,' she said, in amazement. She must have been pointing to one of the small boats that brought provisions to the ship.

'No, that's ours,' another said, waving a hand at a bigger ship.

'Or so someone told me. It's not that bad really,' she said, doubtfully.

'Well, it's bigger than what we came in this far,' another girl said, deciding to try out a sprig of optimism.

The girls gathered together on the deck. When the final whoosh was made – 'That's the last,' shouted a sailor – a bewildered silence descended. Charles stood before them with his list and called them closer together. They did as he said, eventually. As he ticked off numbers, they took their places in the new line, which was weaving under the myriad of ropes and flapping sails. He was occasionally distracted by how childlike most of them were. Too young to be alone. But this was not his business. They were here now. He would address the older ones – some of whom were almost twenty. Maybe they could look after the younger ones. He began to rearrange, he would put one twenty-year-old beside a younger girl. But that didn't work as he soon ran out of twenty-year-olds.

'Shush, shush, let me think.'

He began again. His influenza had not yet dissipated. 'Shush, hush, you over there, stand out.'

A girl said, 'Shush, shush, let him think.'

The girl wore a blue hat and the rim of it fell too far over her eyes. Either it was made for a bigger head or she had become even thinner since leaving the workhouse.

'Now, let me see ...' Charles shouted out names and pointed those named towards the entrance and down to the hold. Someone else down there would look at the number and place them beside their sleeping spot.

'Stand where you're told until I'm finished,' he said.

'This is our room,' a girl shouted up when she had reached the hold. And so it would be called their room.

'It's down here below the boat,' she called up.

'Shh ... that's enough.'

43

The matron moved along with the list to sort the sleeping spots. Girls looked at her as she read out the names, wondering when they would be called – they were getting used to lists. Places were given to Honora Raftery, Anne Sherry, Julia Cuffe and Bridget Joyce. Charles had noticed her early. She had a delicate look. Her bonnet was still white and had a satin ribbon. Her hair did not need to be cut. She did not walk, but inched her way forward. She was not the sort of girl a person would normally notice, the quietness of her would put her at the back of any line of vision. When he spoke to her, she either pretended not to be listening to him or she really didn't hear him. Her gaze was so far away it was painful and could stop the task that needed to be done. He could not contemplate it. But there were moments when it mended itself and she looked straight at him, briefly, before finding another distance. He put her beside Honora Raftery, because he had noticed her too. He had noticed Julia Cuffe, who made a noise every time she moved, and whose very presence dared him to do or say what, he did not know. But he had others to think of, so many others. Anne Sherry was placed next to them in the bed because she was standing beside Honora Raftery. 'It won't be too bad,' Honora said, looking at their bunk. She had shared a bed before – there were ways to make it less crowded. She touched the bed cover and turned her back on the others, she would have to learn not to think about Florrie.

'You can take off your bonnets,' Matron said.

The job was done as best he could. When the last girl had been shepherded down, Charles briefly looked into the hold to make sure the matron and sub-matrons had their jobs under control. He would now visit the other passengers – four families from Desertcreat, Tyrone, from Castledermot,

Kildare, from Kilnoe, Clare, and from Banagher, King's County. One of the women, Mrs Johnstone, was pregnant. Charles had to believe the baby was not due until after the completion of the journey, although he was not sure. There were also six single females from various counties, and the Dublin widow with her two children. These grown-ups might act as ballasts to the behaviour of the young girls. He hoped for this, but his mind did not have time to contemplate how that might work. And although this business created its own struggle, it also created an air of authority, which was useful, not only for its own sake and the order it imposed, but also because it relieved him of any nervousness he might have felt. When he accepted the post, he had not understood how shocking the picture of them would be.

Charles went to his quarters. It was a small room but with adequate space so long as he kept everything shipshape. He noticed the desk in the corner, always a comfort to see the makings of an office, he thought. He laid out his clothes first, then his papers. He found his log, his personal diary, got his pen ready and sat down. He would have to think more about these girls, make some sort of plan. He had read stories of some of their predecessors, hauled into open courts by their employers and handed back to the authorities. Humiliated. And worse to come, perhaps. One could not think of the perhaps. Too much despair got in the way of action. The ministry had not given Charles newspaper cuttings about the arrival of the ships that had preceded him, but rumours had come to him, and he had thought it best to appraise himself of the current opinions so he was prepared. But now he was not so sure. The articles before him were mired in a vitriol of a kind his soul found hard to take. They not only showed a lamentable level of sectarian bitterness, but also manifested a barefaced hatred of these helpless orphans. How could one have so much hatred for those with so little power? No power, be honest, he said aloud to himself, not an ounce of power. It was hard to imagine that men sat in paper offices in new cities and poured out these words. That a man could sit with his belly full and let slide off his pen such squalid insults. How could that be? One editor delighted himself by saying that their domestic expertise might stretch so far as to know the inside from the outside of a potato. He thundered on, picking up new insults with every dip of the pen. He poured scorn on everything about these newly landed girls: their place of origin, their beliefs, their tongue, even their looks. He feared that if they bred children the looks would pass on. According to him they were useless, stupid, ignorant and unmanageable. Charles pushed the papers to the back of his desk and wiped his hands. This was more than unpleasant. Such casual hatred was debilitating. He pulled the papers back across the desk in one motion and tore them into shreds.

He felt somewhat better. There would be action here, on his ship. And these girls would show them when they got there. He would fill their days up as best he could, which would be hard because they were their days, not his. Just because he would be beside them in close quarters for such a long time, did not mean he could live their days for them. But about one thing he was determined – he would train them. Come hell or high water, he would train them so they would be fit to work. Not only would they be able, they would know what was required of them. Three months might not be enough time, minus days of seasickness, but it would have to do. There was no reason they could not learn the rudiments of domestic duties. There was no reason why they wouldn't want to. He would also feed them and build them up. They would be grateful for their training, it would make their lives better when they got there. And they would be liked better for that. No employer would bring any of them into court to hand them back. At this point in his effusive plans, the girls became his. Not *the*, nor *those*, but *his*.

He took out his translated books. They might help. His mother had the title for the book she was just beginning. His mother and father were in Italy now – where the sun cast perfect evening shadows that sank into calm nights, allowing the day to spring open with more sun and to follow a rhythm, a perfect rhythm. The name of his mother's book was, at least for the moment: *'Nature and Attributes of the Feminine Soul'*. Where were the feminine souls? They were not easily seen today, but they were there. And they could be trained. Charles didn't know the girls also had to be healed, cured of what had happened them. But even if he had known, he couldn't have done anything about it. His parents in Italy. The perfect evening shadows. He got up from his desk with a sigh, this would not do. He must begin.

Down below, almost two hundred girls moved about a little, whispering to each other.

'That girl wasn't right about the number of days,' Anne Sherry said.

'Which girl? There's plenty here,' Julia Cuffe remarked.

'The one who was beside you outside, before we got in here.'

'Oh no, couldn't count, that one,' Julia said. 'Probably hadn't got to that at her school, or only knows it in Irish. Just as well she's not in charge of anything.'

Honora was going to ask what number of days the girl had said, but decided against it. They would know soon enough.

CHAPTER 8

In Charles Strutt's mind, it was important to manage the girls in such a way that they did not know they were being managed. In each group he would decide on one girl to speak for them. Of course the groups would be arbitrary, existing only in his mind to help with the smooth running of things. That core person might have to change, as responsibility turned some into tyrants while others flourished when given it. That was why he would not inform any girl of where he was placing her on the ladder in his mind – he might have to alter the place she held.

He would not yet try to remember all their names, there were far too many of them, and too many that were similar. He knew there would be a way in which the names would come to him. Often a name would attach itself to a person because of an association, although he would have to be extremely careful not to let it slip. Charles, with his understanding of translation, was doubly conscious of the minefield of naming. Didn't he spend hours searching for the correct word? Translation was like a ship really, smooth sailing, through leagues or miles of water at the speed of knots, with the danger to follow the presumption of such calm. But thinking of these things would not get the decks cleaned.

There were lots of duties to be remembered as well as names. He had the dispensation matter sorted with the

Romish priest – he would have to inform the girls of that. The priest was accepting, knowing full well that fast days could not be observed at sea. It had merely been a matter of courtesy, neither of the men actually believed a priest might say no.

Charles moved the lists about on his desk – they would be the backbone, the soul, of his operation. He would have to bring some variety while still retaining their essence. He had worked them out as if this ship would sail at a good pace, straight the entire journey, on course, never baffled by wind or current change. It was the only way. The countenancing of setbacks would lead to indecision and confusion. He had rotas organised for sewing, lessons, singing and dancing. Washdays would be strictly Mondays and Fridays, weather permitting. Washing would take place early, so as to allow the linen to dry before being put away at night. He knew this would cause astonishment among some, who would never have entertained the idea that one could wash and dry linen on the same day. What weather! There would be no washing hanging about between decks on non-designated days, no flapping irregularly creating a sense of untidiness. Charles had thought of many routines that, when put together, would be the foundation of as smooth a journey as possible, barring disaster.

The washing of the decks would be a strict part of the training. Of course, during rough weather, the crew would be very busy. During the first bout of seasickness, which he hoped wouldn't last beyond Madeira, hot sands would have to be used frequently. He knew how this was done: the sand was placed in stoves and heated to two hundred degrees, then spread an inch deep on the affected areas, and when the area was perfectly treated the sand was collected for reuse. He would not have to do this himself, but would have to make sure that it was done properly. Hopefully the captain and he would be able to establish a good working relationship. They would no doubt have differences, but, with luck, these would be kept to a minimum and would not become explosive. They were both of the same mindset with regards to the conduct expected from the crew – conduct that would have to be diligently policed. Charles knew this had not always been so on ships of this nature that had tread these waters before him. The stories had been heard: how some were fed more than others, how food had been appropriated, and worse. But not here. He would see to that.

Every mess on this ship would consist of eight and would have its turn to be first on the list for serving. Each one would have its own utensils, iron ladle, large tin oval dish, two tin three-pint pots, one two-gallon water keg, a potato net, pudding bag and towel. Each mess would have a planned menu, the ounces clearly measured to eliminate errors. No mistakes were going to be made here.

'No one, and I repeat no one,' he said to the cook, 'is going to get thinner on me.'

Each girl had already been assigned a bolster, blankets and counterpane, a large linen bag, a knife and fork, two spoons, a metal plate and a mug. Each girl had the utensils to eat, and eat she would, providing of course that she was not sick. How he dreaded the Bay of Biscay. Would the girls be good to each other then and care for the sick among them? Yes, he was sure that they would.

Already his bright thoughts from his train journey to Plymouth were mirrored in the changed demeanour of some of the girls. He couldn't be sure if the changes had occurred among the most forlorn looking, but then he did not know or remember who had been the most forlorn. He would never go back to not knowing these girls. Of course he still didn't know them – he knew only a few names even now, and he couldn't tell the difference between most of them. But he knew the overall look of them better than he had when he first saw them. And he would get to know them even better. Though not during sick days. The sick ones would remember him as ministering what little there was – sage, arrowroot, preserved milk perhaps. He would not remember them before Biscay anyway, that was too soon. They would merge into one for him, berth number after berth number. When they were better, when life had begun to return to their cheeks, they would look different from when lying curled on their sides retching, different enough to give him something to recognise. And the experience, that of the sickness and the care, if they could remember the tending of others, would leave a mark of its own on their faces.

Charles Strutt and the captain and crew and matrons and sub-matrons knew the sequence of events to be followed each day.

Doors open at five thirty. The well-enough girls would have two hours in which to wash, dress and make themselves generally presentable. As soon as the weather got warm enough, a large bath of seawater would be placed under a tent and they would be able to immerse themselves between five and six in the morning. The officer on watch would be summoned to test the tea or coffee, to pronounce it fit to drink, and to ring the breakfast bell. After breakfast, berths, tables, lockers and between decks would be swept, scraped and polished with holystones and sand. The ladders would be brought on deck and similarly treated. Plates and cutlery would be made to gleam. The mattresses and bedding would be folded and made dry and clean, weather permitting. The girls would then rearrange themselves, their faces and hair, for inspection. And at eleven o'clock school would begin. Here hieroglyphics would become understandable. Some who could already read and write would help those who were not as proficient, or at least not as proficient in English. Shapes would be made on pages. The maker of those shapes would stare mesmerised by what it meant and that she had done it and had made its meaning. There would be bursts of great joy during this time.

Dinner would come, substantial pies, as regular as breakfast, and prompting another ceremony. And after, tired though the girls might be, classes would resume. There would be more needlework and letters in the afternoon. Materials had been kindly provided by some local women at Plymouth, the women Honora had watched come and go. Some of these women would perhaps occasionally wonder how the girls were getting on, but most of them wouldn't, having given materials to the ship only because their neighbours were doing it. At five thirty, tea would be called, announcing to anyone who might pass that this ship had been well ordered for the last twelve hours.

After tea, when the girls would assemble for dancing and singing, they might whisper the progress of the quilt they were secretly making for Mr Strutt – the shapes and stitches, the size of the squares, the best way to handle a needle. They would have begun the quilt for him because he was theirs now. Judgment had been made. Already. And in the making of the quilt they would stitch in some of their hearts and do their best to be cured. The lanterns would be hung on deck to light the dancers, and between decks for those too tired, too shy, or too sad. At eight thirty all the lanterns, except three, would be doused – after the decks had been cleaned, of course. Girls would then retire to bed. And sigh. And maybe cry. And hopefully sometimes smile before sleeping.

The clarity, the precision and the reliability of this routine would add shape to their days. The girls did not know this yet, which put them at a disadvantage. The future emptiness of their days worried many of them. They did not know yet that they were going to be busy, very busy indeed. It would have relieved them if they had known, and did indeed, when it began to become clear.

The *Thomas Arbuthnot* sailed out at ten o'clock on a Sunday morning, 28 October 1849. A light breeze set it on its way. This good start left very few sick, so passing the ship *The Lizard* that first night brought a satisfaction the crew would not have liked to revel in too much, for fear it might strain their luck. A Russian barque passed them, but then the wind picked up and allowed the *Thomas Arbuthnot* to pass it. Unfortunately this quickening gave many their first taste of seasickness. The journey from Dublin had clearly been less rough than he had presumed. A stunned girl looked at him, he could not remember her name.

'Am I getting sick?'

Charles knew enough to understand the question.

'No, just seasick. It happens sometimes at sea.'

'So I will get better?'

'Yes, you will.'

How strange that the girl had not asked him when. The main deck leaked, water sprayed berths, the sea roughed up getting ready for rage. Charles gave as much consolation and encouragement as he could to the bewildered below. He talked to the captain and between them they organised what cleaning, scraping, and purifying was possible. In some ways

Charles welcomed this early stirring of the waters, giving him a chance to assess the weaknesses in his plan. His eye was keen, he could see the immediate problems and where cracks might appear as they progressed.

The captain worked beside him. He was not sure about this surgeon, he seemed stiffly conscious of his charges as if they were the only thing on this vessel, but then that could be to his advantage. It did not appear he was going to have to spend time keeping order. Unlike his last journey, there would be no routing out of crew from shadowed corners on this voyage, not if this man had his way. He called for two more crew members, and between them they lit stoves and aired the inside quarters as best they could. The captain had not intended to engage in this activity himself, but with Charles bent to it he felt he had no choice. He would be careful in future to control where they met to speak. Charles went back down to the girls to promise them the journey would not always be like this – most believed him because they wanted to. In time they would become used to bad weather and forget comparisons of awfulness. On his way back up he noted as many leaks as he could and put them down for caulking when the fine weather came as promised.

Charles told the girls that the sight of Madeira would bring calm. So confident was he that he was, at this moment, getting ready their books for school. The notion of school on a boat seemed such a peculiar idea that they looked at him and said nothing. What could they say to what they didn't know?

Anne Sherry whispered, 'Well, my mother went to a hedge school, maybe it will be like that.'

'He's nice, really,' Honora dared.

'He could be worse I'm sure,' Julia sniffed.

'I think he's nice … I think,' Honora said.

Bridget Joyce, who stood beside Honora as often as possible, said nothing.

It was in the afternoon that Charles first caught a glimpse of it, the height of the hills reaching up out of the water. He focused his eyes carefully to check he had not made a mistake – it would not be good to tell his passengers about the sight of land and then discover that he himself had suffered a dreaded illusion. But no, that was it, that was land, and the water looked more ironed out because of it. He took a map to the girls. Although all of them had been to school at some time, there had of course been huge disruptions in their education. It was impossible for Charles to decide whether it was the disruptions or the issue of language that made them stare at him sometimes, as if they had no idea what he was talking about. He could not help being aware too, that they might not be as open with him as he presumed. Bearing these things in mind he unrolled the map. There would be those who could understand the notion of representation, and those who couldn't, or perhaps deliberately wouldn't. Maybe they would have been interested in an academic or dreamy way inside the four walls of the school close to their homes. Maybe now they did not want to understand the vastness of that water, the length of time it would take a letter to travel. The truth of the distance might be too catastrophic. They would know that forever it would only be letters that would go home, never them. There were also those who did not want to see themselves on large maps, a smaller contour of life being more suitable for most. But he would show it to them, because he believed they were entitled to know. He tacked the map to a beam. He was surprised as they flocked to him, the girls crowding close to see.

'What does scale mean?'

'It's not literal distance,' Charles answered.

'What's literal?'

'I'll explain later,' he said.

'Go on, sir,' a girl said.

He had not heard sir from them before that moment. It was a pity he could not remember more names.

'Here's Madeira. Let me show you our proposed route. We go this way,' and his pen traced the notional planned way. 'We move out here, do you see, towards Brazil, because we must get with the winds. It might look as if that would be better,' and he traced his pen down the west coast of Africa. 'But we could not do that because we would hit the doldrums and sit for days upon days without moving. This way we should be travelling all the time. Even if sometimes slowly.'

'What's the doldrums? I thought that was before getting sick.'

'Shh ...'

'If we were in there we'd see land, wouldn't we?'

The girl's voice had longing in it. But another chided her, 'Yes, but what would be the point in seeing land if we couldn't be on it and we were going to take longer.'

Another girl pointed, 'Is that Ireland?'

'Yes, indeed it is.'

The girl was pleased.

'It looks small,' said another.

Anne Sherry pointed and said, 'That's Australia?'

'Yes, that's the west coast, we are going to the east coast, Sydney, here.'

'So, if we've travelled what distance? And how long since we started? And we have that far to go ...'

There was a murmur of calculation.

'That means it will be ...'

'I think it's too soon for that,' Honora said, looking at the map.

But someone whispered, 'Nearly a hundred.'

'Don't be silly. You couldn't be on a boat that long,' another voice said.

Some girls stood on the tips of their toes to see who had said that.

A silence descended and all the eyes turned on him.

'Let's come back to Madeira,' he said.

He showed them the equator and the tropics of Cancer and Capricorn. He showed them latitude and longitude. He got quite carried away before he noticed the bewildered looks on some faces. He really would have to get to know more of their names.

'Will you be going home, sir?'

Before he had time to answer a girl said, 'My brother is coming out to me.'

The others turned their heads to her and it was hard to judge whether their communal look was one of envy or scepticism. Charles began to roll the map. There was a murmur of disappointment, which could have come from a desire to still place themselves on the map. Or from annoyance that the respite from routine was broken.

'I'll bring it again,' he said.

That night after bedtime when the noises had subsided, Charles walked on deck. He looked out to sea to where he fancied he could see flickering lights and candles on the island. It might have been nice to stop, to get one's feet on the ground, even briefly. To let the boat nestle in the dock, where the workers, unhampered by the temper of the weather, could tidy up its loose ends, patch up its injuries and get ready for the next lot of seafaring. But that might be too hard on these girls, too hard for some of them to come back on board. He watched the lights until they were tiny stars thrown on the edge of the ocean. It took some time for this fading to happen. Then the dark around him thickened and the only lights to be seen were the ones still lit on the deck. He thought he heard a noise and wondered if perhaps it was a girl out looking too, without permission. Still, if it was, she was quiet. He turned his back on the sea and headed into his room where he thought he would have a drink. He passed Honora but didn't see her. She had slipped out from the darkness below, unable to turn into sleep. She rolled herself into a small bundle under the ropes and looked up through them. She wanted to believe this was the same sky that was over the home she had just glimpsed on the map, the one she had been taken from and would never see again. That became clear the more days passed. Who could ever come back from so far? If she could believe it was the same sky surely that would help. It would be good to get a map too.

CHAPTER 9

On the following morning Charles called the girls together to begin the first washing day. He knew it would throw up its own difficulties, but then every new ritual had to find its feet. This was the opportunity to have one of the main lessons of order taught. Here are the rules ...

'Here we go again.'

That would be Julia. He could see that some of the other girls also found the rules harsh. A sulky look came over some, but they put it away from their faces when Charles looked them in the eye. Maybe he had a point about slopping water and people falling.

'If we fell and hurt ourselves we could not come up here at all. We'd be stuck down below all day,' Anne Sherry said.

The second washing day went more smoothly, girls even appearing to have moments of satisfaction with their completed tasks. But there was still work to be done to get the ritual flowing better. He had decided he would postpone taking up their trunks from the hold for examination – a few more successful washings would need to be achieved first. They would have to learn order before that happened.

When the men did lug up the boxes, and when the girls saw their names still there despite the sea, a few of them cried and others used that to cry as well. Sometimes it was good to have something to start crying about. Julia never cried – she wouldn't satisfy them, she thought. She couldn't figure out who 'them' was, but she wouldn't satisfy them no matter who they were.

They tripped in the small spaces left between the boxes. They examined their clothes and found out from each other how best to banish mildew. Seeing their belongings and unfaded names gave them a boost, which matured as the day wore on.

Then Bridget Joyce saw her bird again. She saw it every morning and most evenings.

'Look, it's the same bird. Still with us. All day and all night in the dark. Still with us.'

'How can you tell? Don't be silly.' That came from Cissy Weir.

'It's the same bird, I know it is.'

Her eyes filled up. Charles had seen her stepping from the breakfast line to speak to this bird.

'It may be the same bird, it may not,' Honora Raftery said, which seemed to settle the argument.

'It's the same bird,' whispered Bridget, so low it could only be lip-read.

Charles had already had a complaint about Honora Raftery, although he couldn't be sure if it was actually a complaint. It might have been more that the teller wanted something to report, not to get Honora in trouble necessarily, but more to test conversation and to have something to say to him. Or maybe she wanted to break from the ordered rigor and have a small disturbance.

'Honora Raftery's up on deck telling lies again.'

'I don't think they're actually lies,' Charles said. 'She's telling stories.' He had overheard her.

'What's the difference?'

'There is a difference,' Charles said. 'It's all right to tell stories.'

'Even if they're not true?'

'Yes, even if they're not true.'

The subtlety escaped even him. But his incompetent explanation would have to suffice. He would have to remind himself again not to call Bridget Joyce 'Birdy'. It would be too easy to do that.

'You can go now. Stories are all right.'

The girl turned her back on him.

The first day of classes started with calm waters outside, which helped. The boat clipped through the sea, the sails made whistling sounds, the noise of slapping ropes faded into the wood and the water. The dawn that day appeared sedately over the edge of the flat sea and the light had slowly filled the sky. Charles had seen this as he took a morning stroll. He walked back and forth quietly, never going as far as the bridge to the girls' quarter – he didn't want to wake them, partly because he felt it was better for them if they slept, but also because he wanted time alone to imagine himself without charges. Some mornings were like that, maybe because of a restless night, or a deep sleep troubled by dreams. But it was hard to imagine himself without them now, particularly today as he was worried about the classes. He knew that most had more than the rudiments of English – that had been taken into account in their selection. He had seen them crowd around the map. Indeed he now knew that some of them could perhaps have been destined for more than domestic service, but that could be of no concern to him. Others of them had only the basics of schooling and some had a strange grasp of English – they understood, but put their verbs where perhaps their nouns should be. Or was it the other way about? Or was that it at all? It happened so fast in their speech that he did not have time to examine it and if he asked them to repeat it he suspected they phrased it as it was supposed to be.

Charles would have to decide how to determine class groups. Would it be best to mix the weak with the strong so that they might learn from them? But there were others, Julia Cuffe for instance, who by now had come to his attention often enough for him to remember her name. She would scoff, no doubt. She would have to be put into a class that would make her want to learn, make her want to cast aside all her certainties and approach a search for knowing as if it would mean something to her, as if it could be of use to her, as if she might like it even. But this was hard. Julia had been broken and had put herself back to living by believing that every dark thing that she had seen could be trumped by belligerence, bad language, and scepticism. This quality was so rampant in her that it frightened him. In his first direct encounter with her, he had felt obliged to call her aside because of the way she spoke to Matron. She had an answer for every comment he made. Before he had finished his sentence she had a reply ready. And what was worse than the readiness of her reply was that it was often an answer that one would expect from a more grown person, a person from different circumstances. The conversation began innocuously enough – although when he thought about it afterwards he realised that this is what had provoked his exasperation. He had not intended this to be a conversation, he had meant it to be a reprimand, at the end of which the girl would say that yes, she understood, and then he could have handed down some leniency in a benevolent fashion for which she would have been grateful.

'Miss Cuffe, you cannot speak to Matron like you did.'

'Why not, what's she to me?' Julia sniffed.

'She's your matron on this voyage. She will minister to you and look after you if you become ill.'

'I'm not going to get sick.'

'But if you do ...'

'So you're saying that I have to not talk to her any way I want just in case I get sick? I might get sick even if I keep my mouth shut. I know people who did. Being nice doesn't mean you won't have bad things happen.'

'Excuse me, Miss Cuffe ...'

'Julia'

Miss Cuffe ...'

Charles was forced to raise his voice and disliked the girl in front of him for making him do that. 'Miss Cuffe, as I was saying – and please don't interrupt me – Matron, her helpers, and myself, wish this journey to be as smooth as possible, we are all working to that end. The co-operation and civil manners of all of you is essential to that smooth running. The other girls will be grateful too if we can achieve that.'

At the mention of the others the skin around her eyes softened, but only momentarily.

'Well, am I going to be with those girls forever?'

'What's that got to do with anything?' Why on earth was he answering this girl.

'Now, as I was saying, and may I repeat that I do not wish to be interrupted ...' Charles said, with a sigh.

'Then you shouldn't have brought me here.'

'Miss Cuffe ...'

'Mister, it's all right, I'll be good,' Julia said suddenly, as if it had been her idea. 'But sometimes I won't, because the other girls might need a laugh now and then.'

As she said this last bit she changed the timbre of her

voice, he could not say it was a sneer, it was too light-hearted for that.

So she had decided to be good. She was not doing it because he had used his authority. In fact it was only when she saw that he was losing his authority that she decided to pacify him.

'You will now come with me and apologise to Matron.'

'What do you mean?'

'You will tell Matron that you are sorry for having been rude.'

'Oh I see, I've never done that before,' she smiled. 'So, I'll just stand there and say: I'm sorry, Matron.'

'Yes.'

'What good will that do?'

'It's called having manners.'

'All right.'

Charles was surprised at how suddenly she capitulated. He brought her to Matron. Julia stood before the woman. She straightened her back, patted her dress, and touched her hair. Charles realised, with great discomfort, that she was enjoying this new experience, this saying 'I'm sorry'. She meant not one word of it, but Matron graciously accepted the hollow apology and Charles took Julia back to her quarters. His emotions were high. Julia trotted behind him, a child now. At the door he said, more to himself than to her, 'You're too young to know some of the things you know.'

'Well that's not my fault,' Julia said, grown up again.

Maybe he should have said nothing.

'What happened?' Anne Sherry asked.

'What does a voyage mean?'

'It's a journey.'

'Ah.'

'What happened?'

'Nothing. It's the same as a journey?'

'Yes.'

'Do you come back from it?'

'I don't know.'

Julia sat on her bunk and stayed quiet for some time. Anne didn't like the way she looked.

Then came the sound of a bell, and the girls, remembering Charles Strutt's instructions, moved to their classes. Those who didn't were reminded by the others. And so a stream of girls with neat dresses and no bonnets came up from below and moved towards the tables where classes would be taught. The sub matrons, who had now been designated as teachers, organised seats and lines and looked more confident than they felt. Julia Cuffe's teacher cleared her throat and got on with the class she had planned, concealing from them that she had worked out the exact things to say and how often to repeat them. Matron had told her that it got easier with each class. She needed to wipe her brow but decided not to. The girls watched her intently, even Julia. One of them thought that she could do that too. But when a moment of doubt came to her, she thought no, she would watch the teacher carefully and maybe she could do that in the future, if she was allowed.

There came from the room the steady sound of a voice, warming to the way the plan was working. And there came too, an inexplicable sensation, an emotion, gratification.

CHAPTER 10

The *Thomas Arbuthnot* had been at sea for over two weeks when an unexpected problem arose between Charles and the captain. It was a hot day, and tempers were frayed. Charles wanted to make a wire grating for the main hatch – 'One that can be kept open all day to circulate the air,' he said.

The captain bristled. There had been moments like this before. Sometimes a difference of opinion would erupt between them about such things as washing days, which might be interfering with work the captain thought more important than clean clothes. It had happened last week. The sailors were caulking and so Charles agreed to postpone the washing until the next day. The caulking was not complete on the following day, but he proceeded with the washing. The captain's fury was out of proportion with the inconvenience. He gave vent to his anger, which was not good for discipline. Thankfully none of the girls heard, or so Charles hoped, but you could never be sure, there was always a stray girl around going from one place to another or sitting on a step trying not to be seen, thinking something that was best not talked about.

Nor did the captain like that all the decisions regarding the girls were made by Charles. He was also dismissive of the sermons given by him on Sundays. Charles knew this. And while accepting that he was not a proper pastor, he did think his leading of prayers was not so terribly unworthy, and certainly did not warrant the half sneer on the captain's face. It was difficult to pray when such a temporal thing as a sneer was before you. He had enough things to be concerned about anyway. As he gave his Church of England service on the poop deck, he kept his ear attentive for sounds from below, where the girls, most of them Catholic, were also supposed to be praying. But Charles doused his annoyance. Overenthusiastic pride could explode on a journey such as this. Just when things were going smoothly a crisis could erupt, not just with the girls, but the crew also. And Charles knew that he and the captain would, when the time came, praise each other for reaching journey's end, remembering only the neatness and accomplishment of their arrival. And this would be best achieved if they pocketed their little rages.

Charles said again, but quieter this time, 'It would help the air to circulate?' He inserted the sound of a question mark to allow the captain a degree of decision. It worked. The captain backed down over the necessity of making the grating, although he grumbled a little over the expense and the diversion. Why was it necessary he mumbled, they were young girls, they could put up with a bit of heat, they would be fine. And they weren't paying.

The wire grating was made quickly and cheaply – quicker and cheaper than the grumble. Charles would pocket that too. But he would have to learn how to get the captain on his side, to avoid shouting matches that could frighten girls. He went up on deck and watched Bridget Joyce whispering to her bird.

By now there were many strange birds so she had several choices. There were small ones and big ones, white, grey, black, and ones full of plumage, ducking and diving, flying beside the boat or flying at it, swooping their bodies in time with the flap of the sails. Bridget did not mind that some people knew she talked to them. But today she was also interested in a great whale that was following them earnestly but without curiosity. Charles told her as much as he knew about them, and she occasionally looked at him in her way and then back to the whale.

'Are you liking classes?' Charles asked.

'Yes. We have books at home.'

'And where is home?' Charles used the same tense as Bridget.

'It doesn't matter now,' she said, and went back to looking at the whale.

He wasn't sure if he had made an unforgivable intrusion into her world.

'I like the map,' she said. 'Birds fly whatever way they want through the map. They don't care. But they always know where they are going. See the way they take off. It's like the way a hat takes off from your head in the wind. But the hat falls. They don't. They're made to fly, they trap the wind and use it. It's like swimming. It's like us on this boat. We're flying through the water, they're flying through the air. I like it best when they're above my head, like this,' and she put her head back to look at the birds above her.

Charles did not know if he was expected to answer this.

'Did you look at birds at home too?' he asked.

'Not as much. There was more to do.'

'Would you like a glass of lime? I could get you one.'

'Yes, please.'

Charles was suddenly afraid and was glad to have something practical to do. He brought Bridget down after she had finished her lime and put her beside Honora.

That evening he filled his log, all quiet below after a placid dusk. But early the next morning an unheralded storm blew up suddenly. It followed after what had been an unsatisfactory windless two days. It tossed their ship and the equilibrium that had worked itself into their, by now, acceptable days of cleaning, eating, learning and dancing. The dancing had worked out well, except of course during storms. Complaints and necessary punishment too were now down to a minimum. Cantankerousness among the few was becoming bearable. The off days of individual girls were diminishing into the whole. But this storm caught them unawares, and for that very reason, brought a sharp edge of hopelessness with it.

Bridget Joyce was not surprised by it, she had been expecting it. The birds had told her the previous evening, in particular the tern that fluffed the feathers on its chest when expecting a change. So while others cried at the ferocity of it and tried to keep themselves strapped into their berths – pointless with all the getting in and out to be sick, if they could even move – Bridget lay on her bed, her body straightened and thought about the birds. When it eased somewhat, she would go back up to find out what they were saying now. They were lucky it was daytime. It never seemed so bad when there was light outside. Even if they could not see it in their quarters below brightness, they knew it was there. The boat rolled and slid and groaned sometimes when hit by a particularly large wave. Doors banged, cups and the small belongings of girls could be heard thudding to the ground. The breaking glass tinkled. Below, even more below than the girls, one trunk had freed itself and hit the others sporadically as it slid from side to side. The girls tended to each other as best they could. Those with sturdy stomachs helped those who had succumbed to dry retching. And just when it looked as if it could not get worse, the storm turned itself up and became even more frightening.

'Are we going to die?'

'No,' Charles said. 'This is now the worst and it will get better soon.'

This was the part of the sea that Charles had forgotten.

The awfulness was apparent in their faces, and yet Honora felt this dreadful day did at least break up the hours. It gave her something immediate to deal with and took her mind off the savagery of what had happened to her and the rest of girls around her. She did not say this.

A slight abatement came and grew in the water. Charles made a consoling announcement about the now foreseeable end.

Honora went up on deck. She had to use all her strength to open the door, which was being buffeted by a ferocious wind. As she struggled up the stairs, distastefully putting her feet down as best she could, a magnet appeared to pull her stomach up to her throat. But once on deck, watching the horizon, there was a reasonableness about the storm. One minute she saw only sea, and a few moments later only sky. But it was better to watch. Up here she could count the number of crashing waves and corrugated bounces that it took to achieve the change in view. Up here, the noises of the sick had space to waft out and away. And up here she could see the gradual levelling of the bumps.

The birds were still swooping, but occasional dips looked like a cavort, as if they knew the end was in sight and that no great harm had been done. As she made her way back down the stairs she peeped into the room that was their eating quarter, and saw that the crew, who had no doubt been lying down themselves, were beginning to ready the tables. Still holding firm against the gravity in the middle of the floor, they prepared as best they could. Some of the girls could now swear by the best spots to stand during a storm, having watched this trick. They were wetting cloths to put on the table to stop the plates, mugs and cutlery from sliding – whoever turned up to eat must be made comfortable.

'That will be the last one before the Cape,' a sailor said in sympathy as she passed, moved perhaps by the look of her and the knowledge that his daughter was safe in bed on a floor that did not move. Honora believed him about the last storm, it seemed the hopeful thing to do.

And then the sea calmed. After checking the condition of his charges, Charles surveyed the damage. Almost half of the lanterns were broken and gloom threatened. What if the girls could not see at night? How much more difficult would that make the remainder of their journey? They were not even close to halfway yet.

'What will we do for light?'

There was always a voice to say aloud one's worst fears. He would have to come up with some way to fix the lanterns. So he got bottles and tied a string tight where he wanted the neck and bottom cut – it was worth a try. Girls watched him silently.

'I know what you're going to do next,' Julia Cuffe said.

The sound of her voice saying a normal thing encouraged him greatly. He wondered if he should ask her what she thought he might do, because in fact he wasn't sure. But he stopped himself, because a reply might push her back against her own wall. Charles twisted the string and rubbed it patiently around the desired place of friction until the line got hot. Yes, this was how to do it. Patience. He must not rush. He concentrated on not breaking the glass before it was ready. Some girls smiled as they saw the progress. They all stayed quiet. Then he doused it in cold water, achieving, in most circumstances, an almost clean break. He then fitted this regular globe into the lanterns. All was light again. The girls still watched, then clapped, as each lantern got its new cover. The joy destroyed the memory of the storm. Bridget Joyce whispered that he had made light. It pulled him up straight, because in truth, he hadn't been feeling too good that day.

Charles went downstairs and wrote some letters, which he would give to the next ship they met wending its return journey to England. As he wrote, he thought himself lucky that he had people to whom he could write. He went back upstairs and was especially nice to the girls, forgave those needing forgiveness and made an extra effort to speak to the shy.

'He is nice.'

'Nice enough, you're right.'

Julia Cuffe didn't make her usual sound.

CHAPTER 11

Charles wrote in his diary that nothing much of note had happened for a while, other than a small problem about Sunday service. Charles liked when nothing much of note happened. There were of course the usual little things, the Sunday service being one of these. One of the sub matrons, who should have been keeping order while Charles preached, was either too busy or inattentive to quiet a few noisy girls. It wasn't as if it was a difficult job with so few girls at his service. Charles confiscated a lime juice – any slip of order now could quickly undo all the good work. But later that night while out checking the decks he relented, and decided that the small gesture was all that was required. It hadn't been a serious derogation of duty. Getting the balance right required flexibility. It would be forgotten about, though learned from, by next Sunday. As he was thinking about this he tripped over an errant steward, who was in irons, but already getting his apologies in order, having decided that work of any and all kinds was preferable. Charles bade him goodnight then engaged in a few pleasant words.

'You won't do it again,' Charles said. The tone of the words gave the man some ease and he got his apology polished. The next day, happily back at work, he was most helpful in the landing and gutting of a shark. Out here at sea all kind of things reaped their own rewards. They would have the shark for dinner. There had been little variety of food, so this would be useful for the relief of all their palates.

Thus they sailed, bobbing their way across the Tropic of Cancer, out of sight of Senegal and Sierra Leone and Gabon. Charles imagined these places on deck at night because that's what would have been close if they'd been going south straight along the west of Africa. Sometimes he longed to see a light that was not that of another ship.

The dancing nights were now well organised. On the first night there had been a bit of consternation.

'We have no boys to whistle,' Anne Sherry said.

'Can none of us do it?' Honora asked. 'How do you do it?' She puckered her lips and blew but no sound came out.

'We're not supposed to whistle, we're girls,' Anne Sherry said.

'Why's that?' Honora asked, never having heard this before.

'A whistling woman and a crowing hen, are neither fit for God nor men,' Julia said, and laughed out a huge gleeful sound.

'It gets you into trouble, so I'd better do it then,' she added.

She pursed her lips, blew out a few melodic notes, straightened her back, fluttered her tongue and flew into a piercing sweet sound that echoed through the ropes. The sails slapped to it.

But then a sailor's voice was heard shouting, 'No whistling on a boat. Do yiz not know that, calls up a storm. And anyway, a girl could get a beard whistling.'

This brought much laughter from everyone except from Julia, who said, 'God yiz would believe anything.'

Honora stuttered into a lilt, and more girls joined in. Many of them could do it well, some better than others, and from this night on they were often dry mouthed by the time the evening was over. In the beginning some girls had stood at the edges while the better dancers, the girls maybe one year older who had been to a dance at home, took the centre of the floor. Or a girl might sit and watch because that was what she wanted to do – to be riveted by someone else's movement. But gradually most girls filtered in, seduced by the joy that came of its own accord when you learned to let your feet and shoulders move to the sound of notes. And a girl might learn for the first time, if she was one of the very young ones, that once her feet and shoulders were in time with the lilting, an entire flash of heat could radiate out from a small spot near where her heart was, and she could be overtaken with a throatful of joy. What would God have thought if he could have seen a ship like this at night, flapping sails, the light dipping as lanterns swayed, the sound of voices making music and the sight of girls with long dresses dancing, tripping their steps into each other's.

It was the day after a dance that they met the *Duke of Bedford*. It was always an exciting time, seeing a ship that seemed to be making straight for them. The girls liked to watch the approach, the sails waving towards them, getting closer and closer. They would stare at the distance getting smaller and wonder where the boat was from and where it was going. The crew would not do this, being used to the notion of ships on the sea, but they did not interrupt the staring, there was something entirely private and perhaps sacred about every girl's looking. The boat pulled close and the two captains spoke through a trumpet. Not everyone could hear what they said because the wind and the swish of the sails cut up the sounds. The girls stayed quiet to see what they could pick up, they could check with each other later and put the bits together and maybe come up with something that mattered. They were stopping longer this time, their captain boarding the other boat.

'Oh look at that, I hope he doesn't fall.'

He went on board for dinner, as was the ritual when time and conditions permitted. The last ship they had met had come past them in the wind and no one had stopped. They had simply shouted greetings and a man on the other ship had held up a baby.

'Look, it's a baby,' they cried.

'We speak the ship, did you know that, we do not speak *to* the ship,' Anne Sherry said. Her English was getting better and better the teacher said. But even people whose English was very good might not know that, you had to be at sea for a long time to learn some things.

The captain returned from the dinner with presents: two sheep, a pig and a dozen fowls. Their palates would be truly spoiled now. He also had a newspaper, which could be taken to the classes when he was finished with it. It was while the boat was still at a lull, while the creaking and lapping of the two vessels were married, that Charles gathered some girls near him and told them about the changing of the stars. They would see it soon, maybe tomorrow night, if the sky was very clear.

The fuss of the other ship was a welcome distraction, and Charles was glad to have his letters taken from him on their way, particularly the letter to his mother. He watched the ship disappearing, bearing his news that would arrive in Italy, where the sunlight was even.

On the following morning Charles wondered if it had been wise of him to mention the stars, there seemed to be an air of consternation about, among the younger ones especially. He wouldn't have done so if they had not been lapping beside another boat. One had to think carefully about what information one imparted, but a moment of rest, or the togetherness of boats, could put the tongue off guard. Oh well, he would just have to make sure he explained it properly and comfortingly. He would use the map to illustrate. They would examine it today, find their latitude and longitude and then tonight, after dancing, anyone who wanted to could stay on deck with him to read the sky.

'Are you staying?' Honora asked Julia.

'Might as well, might tell us something we'll need to know. What do you think?' and she laughed out loud. 'What do you think, Honora?'

It was a clear night. Perfect for seeing the northern stars fade away and the southern stars rise into view. Charles pointed to what was the familiar and the girls stared in awe as they saw the change. Although in truth, some of them were pretending in order to keep Charles happy. They did not know their own sky well, certainly not as well as he did. Surprisingly, it was Anne Sherry who was most moved. Surprisingly, because she was generally most in control of her thoughts and emotions.

'Imagine. Even the stars won't be the same,' she said. 'It's like leaving again.'

'Don't be silly, we've already left. You can only leave once,' Julia said.

This was what Charles had wanted to avoid. He hurried them below. After they had settled, when the last noises seemed to be over, he walked back on deck and had another look at the beautiful stars by himself. Yes, he could imagine travellers addressing them, those who thought they would never see them again. And he could imagine how possessive one could become about your stars only when you were leaving them. He went down below. He could hear a girl crying, but that was not unusual. Most nights there was at least one. The girls had a way of letting her cry for some time before someone would go to her. Indeed, those closest whispered over the sobs for a while before providing comfort for whatever sadness had overcome her. He heard the whispers.

'Why's she crying? She doesn't usually.'

'She says that even the stars will be different.'

'Oh, what the hell difference does that make. Everything will be different.'

'Still, I'd better go over to her. She's only young.'

'What age are you?'

'Sixteen.'

'Oh.'

Charles walked away. Maybe he could write more letters. Perhaps they would meet another ship on its way back.

CHAPTER 12

On the following day Charles let the girls know about the equator ceremonies. Perhaps telling them about the stars had been too much, but they would definitely need to be forewarned about the equator carry-ons. He unfurled the map again – the girls seemed surprised that they were so far down. They had travelled unfathomable miles and were still going. They felt tired just thinking of it. The sun was now so close it could almost be touched. The girls put both their hands in front of their eyes when they came up in the mornings to stop themselves from being blinded. The few thin clouds in the sky seemed to be in an almighty hurry, casting only a momentary shadow, as if they were dancing past the light.

Charles showed them exactly what their latitude and longitude was.

'That's not bad,' one of them said.

But Anne Sherry still looked at where Australia was, he could see her out of the corner of his eye, her gaze fixed on it. Although surprise for non-seagoing people is part of the joy of equator ceremonies, in this instance, he thought it best to give them a little information, partly because the act of looking forward was good for them, and also because he did not want them to be frightened in any way. He was still at times taken aback when he realised again their ages, and last night had reminded him of this.

It was a very hot afternoon, as one would expect, when a sailor shouted, 'Now!' and simultaneously a trumpet bellowed out its noise. There was a sudden shouting and bustle from all directions, members of the crew enthusiastically throwing themselves into their production, as much for themselves as for their passengers. Some of the young or nervous girls clutched the hands of others, unsure of what was happening, unprepared for the make-believe. Dressed up people were also coming over the side – Neptune and Amphitrite, the constables and the barber, all boarded the ship.

'From where?' some girls shrieked. 'Where did they come from?'

The visitors approached individual girls and asked them questions. The girls stared at first, then tried to get an answer out as they realised what the game was. If the answer was not correct the girl was ducked in a large tub. It was hard for Charles to tell if a girl wanted to be ducked or not – if she was shy or afraid, or if there might be a feminine reason for her shouts of 'No, no, no'. But all in all, he thought the celebrations had been enjoyed by all. There was a general sense of lightness and smiles on faces. It resembled a visit to any of the best theatres.

The crew then hoisted a lit tar barrel over the side and everyone – crew, girls, captain, Charles, Matron, sub matrons – watched for miles as it floated and burned its way into the heat that surrounded it. Charles allowed the girls to stay up later than normal that evening, to see the last flame of it in the instant darkness.

As the tired girls made their ways to their sleeping quarters, he overheard some of the voices.

'She said that was a story for the equator. She said her father carried stories. How could you carry stories? And she says that she's going to do that too, always going to carry them. No matter where she ends up.'

In the dark he couldn't make out who had said it.

'My mother and father are dead.'

'Mine too.'

'But someone said we can get married when we get there if we want. I can't remember when I heard that, if it was before we left home or not. Maybe it was when we got on this boat.'

'Get married! Wouldn't that be funny.'

Mercifully, the days began to cool a little as they moved away from the line of zero degrees. Out there at night Charles thought of the names of African countries. He knew the coast well. It seemed better to think of it than this long stretch of water. And there was talk now of steamers, who would go that way, stop for coal in Cape Verde and Cape Town. The passengers would maybe see coasts occasionally, would get off at some ports and put land under their feet. There was talk of it and, although some said it was not possible, others pointed to how new and great things were being made every day. Things were changing in leaps and bounds. Charles thought he might like that, being on a steamer down the coast of Africa.

Charles was at his desk when a sub matron came running to tell him that Mrs Johnstone had gone into labour. He had noticed her almost due on the last day the boxes had been hoisted up on deck. He had suspected this would happen, that she was closer to her time than he had been told at Plymouth. Her face was bronze and set in dreaminess as their boxes were hoisted up on deck. She showed no interest in what was in her family's box, but watched attentively as her husband did the necessary checking, airing and replacing. Honora Raftery had got her a chair on which to sit, her solicitousness suggested that she too sensed a coming event. Charles thought maybe this would bring her good in her own life. Mrs Johnstone asked for one picture to be kept out, a black framed drawing of a stern-bonneted woman, her mother, Charles presumed, and allowed her to keep it with her. He did not like birth at sea. Yes, the luck it could bring tempted hope, but many things could go wrong. He hoped for a short labour and one that would not be too wicked.

The birth went as smoothly as even a land birth can go. Charles suggested to Matron that she ask Honora to help with minor tasks that might come up. It seemed right to ask her for assistance.

'But keep her on the outside of things.'

He needed the sub matrons to be extra vigilant on deck, the hint of the occasion could otherwise lead to breaks of discipline that might have unhappy consequences, so he felt it would be better to ask one of the more mature girls to assist. The matter seemed to be proceeding well – although in truth it was hard to tell whether the experience was worsened by virtue of being at sea, only Mrs Johnstone could say for sure, and she wasn't talking at the moment. There was heaving and moans and short cries, but all in all it was a well conducted, uncomplicated labour. Everyone was doing what they had to do, mainly waiting for the woman to have more and louder pain.

Honora was standing behind Matron when a sudden piercing scream replaced what had preceded it. She felt herself become faint and light-headed. She felt her equilibrium threatened. But then a kind of excitement steadied her. Standing so close to a beginning filled her with hope, she took a deep breath in sympathy and willed and willed with all her heart that the woman could keep it up, keep it up.

She knew she was ignorant of what birth was, she knew more about death, but that didn't mean she could not wish with all her might, and that these wishes could not impart spirit. She peeped out from behind Matron's back. Mrs Johnstone opened her eyes and caught the look that was passing over Honora's face. As if in answer to it she screamed, 'I will, I will,' then emitted two more shouts.

'Almost there, almost there,' Matron said in mantra. 'Almost there.'

And a rounded head with hair on it began to appear. Honora wanted to move but couldn't. She felt rooted to the spot, shaken by small sobs of joy. The baby slid out in time with what now seemed like skirls of joy from Mrs Johnstone. A baby girl, whose address would never be Desertcreat, County Tyrone, was born.

Mr Johnstone was brought in. Any secret worries he might have had about this extra responsibility were well and truly buried, his mouth turned up in a smile that was glorious for those who beheld it. Mrs Johnstone lay back exhausted.

Charles ordered a tasty treat to be prepared for her. 'Some arrowroot too,' he said, 'and plenty of sugar in the tea.'

On his way to see the cook and check with the sub matrons that nothing untoward had happened, Charles looked out over the deck to thank God. It was a moment that did not have the formal recitation of prayers, but was no less profound. He noticed a large group of porpoises diving to their own joy. He would have to tell Bridget about them tomorrow.

CHAPTER 13

The *Thomas Arbuthnot* was fifty-seven days at sea when Christmas came around. More than halfway, Charles hoped. The weather was not always clement coming up to the day itself, the girls often having to walk barefoot to better plant their feet on deck. It so happened that the day coincided with being well off the Cape of Good Hope. Charles had not made too much fuss about that when showing the map the last time, wary after the issue of the stars had caused some distress. Perhaps it was best not to highlight the profound parts of their geography. The bad weather, the buffeting about, the wet decks, all called for their own concentration. Honora thought she could now determine when a new storm was gathering, when the boat would begin to tip this way and that. Sometimes she longed that she might sleep through one, it would mean one less to go. Because like labour shouts, there can only be so many storms in one journey. Honora had learned much that might be useful for her new life.

For Christmas Day, there would be extra cooking, and Charles intended to include the girls in as much of it as possible. In fact, all week girls had been taking turns helping to prepare puddings and other small treats. Still, it would be displeasing if the change in routine allowed any slips in behaviour, so care had to be taken to put a stop at the reasonable end of excitement. But it would be an opportunity for the girls to show what they had learned in their cooking classes and how well they could now serve the tables. Matron had said he would be surprised. And Matron was not one to give praise lightly.

'I think you will be very surprised,' she said.

All these plans were working out well, which was why Charles was particularly agitated by the previous night's noise. The day had gone as normal. The heaving of the boat had given way to a surprisingly pleasant slipping along, the creaking of the timbers kept time with the steady pace. Fifty girls had baths that morning, the noises coming from under the bath tent had been as usual – the cantankerousness of some melting into the water with resignation, shouts of glee emanating from those who loved the ritual. Charles had attended to a few loose ends, which had been put aside because of the recent temperamental weather. The talk was of Christmas and it seemed lighthearted enough. The girls had grouped in small numbers to prepare for their usual dancing, he thought. There hadn't seemed to be any particular dangerous emotion afoot.

Charles was leaving the deck to go to his quarters when he heard one of the older girls shouting out to the sea. Her face was not towards the deck. She was hollering so loudly the words could be heard perfectly by all who stood ready to dance. Her voice even carried above the sound of sail and water and wood. In fact, it seemed caught in the wood, as if the timber was echoing it back to her.

'The ship has well rounded the corner now. There's no going back.'

He heard that much. He had specifically decided not to do the map that day. But clearly his teaching had led to learning of its own, which in normal circumstances might have gladdened him.

She followed with another wail of a sentence – she seemed to start high and go low. It was hard to know what effect, if any, that she intended to have by making this noise. But hot on its heels followed the slowest, lowest, moan, which moved up first one pitch, then swelled into a second, gathering a scream under its echo, and rising further, if that were possible, into the most ferocious howling. Everyone was now involved in these gutturals, weeping for their lost land and their families, immersed in their threnody. Charles stood rooted to the spot, helpless in the face of this terrible sound, the hairs standing up on his neck. It would have to stop. It seemed to him to be the erasure of hope. The tone was eerie, poignant and frightening at the same time. The parts of the singing – if that's what you could call it – melted into a chorus. Then the first girl began another stanza, which moved up ahead of what all the others were now singing. He saw a wildness and a mournfulness about them that he had not perceived before. As he watched, it moved down again to a harmonious note in a doleful tone. It seemed to him – suddenly aware he was an outsider – that the sound was splitting time itself and pushing a canyon into it. Perhaps if he left them the sound would die of its own accord, fade out on the wind. But it continued, seeming to have no end in sight, so he stepped in for fear of where it might lead, because how could such a wailing not end in disaster?

'It's only a *caoineadh*,' a girl beside him said. 'A lament. It won't do you any harm.'

'That's the *gol*,' said another, as the chorus started again and appeared to be passed from one set of girls to another.

He would have to act. He galvanised the sub matrons, one of whom had joined in herself.

'Break them into smaller groups. Now,' he said, harshly.

He ordered the sub matrons to pick selected girls and warn them that there would be no pudding tomorrow if this noise did not cease immediately.

He called some others to him with the intention of encouraging them to laugh at the wailers. He saw this as a possibility because one girl had started to do that herself without his prompting.

'But they don't mean any harm to you, sir.'

It didn't matter. They would have to stop. He told more girls about the danger of the pudding. Gradually the noise subsided. Thank God. The last few who were still lost on the sound came abruptly to an end and looked at him strangely. But what puzzled Charles most was that in the next moment, having looked at him with a certain amount of resignation, the girls, led by the three who were last to stop, burst into a loud joyous song and ran together into the middle, kicking their feet this way and that, hitting their heels off the wood and laughing loudly.

'See, it's all right,' the girl beside him said.

And in a flash he saw an understanding that was much too old for her, almost as if she was forgiving him something.

Later in the night Bridget Joyce took ill. She raved in fever. She spoke in tongues.

'That's not tongues, it's Irish,' Honora Raftery said, when Charles voiced his concern about not being able to understand what the patient was saying. She wanted to pick flowers. Daisies.

'I want daisies.'

'But there are no daisies at sea. It's not possible, Bridget. But you'll get daisies when we get there. Honestly you will,' Honora consoled.

'Are there daisies in Australia?' she whispered to Charles. She did not want to lie to Bridget.

They cooled her forehead with damp cloths, and gradually a semblance of normality returned to her body. It was the wailing noise, he knew, that had brought it on, but decided not to labour the point, best leave it be. When Bridget finally drifted into a mumbling sleep, Charles picked his way quietly to check as many girls as he could, without waking those who were already asleep, having tired themselves in a terrible emotion.

Christmas Day was needed after that. Although Charles felt a little shaky, the girls appeared to have put the experience behind them. In fact, they acted as if nothing untoward had happened and gradually the almost total cheerfulness of the group lent its support to him. He too got on with making the best possible day out of this. The captain made a ceremony out of giving him a present and the matrons were then given their gifts by both the captain and Charles: a leg of mutton from the captain, a bottle of wine from Charles. He made five bucketfuls of punch to help the spirits of everyone over yesterday and into the present, today, and the future, tomorrow. No more mention was made of wailing.

The food was even better than expected, with unparalleled variety. As well as the originally planned menu, the cook had harvested anything that might make this a special meal. One of the crew had again hooked a shark and it had been cooked – it was a strong, rich, white fish, well cooked in butter. There were also some small birds that had been caught in the rigging. The girls both helped and served to a very high standard, he thought, and he allowed them to stay up until after ten o'clock, making moderate noise. Their conversation rose and fell in pleasant time with the noise of their travels. Then, without fuss, they went to bed with no further incident.

'That's the first one,' Anne Sherry whispered.

'Shh. Let's not think about that,' Honora whispered back.

CHAPTER 14

The ship headed for its last stretch, Charles more aware of this than his charges. In many ways they had become used to the boat, and although at moments they longed to be off it, collectively they now lived as if this journey had no end. Charles knew this state of affairs would change. But not just yet. There was still time to be done and the calmer they remained the better. Meanwhile, the girls got on with making the quilt. That too had developed at a good pace. Girls who had wanted to be dogmatic about the way their mothers had done it had given up. Either they had realised that everyone was entitled to do their square – even if some of them were uneven and perhaps marred the overall look – or else they had decided that their desire for the greatest colours and matches would have to wait until they were doing their own in their new home. Some girls knew that the quilt didn't look perfect, but they couldn't point out where it had gone wrong, which patch sat up too high or had ungainly stitches.

'But if you hold it far enough away you can't see the mistakes,' Anne Sherry said. She still stayed close to Honora Raftery, but not so close it was noticeable and she ventured opinions more often now.

'And it's not supposed to be as even as embroidery.'

Julia Cuffe had become more sullen.

'Why won't you dance anymore, Julia?'

'I'm saving myself, amn't I, for when there's men.'

Charles wrote in his diary that again nothing untoward

had happened for the last few days and they were making fair speed. He looked at the pages and noticed how sparse and perfunctory his entries had become. He was wondering why that was when Matron called for him – he should have known never to presume there was not a drama waiting to erupt.

'One of the boys from the Kildare family has swallowed a pin'.

'Swallowed a pin! Oh for God's sake how did he do that? Never mind, the how is not important now.'

Charles gave him plenty of biscuits to eat and then a sharp emetic. That would sort the matter out. His brother, upset at the attention not being given to him, asked if he could go to see the girls' quarters, so Charles, in a fit of amusement took him down.

'Now, here they are.'

The boy was suddenly quiet, not so brave now, faced with so many girls, who rose to the occasion and decided to have a little revelry. Even the quietest of them got a pinch in, but quickly snatched their hands behind their backs, looking all innocent. The boy said, 'Thank you,' quickly, clearly having realised that his request may not have been such a good plan. He went upstairs and advised the other boys not to want to go there. The pin was passed by now. He thought it better to talk about that and ask his brother if it had been sore.

Then there was another storm. Short but sharp. The girls were giddy because it ended so quickly. It began at noon but was over before the bell was rung for tea. The cook had kept some of the midday meal, which had not been touched, and which they ate now. As they walked over the newly holystoned deck, they delighted that the storm was over.

'That was so short.'

'Maybe they'll stop altogether now.'

Girls rustled into their beds, mostly content. Some were beginning to think ahead, those who would be worriers. Sleep was descending when a girl called Rose in the far corner jumped from her bed and started to cry. Another went to her aid, but this second girl began to cry louder.

'Rose Larkin is dying, Rose Larkin's dying,' she wept.

Honora and Anne rushed over. They were older and knew what was happening. This was not the first time this scene had occurred on the journey, but it was the first time that it had happened at night. It was surprising that the younger girls had not become aware, but it was also surprisingly possible to hold on to certain privacies, even in their cramped conditions.

'Shssh, she's not dying. She's not dying.'

'She is, she is, she's bleeding to death. Look at her blanket. Rose Larkin's dying.'

Rose Larkin waited to hear what Honora Raftery and Anne Sherry would say. Then she would know if she was dying or not.

Cissy Weir shouted, before Honora could get her explanation properly ordered, 'That's just a thing girls get.'

'What thing.'

'There're rags for it.'

'What thing?'

Rose Larkin had stopped sniffing now, she was glad she was not dying. Her first helper was silent, glad that there were other girls who did not know what was going on. She hid behind their questions. But what thing could it be?

'It's a thing some girls get. What's it called?'

'It's a thing all girls get.'

'All girls! Don't be silly.'

'But what is it?'

Then Matron arrived, to Honora's relief. Someone must

have run for her. Matron told the girls to go back to sleep and went and sat on the side of Rose's bed and whispered an explanation to her. She did not want the younger ones to know before they needed to. Yet as she sat there she wondered if maybe it would not be best coming from her before they went to their new lives, because there was no guarantee they would be told with even a modicum of kindness. Luck would decide that – who hired them or who didn't.

Charles continued to write in his diary. He wrote about recaulking and winds and speeds and how to keep decks dry and private words about the captain. He grumbled on the pages that he had had to replace some of the upper boards on the fore lattice work to prevent some of the girls from talking too much with the sailors. He didn't mind a small amount of talking when it was necessary and fruitful even. They would have to mix with men very soon, unprotected by a father or a brother or a mother. Though not too much talking yet, not on his watch. But his annoyances were short-lived. He noted that Bridget Joyce was beside herself with joy when an albatross landed on the deck. There were hot days, wet days, light winds, cloudy sultry days, bad travelling days and days when great progress was made. Gradually the time of their sailing was shedding itself.

As the time rounded into the last week, little disturbances manifested themselves. But Charles knew these were not an actual return to original behaviours, but more a result of fear and nervousness. All in all, his girls were much better behaved than when first boarding. They had acquired many good habits and some had even mastered literacy beyond his wildest hopes. He counted the achievements, while still preparing for the impatience and apprehension that seeing land would bring. And as it began to come into his sights he blessed them, truly his girls now.

'Land ho! Land ho!' a sailor shouted.

'You can see it, you can see it. In the distance you can see it,' a second voice, that of a girl, was heard shouting at five in the morning. And a huge rush came out of beds.

'Wake up, Honora, you can see it.'

And sure enough, up on deck, you could see the faintest glimpse of lights twinkling as the dawn gathered itself together. They were afraid to be sure. As the sun rose, definite traces of earth could be seen, a line that had to be land. Full dawn came and lit up the entire world. No one wanted to have breakfast in case by turning away to go inside the land too would turn its back. But Charles insisted. And as they trooped in they looked different somehow, there was expectation on their faces.

These were the last days at sea and they had a bewildering busyness about them – seeing places in the distance that Charles or the matrons named for them and paying special attention to their washing and trying to contain themselves.

'I can smell things from the land,' a girl said. And sure enough others smelt them then too.

Unfortunately they would have to go around Van Diemen's Land, the wind not favouring them. When they saw the south-east tip of it, he took the time to spread the map out again.

'Van Diemen's Land, my uncle's there,' Julia Cuffe said.

The other girls looked at her with new curiosity. Charles momentarily thought of the history of some of his charges. But that was before and there was too much else to be done now. They sighted the Mewstone. They passed between the Eddystone and land. Charles pinned the map up again. Julia Cuffe was not to be seen when he was doing this and then he heard a shout. He ran on deck. She was standing below a sail shouting at the land.

'Can you see me, can you see me?' she bellowed.

Charles went to her, uncertain how to approach this outburst.

She turned to him, laughing hysterically and now screaming, 'You'll not make a good girl out of me.'

He did manage to calm her but decided that punishment might make the issue worse. He put the map away – it had a habit of causing trouble. Then there was the Pillar Rock.

'Van Diemen's Land, I know that one,' said one latecomer to the news.

Charles relented and put the map back up.

'There's not many names there,' Anne Sherry said, pointing to a long stretch.

The wind had now become baffling, leading to incipient frustration. The waters went calm. The girls watched the sea. They peered out, hands shading their eyes to see more land. Once seen it was a severe disappointment if a mist or a change of direction took it away from them. Charles would have to arrange a new way of keeping order because the excitement had lent a certain carelessness to the washing and keeping clean of the decks. He did not want the cleanliness, so hard achieved, to fall at the last hurdle. A foul gale then blew up and the girls were sent back down. That night those who could not sleep heard the crew worrying about the martingale stay chain, which had broken and was endangering the flying jib boom, the boom and the foretop mast. They were trying to forget these words.

'You can see The Heads. Mr Strutt said you can see The Heads,' Honora told them the following morning, unsure of what she was speaking about, yet wanting to believe that The

Heads might be a good sign.

The ship moved on. It rounded into the choppy water. They could see yellow sand and trees, so many trees. Some had green tops, some white. This getting closer was watched quietly. The birds, dressed in the most spectacular colours, began to arrive. Bridget Joyce grew flushed with awe. Matron called the girls to assemble to present their quilt to Mr Strutt. Everyone was very proud.

Now there was the final cleaning and washing, the taking up of trunks, the airing and viewing of clothes. The water shimmered, not like sea at all. You could imagine touching land.

'We're in,' came a short shout. And then the most bewildering thing of all happened, on Sunday 3 February 1850, the ship came to anchor near Garden Island, just as dusk was settling.

'You can take your cutlery, plate and linen bags with you.'

'Can we? Really?'

'Yes, I think you can say they're yours now.'

'Thanks.'

They tidied them away, the first of personal property, other than clothes, ever to come to them.

There were sounds of people boarding, and the girls went quiet. The inspectors began to check the state of the ship and were truly astonished. They eyed the girls. The girls eyed them back. The inspectors set up a table where complaints could be taken. They knew this could take some days to accommodate. No one came to the table. The doctor came and declared that all was well with the girls and whispered under his breath it was a pity he couldn't have said that about the other ships.

Charles Strutt said, pleasure all over him, 'They are fatter now.'

CHAPTER 15

With much noise and shouting, Charles Strutt's girls came off the *Thomas Arbuthnot* into small boats. As they rowed away, some of them looked back at their big boat before gradually turning their eyes towards land.

'I didn't know that a ship could go through water like that.'

Others turned to look at the girl who had said this. She blushed.

'I mean before,' she said, 'but I do now,' and she too turned to look at the approaching land.

'If we survived that we'll survive anything,' another said.

'We're young,' Honora said, like an old person.

When they reached the quay a man checked them off a list just as when they had boarded so long ago. But this time the unsteadiness in their feet was caused by solid ground – how it came up to meet the soles of their feet, which were now used to the movement of water. They looked at where their shoes landed. They were wiser too. They had lived an unlikely ninety-nine days and nights. And they were fatter.

'Or at least not thinner,' Honora said to herself, running her fingers down her ribcage.

The going through the door of the boat had been different in another way – Charles knew them, knew their names. He did perhaps call out Bridget too often.

Honora, Anne and Bridget stayed close together. Julia

meandered off for moments but kept them in her sights.

'Well there we go now, Australia,' she said to herself.

The new noises were overwhelming – shouting and scraping as the trunks were hauled out. Honora remembered Plymouth, but only for a brief few seconds. Charles called for the girls to stay together and near him. There was no need. They had no intention of wandering far from him.

After further discussions with the captain, Charles lined the girls up, three in a row. He arranged for the sub matrons to be sprinkled among them and started the walk towards Hyde Park Barracks, he himself leading the way. A sort of chatter grew, ebbed and flowed in semi-tones, and sometimes went quiet to allow a loud bird to squawk in answer.

'What's that?' Anne Sherry squealed, pointing behind a bush.

'What's what?'

'It's gone,' she said, deciding not to trust her description of what she thought she had seen.

'It was like an animal with a baby's face. I think. But it had fur over its eyes. I think …'

'No it wasn't, couldn't have been. Don't be silly.'

Maybe she had just imagined it.

'What's *that?*' a girl screamed.

Bridget trained her eyes towards the sky and the tops of the trees, and what she saw there took her breath away.

The girls coiled up the street, their hats bobbing and flashing colour. When they came to the gate of the barracks, Charles lined them up in a straight row. Some stared in wonderment, some in fear, at the imposing building. Little spurts of fright were kept under control. This is where their feet would tread the same footsteps as Caroline Chisholm, of whom they still knew nothing. Charles led them to the dormitory where iron beds had now replaced the convict furnishings, although a few hammocks still swung from the rafters.

'What's that?' Anne Sherry whispered.

'I don't know,' Honora said, suddenly tired and overwhelmed by all she didn't know.

The room was big, so big, the girls having now become used to bending their bodies to fit the boat. Their voices bounced off the walls. The echoes came back to them. Charles waited until all of them had been assigned a bed before he explained that he would now be leaving them in the care of the authorities.

'But you're not leaving us for good?' a girl asked.

'No. I'll be back tomorrow,' Charles replied.

That would have to do for now. He would have to tell them gradually that he would not be here with them, that he would only oversee their relocation into their new lives.

'He'll be going back,' Julia said.

'Shh ...' Honora said.

The authorities – men and women the girls did not know – ushered in people of the Catholic cloth, among them a priest to remind the girls of their fast obligations now that they were not at sea and to hear their confessions. But what could these girls have to confess?

Charles walked out the gate and set off to visit people he knew – officials, dignitaries, and an old emigrant from his previous ship whose address he had. He did not look back, best not to. He needed a plan for these few days. Sudden idleness would contrast too much with the last three months, and anyway, he was used to plans by now. He gazed at the animals around – they seemed to be performing for him. He would have liked to touch some of the smaller ones, but thought it safer not to. Charles enjoyed the walk, loved having his feet on the ground. He tried not to think about the girls. They were in safe hands now. At least until the hiring began.

Back at the barracks the girls made new arrangements among themselves, mindful of the order required for the smooth running of large numbers. Those among them who needed it were worried about the lack of a safe place to dispose of their menstrual rags, and so hid them under the floorboards as best they could, where they would live with the rodents for many years, undiscovered until renovations were undertaken one hundred years from now. Living in rooms, on land, had to have its own rules too, and they used what they had learned on the ship to calm the beating of their hearts. And they tried to sleep.

'Are you all right?' Anne whispered to Honora.

'I think so. I'm going to see tomorrow if I can write to Florrie.'

'I'm not going to write to anyone,' Anne said. 'I don't see what good it would do.'

'Will we be able to walk outside?' a voice whispered.

Another said, 'If it's not too hot, I think so, but not far. You wouldn't want to go far.'

'Go far? Well, that's something to be worried about now,' said Julia.

In the morning the nuns called again to continue their praying, some of the girls wishing the prayers to be over so they could rush out and see Charles who they had just seen coming to the door. They wanted to ask him about the rumour of Yass – where was that and how many were going?

'One hundred and eight,' he said.

'And it's not only Yass, it's Gundagai and places around there. More or less south-west of here. Now remember, we will have to travel by horse and cart on road or track, for a number of days and nights, possibly two weeks.'

One hundred and thirty hands were raised. Wherever he thought fit to bring them would be all right by them.

'We will be sleeping in tents, which will be put together as best we can. And we will be travelling through bushland,' Charles said, hoping to change some minds but only two girls put their hands down. Charles would now have to choose who of the surplus twenty or so would stay in Sydney.

He called them to him – he tried to choose girls who had lived in towns, he would prefer to get their agreement rather than tell them they must stay here.

Anne Sherry said she definitely wanted to stay in the city. Honora Raftery looked surprised.

'Would you not prefer to go to a place in the country?'

Anne looked embarrassed. She turned her eyes away from Honora.

'No, I'd prefer to stay here,' she said.

Julia Cuffe had not volunteered – she was still moving about around the edges, sometimes quiet, sometimes making scoffing noises. Charles thought that Bridget Joyce might be better here, he would talk to Anne Sherry about that, now that she too would be in Sydney. There were other Bridgets who would suit life in this growing city better perhaps than the country. Molly Plunkett had cried, 'But I want to go to the country. Maybe it will be better ...'

'But it will be a rough journey, with the possibility of bushrangers. And many of the places for work will be very far from others, not like here.'

'What are bushrangers?'

'Like pirates on the land,' another girl answered. She was still at sea.

'But it might be like home,' Molly said, and cried again when she said the word.

'Molly, you're terrible silly, it won't be like home ...'

But another girl added, 'Well, it might be more like home ...'

Charles would also have to see if any were needed in Brisbane, and if so who they would be.

The hiring of the girls chosen to remain in town now began in earnest. A woman came to the landing and ushered the first six down the stairs. Wearing their bonnets, the girls nervously went into the room set aside for the purpose of viewing. One girl cried, others looked on with hope on their faces. That man seemed nice, that woman appeared kind.

A tall robust man came into the hall.

'I want one of them, no two of them. Find me two,' he bellowed in a voice that carried to the ceiling.

He had decided to take on the editor of the *Herald*, who had again lambasted the orphan girls. That was how he would show him – hire two of his own.

'Yes, Commissioner,' said the woman directing the girls.

Charles might have liked to make a suggestion, but the authorities here preferred to make their own judgments. In the room the hirers looked the girls up and down, checked their references, spoke some words. More girls were brought down. Some of them looked at the floor. Some dared to raise their faces – Julia Cuffe looked one and all straight in the eye. Anne Sherry was the first chosen for the commissioner, and Rose Larkin the second. They were led out and up the stairs again and more girls were brought down. One of them was crying.

'What's wrong with you?' a matron asked, trying to put some care into her voice.

'Nothing. It's just that at home the animals don't kill you.'

'Who has been telling you nonsense?'

'No, it's all right,' the girl snuffled. 'I'll learn which animals to stay away from.'

'Good girl. Now dry your eyes and come down with me,' Matron said, and led her into the room of hirers.

A ritual of goodbyes began. Despite being fearful, they always ended with an expression of hope for each other and themselves. Then the girl walked out with her trunk, her bonnet firmly on, beside a man who would be her new master. Most of them did not look back when they came to the street – perhaps because they forgot, now being taken up with new thoughts, or perhaps because they were afraid to show what was on their faces to anyone who might be there watching. One by one they went, until it was time for Charles to ready his charges who were travelling to Yass, Gundagai, and places on the way if they were needed. And maybe a little further. There was plenty of work to be done. There were new settlers and men who had freedom now, who had gained squatters' rights and had houses to run. And there were banks opening and hotels that could have a girl in the kitchen. But not in the bar, he would not allow that. There were many Irish there already in these places, places that Charles had never even heard of. This would be good for the girls.

'How many Irish?'

'Some. I'm not sure.'

But plenty of work, of that he was sure. This was why the request had been made. The remaining girls now put on their bonnets firmly and walked out of Hyde Park Barracks.

CHAPTER 16

The first night of the journey was spent on a steamer to Parramatta, on water so unlike the open sea, on a ship so unlike their own. At Parramatta they stayed in a depot, an old convict barracks quite like Hyde Park.

'Another barracks,' a girl said, 'you'd think we'd done something wrong.'

'But we've got a big room, look at the space,' Honora Raftery said.

'I suppose you're right,' a voice from behind her replied.

She missed Anne Sherry and Bridget. She even missed Julia.

In the morning they collected fourteen drays to be drawn by teams of horses over half-roads, roads, and no roads, to their final destinations. Honora, for the first time in months, thought it smelt like home – horses smell the same. But best not to think about things like that. Food would have to be cooked, a rota organised for eating. These familiarities were welcome to the girls and they organised themselves into groups. Charles told them that care would have to be taken about biting insects – those dangerous and those not – although who could possibly know which was which.

'We'll learn,' Honora said.

Oh, you will, Charles thought, more than you can imagine. He laid down the rules of their journey and no girl thought to disagree. Provisions for the first few days were collected. Honora was put in charge of keeping the food as cold as possible.

'We will stop at various places to replenish our stock,' Charles said.

Sleep was fitful and disturbed that first night on the road, the open air was strangely more frightening than a ship at sea. Horses made their own noises too, adding to the peculiar bush sounds. The sounds came from all directions. And just when it seemed they could agree on a direction and what they might be, they merged into one unfamiliar cacophony coming from everywhere.

'The animals are all different.'

'Will there be no animals like at home?'

'Maybe rabbits. That's all I think.'

'The man said there are no rabbits here,' another girl whispered. 'Nor daisies,' she added.

They thought about that, and decided they could get used to that too, along with everything else.

The compensations of more room for movement soon became apparent. It was a strange feeling to be able to walk a distance from the other girls – keeping them in view at all times of course. And it was at night that they learned just how different the stars were. Now they were on land and had ground below them, you would think some of the sky would be the same.

'But it's a different hemisphere. Remember the map, can you remember the map?'

They could.

'Remember when we crossed the equator? Well, since then we have been in the Southern Hemisphere.'

'I see.'

'There are only two hemispheres, isn't that right, ours and here?'

'Yes, that's right.'

So for the next two weeks, Charles and the girls wound their way across the strange-coloured country. There were different ways of dealing with this – wanting to know how long the journey was to be or not wanting to know. The girls stared at the never-ending tree-covered hills, smelled scents of dryness, and tried to cool themselves as best they could. They watched the animals that came close and they learned to sleep at night, lulled by noises that did not now frighten them unduly, even if they did not reassure them either. There was always something new to the eye or ear or nose.

During their journey they were to encounter an obstacle. One dray was passing another when a harness loosened and the two horses collided. Two girls jumped, or were thrown, and a wheel went over them. The two injured girls had to be left behind in Camden in the care of a medical officer. Charles did not like this one bit. He would have to write to the girls and keep their spirits up. He was very suspicious of the local surgeon magistrate, but he had no choice. All he could do was try to keep in touch. He supposed that they could now be hired close to Camden once they had recovered.

The journey continued. The fourteen drays following the one in front, each with its complement of girls watching the strangeness of this new country – the shape of the hills perhaps, which sloped and stretched as far as the eye could see, or the colour of the trees.

'White. It is white. Who ever saw a white tree?'

'Well, now you have.'

'And check your shadow, it falls a different way here.'

But no one could remember how it had fallen at home.

The heat was dry and thirst was ever-present and fresh water was not easily acquired. They saw their first kangaroos, emus, wallabies and wombats. Charles and the men named them as best they could. Girls laughed uproariously as they watched the kangaroo leaping past them in the most ridiculous bounds they could have imagined. But the grace and speed mesmerised them. Yet laugh was what they did most – put their hands over their mouths and shriek with excitement that such an animal could exist. It was the birds that astonished them most. Particularly the parrots, the cockatoos and the lorikeets. Luckily Charles had learned some of their names. When they talked of birds they thought of Bridget Joyce, who had been hired out to a magistrate in Sydney. And in the talking they hoped she was well. She was one of the girls for whom Charles feared most. He could not bear to think too much of what might go wrong for her. He would check on her when he got back to the city. But the girls couldn't keep thinking of the others they had left behind in Sydney, it might make them think of the fact that they too were nearing the day when they would be left behind. It was best to keep gloom at arm's length. They knew that well now.

And there were more troubles. Rain made some of the tracks so wet that horses fell. Girls got sick, though not as sick as at sea, and they soon got better. One horse left for good, wandered off in the night. Still, progress was made.

The girls saw their first black people. The sight caused them less astonishment than Charles had expected – it was just another new thing. They collected new things with ease now. And until someone tried to make them believe otherwise, they had no more reason to fear a man who was black than a man who was white.

Picton and Mittagong were left behind. Then on through

Berrima and across Paddy's River, which caused much merriment and wonder. Who could it be named for? Then Marulan and Goulburn. Charles wrote in his diary 'One of the girls discovered a relative, so naturally we left her there. I like the town, even though I was not predisposed to the place, having read one of the editorials'.

A few more girls were needed too. It was here that one of the better readers found out what the local newspaper had printed about them. One of the men driving the horses must have had a paper. An ex-convict could be well learned.

'This is about us,' she said, more in amazement than hurt.

The words – barefoot little country beggars – like the ones Charles had read before, were altogether unseemly, insulting and untrue. He did his best to explain the tirade away.

'It's as much to do with a fight between here and London,' he said. 'Some people here think they might end up with too many dependents, which London should be caring for. You are caught in the middle of that argument.'

'Why would that make them say this?' She hit the paper with the back of her hand, a gesture that had been done by her father before he had died.

'It's difficult to understand, I know,' Charles said.

'Not for me it's not,' the girl replied.

Charles did not answer – he did not exactly understand her inflections. But he did get the girl to promise not to divulge such useless words to the others.

So their cavalcade went through Gunning, showing bits of colour and bonnet here and there.

On the evening of 1 March 1850, the caravan of horses and girls pulled up three miles outside Yass beside the blue river. As they had been rounding the hill down into the beginnings of the town, Charles had pointed it out to them.

'We'll stay there tonight and you will have plenty of water to dress for tomorrow.'

But when they came to the river it was not quite so blue as it had looked from a distance. Still, it was water, and easy to approach for washing. Charles let the girls stretch a little while he checked his own belongings, wrote in his diary and put full stops where he had hurried and been careless before. With the help of the horse drivers he then assembled the boxes. Privacy was garnered in whatever way possible, so that the girls could wash, dickey up their faces and make the best possible entrance into the town. They made a lot of noise doing this, filling the air with nervous excitement.

'Are you ready?' Charles called, after what seemed like enough time. They came out from behind the makeshift curtains. Some of them looked beautiful, milling around the river, but they wouldn't have known that. It would have been better to have a room for the washing, and yet maybe this public baptism together was a good way to begin their new lives. Honora patted the dress of the girl beside her.

'I like your dress,' she said, as if they had many of them.

'Are you nervous?' the girl asked.

This was a more unusual question than might have been expected. These girls had an understanding that they must indeed be nervous, but that mentioning it might not be such a good idea. The other girl might be calm that day, and upsetting this would not be appreciated. But then again, the worst had already happened, so now was the time to hope, maybe? And if that day was a day of hope, it certainly would not be good to be reminded that it was not so for everyone else.

'I am a bit,' Honora said, 'but I would like to be there, not still going to be there.'

She repeated to herself what she'd just said to see if she understood it, to see if it made sense.

The other girl said she wasn't nervous now. She was busy mapping out love already. After the period of consistent meals, an optimism had begun to shine on her with every rising sun.

'But I prefer our porridge,' another said, as if this might be her last chance to be understood.

'You'll get used to the other,' they chorused, comfortingly.

'I know,' she agreed sadly.

And the girls set to putting their best foot forward. Bonnets and dresses again strode into the streets. People came to look. The line of girls moved towards their lodgings.

Over the next few days the hiring began. Men and women walked into the room and surveyed what they saw, picked what they wanted. A girl for here in Yass, two girls there, three there, a girl further out. Mr Corliss came into the room. He looked, but only a little, it seemed rude to look too long at girls with bonnets on, most of whom were looking at the floor. Mr Corliss preferred to speak to that superintendent man as a way of doing business.

'I'll take Honora Raftery,' he said.

'Yes,' Charles said.

He hoped it was the right place for her. Mr Corliss certainly seemed civil enough.

As he did with all the girls, Charles spoke to Honora alone before she left.

'Is there anything you'd like?'

'I'd like a dictionary,' she said. She had been thinking about that in the classes on the boat, but had forgotten until now. 'And a map,' she added, remembering the shape of her home.

'No, I mean at this moment, is there anything you need?'

'No. I'm all right, I think.'

Honora walked away from the hiring room. She wondered too long about whether she should look back, and by the time she had decided she would, they had crossed the hill and it was impossible to see the barracks.

The following morning Charles felt an emptiness – it was inevitable that some of the girls would have become more a part of the every day than others. He would have to organise some entertainment for himself this evening, something to lift his spirits. He would accept the invitation to the Catholic priest's house. The man was more cultured and humorous than his Protestant counterpart, and while Charles would find some way to accommodate both, this evening he needed levity.

On the morning, two unwelcome advances for wives had to be dealt with, and this was done swiftly. Charles Strutt's desires for his girls had to be reiterated. Not every man to arrive with thoughts of marriage would be suitable. More farewells had to be performed, and the number of his charges dwindled. Pastors, priests, businessmen – some fine, some doubtful – were visited and sized up. Two girls went to Ryan's out at Galong.

'That's the best place.'

'No, I heard he was cross.'

The underground movement of rumour had untold pieces of information already gathered – as if the news flew in on the clouds that passed over them. The numbers dwindled even further. Forty girls had now been hired and fifteen promised. It was time to head off towards Gundagai with the last forty-five.

After disposing of the surplus horses and letting go the

men who would no longer be needed, Charles set out. There were the further miles, the further mishaps, and some sore throats in a blazing heat. Through Bowning, Bogolong, Jugiong, and hence to Gundagai, where the hiring began again. One evening Charles wrote in his diary that there were only ten girls left. And some of them were for Wagga Wagga. And then there were four. Soon they too were gone. Charles could not bring himself to record the sentiment of his last farewell.

On his way back through Yass he was alarmed to hear from one of the horsemen at the barracks that Honora Raftery was missing. He rushed to the house of her employer, whom he discovered was also missing. He became deeply concerned. He sent for the cook. Much to his relief she told him that Honora's master had taken her to visit one of the other Irish girls, having become anxious about the depth of her loneliness, and thinking, correctly, that this visit would reassure her. Charles himself felt reassured by this. Surely these people would be good to her. He would have liked to have seen her, maybe checked what showed in her eyes. Perhaps another time.

Charles passed the church on his way out of Yass, having begun his journey back to Sydney. He foresaw weddings, christenings, and funerals at the end of what he hoped would be good lives. He wished prosperous and kind times for them. The troubles on the journey back were welcomed – diversions to help him with the necessary shedding of the lives he had now entrusted to strangers. The *Goulburn Herald* had a different story now. Good news of his girls was filtering through. He would post it to Honora Raftery at the earliest opportunity. She would somehow get the new story out.

CHAPTER 17

On the first morning of Honora Raftery's new life she was woken by strange noises. The kitchen was working itself into a clamor and the cook had decided to allow Honora to start late, but only today. The metal of pots hitting together and the cook's clearing of her night voice were both making inroads on the natural dawn sounds of outside. Soon the birds would have it all their own way. The sun was still shy, brightening the landscape gradually, throwing light benignly on corners that had darkened for the night, as yet showing no signs of the impending mercilessness that it would burn on people in only a few hours. Honora registered the noise of an approaching horse and shouts from the man on top of it. She knew she would have to rise now. Although she had become worried in the night, she got up and dressed as confidently as she could. She tried not to think of her mother and her father on this morning – the thought of them had more to do with the unveiling of her sleep than anything else, because her mother and her father had never been in this picture, had never seen any of these things out of their small window. They had not known the smells or the colours out here, or ever even had to live in a sustained manner in the language that was now making itself heard from the kitchen and the yard.

Honora walked across to where the kitchen was a little way from the house. She was lucky in her new place, which was modern for its time, the cooking was not done in the open fireplace in the hut where she was sleeping. The distance meant that if a fire started it could hopefully be controlled and not catch on to the entire dwelling and outhouses. It also gave Honora time to step straight forward – a girl could be blown about in life like chaff, but if she managed to walk properly she could catch on to something and it could become a solid thing. The kitchen had a bark roof and the smell of fire and oats was already coming out the door.

'Good morning.'

'There you are. It's the new Irish girl.'

'Indeed it is.'

'Well, let's get started.'

Honora was sent by Cook to collect wood. 'You'll see it easily.'

The wood was stacked beside an outhouse that had been built on a slight incline. There was another small hill beside it – she would go up there later to see what she could see. But that would have to wait. She examined the pile – the stack of old twigs and cones and strips of bark, which must surely be for starting the fire in the morning. She carried wood back, huge uneven blocks of it. And that was the right thing to do.

'Good on you, that will be a help. We needed that. Now here's soup to be got ready.'

The day went fast, what with getting more wood several times, handing food to Cook and cleaning pots and flat plates where candles were stuck. Honora was sore and tired by evening time. She did not know what time it was when Cook told her she could go to bed.

'You remember where it is, over there,' Cook pointed.

Honora trailed her legs across to the hut, lay on her bed and fell into a deep tired sleep, until she heard the horse again and the sound of the man on the horse shouting and the clanging of pots.

It was a week, maybe, before Honora ventured up the small hill. To her great delight she saw the straggled outskirts of Yass town, she had not realised she was so close. It was comforting to know there were other people not too far away. The hills heaped on top of each other, away and away. She could see the main street of the town, the hotel there. Coming along what was now her road, there were deserted houses, perhaps erected by someone for momentary shelter, or perhaps there had been more of a purpose to them and it had not worked out. Now they stood, scattered like fallen leaves, rusted and dried almost rotten, mostly unnoticed, unless a person was ruminating about things and accidentally saw them for what they might have been. Honora looked at them today and remembered the man from the London *Illustrated News* looking at their house. She had seen him take a pencil and draw. She didn't like it, certain he would not draw it as she would. But it was he who had been sent to draw their house, not her. Florrie did not like it either. But Honora could like these houses. Cook called from the door for more wood. Honora wondered what Charles Strutt might be doing. He had, after all, been a nice man.

CHAPTER 18

Over the last few days Charles Strutt had been visiting and checking on some of the most fearful girls. He called in to Hyde Park Barracks, hoping to find out that none of the girls had been returned, and to see what preparations were being made for the next bunch who were, at this moment, on the sea, not that it was any of his business. He wondered what would befall them. He heard of a court sitting that morning, just down the road, and decided to attend. It would be interesting to see how the law worked in this new place, to see if it would have grown its own necessary variations. Would the men in front of the judge have less fear because what more could be done to them, except of course the flogging. Bad business that, Charles thought.

The first cases being heard were what one would expect to find in a new colony that had on its streets ex-convicts not yet settled properly. Then came the worrying return of orphan girls, thankfully none from the *Thomas Arbuthnot*. The judge dealt with these in a disdainful fashion, showing little sympathy for the girls, but then bellowed at a Mr Arbuckle who was delivering back, with complaint, the girl who was working for him.

'Mr Arbuckle, this is the third girl you have returned. Am I to believe you are a very unlucky man to have procured three times, *three times*, an unsuitable and lazy housemaid?' He fumbled and found some papers. 'Yes, three times.'

Mr Arbuckle made to reply.

'That was merely a rhetorical question. I do not expect nor desire to have an answer from you. Understood?'

'Yes, Your Honour.'

'Am I to believe that this is your fate in life, such terrible luck, and yet you do not appear to me to be a person of ill fate. So this may lead me to believe it is you who is the problem. Could it be that you are an unreasonable employer?'

There was general laughter in the body of the courtroom. The judge glared and all went silent.

'So, Mr Arbuckle, I will indeed relieve you of this third girl. And perhaps this is her lucky day. I will also inform the authorities who deal with these orphans that you are not to be given any more. Next.'

The judge addressed the clerk, 'I suppose the next are from more drunkenness,' he said in a resigned tone of voice.

There followed more cases and Charles was about to leave when to his horror Julia Cuffe walked through the door. He put his head in his hands and remembered everything about her, everything that had gone wrong from the moment he had first become aware of her.

Julia Cuffe's first trouble came from her ability to mimic, she had tried it a few times in the first week on the ship. It had gone down well at home, before the sickness, so she thought it might get her small concessions once they had set sail. But there wasn't enough room. Nor room enough to create any other kind of trouble. She did try out various forms of diversion in classes, but Charles had removed her without ceremony. She was out the door before she could even figure who told on her. She always liked to know who told, even though she accepted that she had to be blamed. There always had to be someone to blame, it made others feel secure and superior. And that was her path, to be blamed, even if she wasn't at fault. Although she usually was, preferring all things that were forbidden.

'Just bad. She's just bad,' Matron had said.

But Charles had said, 'No.'

He thought that working in the kitchen might be the best for her. But she threw a pan at the wall. He moved her to the laundry room. He moved her to a scrubbing job. He moved her to helping Matron very early in the morning. He moved her to helping Matron very late at night. He moved her to the stern of the ship, to the middle of the ship, to the port of the ship.

'I'm at the back end this week,' she shouted. And laughed. 'Wait till I get to Australia – I'll show you back end!'

Although tempted, Charles did not move her to the hold.

On the morning before the ship was to dock, Charles had brought Julia to his quarters. He wanted this conversation to be had away from other, more fearful ears. And he wanted her to have some hours before landing to think about what he said.

'I wish I did not have to speak to you like this, Miss Cuffe.'

'Oh, forget the Miss.'

'Could you please try to listen, Miss Cuffe.'

'Fair enough.'

'There are strict laws where you are going, you will not survive if you continue to behave in this manner.'

'In what manner?'

'Please, Miss Cuffe. As you know I have tried to show you the rudiments of domestic service, which is what you will be required to give ...'

'Kitchens is that?'

'Yes, kitchens, if you will. And when you arrive, you will

be hired by people who will require you to have at least basic manners, of which you haven't shown much so far. Perhaps that's a little harsh, you may have …'

'Not a bit. Just don't go in for all that palaver. Could I not get a job outside the kitchens?'

'What kind of job?' Charles sighed.

'How would I know. You're the one who brought me here.'

'But you had a choice. You all had a choice, well you could have said no, I think …'

'Some choice.'

'Miss Cuffe …'

She was at it again, interrupting him as consistently as she had done in the first week.

'Miss Cuffe, it wasn't exactly me who choose you … Never mind. As I said, you will be required …'

'Require away. I'm not from Australia.'

'I know you're not. Now. But you are going to be.'

'Going to be from Australia! Don't be daft, begging your pardon, sir, as you say. But I couldn't be *going to be* from Australia.'

'Well, be that as it may, you will have to work.'

'I know that, sir, I'll find something.'

'But how will you find something. You will be a stranger here. There.'

'I thought you said I was going to be from there.'

'Miss Cuffe …'

'Sorry.'

'As I said, you will be a stranger, all right, let's say newly arrived. There are dangers.'

'I'm not afraid.'

'It's not a matter of whether you are afraid of those dangers or not. They're there.'

'These dangers ... What are they like? Are they the same as at home?'

'I have no idea with what dangers you have been acquainted in Ireland, so I cannot say.'

'Have you ever been to Ireland?'

'Well ...' Charles began. He thought that maybe he should say he had lived there for some time. Why was he allowing her to make him contemplate an untruth. 'Look, that is neither here nor there,' he said.

'Oh, but it is. If you've never been there how do you know what dangers we have, or whether they're different to the ones where I'm going.'

At this point, Charles was overcome with the futility of the exchange and decided to get his charge back with the other girls. He worried that perhaps he should have waited until the very last moment before speaking to her. There was now too much time for her to do damage to the others.

When Julia was at the door, he said, 'But really, there are dangers. And I don't want you to fall foul of them.'

'Don't worry, sir, I'll be all right.'

And maybe she would. And maybe she wouldn't.

She was the seventh girl to be hired, by a burly hotel owner who needed a girl for his kitchen.

As she left she said, 'Hey, Strutt, be careful.'

By the time she and her employer had reached the hotel, his eyebrows were up, wondering if perhaps he had not made a mistake. His wife should have come.

It wasn't the mimicking so much that the landlord minded, it was what it meant, what was behind it, what it signified. So he let her go. He dismissed her early in the day, so she would have light for a while. He might have passed her on, but decided not to inflict her on anyone he knew.

At the door, she raised her voice and howled out curses in a frightening language.

'That's enough,' the landlord shouted.

But still she roared.

'Shut up,' he screamed.

But she wouldn't. He ran after her and was going to hit her, when luck intervened and a policeman came by. They brought her to the magistrate. Whatever came over the landlord, he allowed the judge to convince him to give her a second chance.

'Now, young lady,' said the magistrate …'

'Young lady,' sniffed the landlord.

'You are, very kindly, being given a second opportunity here by your employer. Use it wisely. There are dangers out there, do you hear me?'

'Yes.'

'Yes, Your Honour.'

'Yes, Your Honour,' Julia repeated.

Luckily for Julia, the magistrate did not ask her any further questions, thus denying her the opportunity to make him remember her.

'Dangers,' he boomed.

The next time the landlord threw her out, he did so at night.

It is a known fact that everywhere, at any time, dangers are more plentiful at night. Julia made her way through the streets, at first more afraid than she had ever been. But she did not like being afraid, so she straightened her shoulders up and walked past what appeared to be only a few men. Some of them hooted and whistled after her, drowning out the silence of those who simply looked. She made it past them, the echoes of their suggestions making her ears hot. Still, there was always one thing she could do if she ever became hungry ...

In its way, it was dirty work, but it was work.

The next time Julia was brought before the same magistrate, he did not recognise her. And the clerk had forgotten to put her file in front to him.

What would your father think of you?' he mused.

'He's dead.'

'Be that as it may, keep him in your head.'

'But if I kept him in my head he'd clog me up, and I couldn't see.'

'What?'

'But, I'll tell you what, Your Honour. I have him with me. He's right behind me all the way.'

The magistrate fumed inwardly, but still, it was her first offence. She paid her fine.

The next time she appeared before him, charged with loitering, the clerk had remembered to place the file before him.

'Young lady. You were given a good and decent job ...'

'Your Honour, it was only pot walloping.'

The clerk, above and beyond the call of his duty, warned her with a look.

'You were given ...'

'A good and decent job,' Julia finished for him. 'And I never asked to be brought down here to the bowels of the earth for a *good and decent job*.'

The magistrate began to reply, then thought better of it. He dipped his pen in the ink, checked the veracity of a few particulars with the clerk, and wrote a note.

'It's Brisbane for you, young lady.' He bent his head. 'I am signing an order for you to be removed to Brisbane, perhaps you will do better there,' and the judge paused to write. 'What arrangements are there in place regarding the disposal of these girls in Brisbane?' the judge asked the clerk, with only the slightest trace of anxiety in his voice.

Charles winced at the word and wondered if there was anything he could do and then thought not. The clerk said that already many had gone to that city and he himself had not been informed of any huge problems. The judge handed the paper to the clerk.

Julia wasn't sure if she would obey the magistrate and see if Brisbane was any better than this kip, or if she'd give this place another go.

Charles slipped out the door to continue his visiting.

Four days later Charles set sail back home, where he remained for six months before taking his next journey over that sea. On the day he left, girls were burrowing into their lives in all sorts of homes, some happy for an occasional lengthening moment, some not. As he walked on to the ship, hearing the noises of preparation, it was impossible to say from looking at him whether he thought of them, just as it was also impossible to say if girls around this new city, or in Brisbane or in the towns of Yass and Gundagai and thereabouts, stopped what they were doing for a moment, feeling that some tie in them had been broken.

CHAPTER 19

One year to the day after the landing of the *Thomas Arbuthnot*, Honora Raftery got married. A little fast, it may have been thought, but she had found a man who was not unlike her dead father, so there was no need to wait. He was not of the same religion as her, nor indeed of the same nationality, but who was there to tell her that this might be unwise? But how like her father – and who would have thought that possible? Her employer was sad to see her go, so sad that he thought some arrangement could be made to keep her living nearby and maybe providing occasional help, until the children started arriving.

Honora's husband-to-be was a little concerned as their wedding day approached. His late marriage had not to do with a lack of heart, more a lack of opportunity. He had been hopeful on meeting Honora, and was well pleased when she said yes, and even more so when Honora's employer blessed them. But having gained all the necessary agreements for the wedding, he felt let down by what he perceived as nonchalance on Honora's part. But then he remembered, it would be her age.

The day went well – it proved possible to get some of Honora's shipmates together, and David's mates turned up on horses and on foot. The women cried and put away serious matters for the day. And on that night reticence went up in smoke. When David closed the door of their room, Honora knocked him off his heart with her look.

***

One year to the day after the landing of the *Thomas Arbuthnot* a voice shouted out in Georges Street, 'Bridget Joyce, is that you Bridget Joyce?'

It was. But Bridget didn't recognise Julia Cuffe.

Julia was on her way to collect her belongings, having been finally and definitely caught and without doubt on her way to Brisbane, when she saw that flittery one from the ship.

'Well, I'll tell you what, she's more than just flittery now,' Julia said to no one.

'I don't remember you,' Bridget said.

'It's all right,' Julia said, not taking it as an insult, putting it more down to the sorry failed state of Bridget.

'And how are you, Bridget?'

It wasn't seriously a question. Bridget looked at her, not quite sure how to answer.

'It was being despised that I found the hardest,' Bridget said.

Who could despise this wisp of a thing, thought Julia.

'They probably didn't despise you, they just didn't understand you.'

'No, they understood. They despised me. I know what that means.' Bridget took a long breath and looked up the street. 'And I'm tired of speaking English all the time, there's no rest from it. And how are you?' she asked, as an afterthought, remembering that she should.

'All right. I got into a bit of bother and I'm being sent up to Brisbane. The courts sent me.'

'Where's that? Is it near Yass?'

'No. At least I don't think so.' Julia made to move off, but turned and asked, 'Who's looking after you?'

'I don't know,' said Bridget.

It was hard to know if this was true or not. Julia was glad she was fit enough to make as much trouble as got her to court. Moral squalor, is it, Your Lordship? I'll show you yet what moral squalor is.

CHAPTER 20

Charles Strutt had tried to have Bridget Joyce hired by sympathetic people. He had to point someone towards her without them becoming suspicious of why. The work would have to be light and there would have to be room for delicacy. A quiet house might be suitable, with some sensitive female companionship. After the fourth day of hiring he thought he got it right, the magistrate who entered the foyer might be married to the right sort of woman. Of course, he could be wrong. He had seen the most unlikely pairings of people. He made sure that Honora Raftery helped Bridget with her belongings and stayed to wave goodbye. Her trunk seemed lighter than the others, but that could not be. He himself supervised the loading of it on to the carriage.

He turned his back and worried.

At first all went as well as could be expected. But later, the gentleman who was married to the gentlewoman, in this Charles had been correct, had a change of circumstances – twins – so a different kind of help was needed in the house. Bridget was passed on to the gentleman's brother, who wasn't gentle.

In the first house Bridget had woken to the birds. The sulphur-crested white cockatoos began their arguments in hurried, clipped voices and then rose to screaming at each other all over the gardens. The kookaburras ignored them, going about their business of getting worms, occasionally looking up at the racket going on in the tree. Wasting time, wasting time, get on with it, get on with it, they said to each other. And then, perhaps, a lull. And then a long monotone delivery, punctuated by a few impatient squawks. The kookaburras, her and him, had their hunger almost satisfied and looked up again. Bad story, bad story, look he's falling asleep listening. Not the point at all, not the point. Missed the point entirely. Then the coloured galahs took off to go somewhere else, leaving the white birds to fight if they liked – they would come back this evening before Bridget's bedtime.

Before it was time for Bridget to go and help Madam with the sewing, maybe the satin bowerbirds would come to get the blue thread she had left out the moment she had woken. She had brought it up from sewing last night, but knew it was too late to leave it on the window – they would have been in bed by then, their decorating done for the day. And a wind might come in the night to whip it away, or rain might soak the blue out of it, or lightning might burn it up. She had never seen the birds come to pick up her offerings, but they were always taken. When Madam first told her about the blue bowers who decorated their nests with all things blue, Bridget was not surprised. This surprised Madam. But Bridget knew things about birds – the order to their lives, their personalities. In this garden that she could see well from her bedroom window, she followed the lives of the birds, which she now considered hers. But then the twins arrived.

Madam was reluctant to let this slight girl go to her brother-in-law's house, but what could she do? She wasn't, after all, the child's mother, and she had just had twins who would require much looking after. So her husband took Bridget away at night, so as not to upset Madam.

The decline began almost immediately. There was no

window in Bridget's bedroom. In this house they were laying the new concrete outside the house to stop the encroachment of the interminable growth in this bloody country. Growth everywhere. And the noise of them bloody birds. Growth only encouraged them.

The first thing to go was Bridget's tastebuds. She tried to put food on different parts of her tongue, knowing there were taste lines marked out on it. She tried to eat food without taste. She knew weakness would envelop her if she did not eat. And still, she wanted to live.

Then the dreams began to come. At first they were fragments of the past, so jumbled that Bridget woke horribly confused. Her mother on a ship. But how could Bridget know of a ship on which to put her mother? She was not from the sea. And why was her mother on a ship at all? Had she abandoned Bridget? And where was her father? Then the dreams came every night, piling on top of each other. Bridget tried to stop them. Before she went to sleep, after her prayers, she vowed not to encourage them. But in the morning she tried to piece them together, fit them together as if they were broken glass. If she could get the glass fixed, then she would know what her heart remembered when it was resting. She tried, as her eyes opened, to do this mending. She ran after the dream, as a child would follow a kite. But then, as wakening steadied its hold, she let it get away. She tried to use the beauty in it to give her strength for the day, not sadness. And soon she looked forward to going to sleep. Here she could see ladders going up and down, always towards clouds, both above and below. Sometimes a great bustle among tadpoles and frogs, caterpillars and butterflies. A kangaroo jumped in and Bridget screamed, which scared it away immediately, and Bridget's swallows and thrushes got back to their unspectacular soft singing and gentle hopping. Some nights her dreams were full of the colours of dresses – mauve, red, rust, green, with brown thread at the high necks, yellow with a blue sheen, black with a faded pink hidden through it. Or she could have familiar flowers and leaves strewn about. Of course they were familiar. How could they be in her dreams otherwise. They never seemed to be growing – they seemed to be plucked and strewn, the roots of the discarded trees bare. But the flowers and leaves would be fresh. The smell of them often woke her.

One whole night had potatoes, white floury potatoes. Being pulled by black horses, blooming into turnips, slipping down hills. The next day Bridget couldn't eat, no matter on what part of her tongue she placed the food. That evening the scissors slipped in her hand and cut the tip of her finger. She sat staring as the blood dripped on the cloth she was mending. The woman of the house screamed, 'Get her out of here.'

Bridget was brought to bed. She dreamt of thorns.

'Get her out of here. And the noise at night ... I have to hold the pillow over both my ears. I cannot, I am telling you, cannot, stand the noise of her.'

Bridget, by then, had started to talk to her mother. 'Yes, rain is coming in from the west.' She dreamt that she was in her mother, sewn up inside her, her mother's arms around her.

'Get her out of here, I'm telling you. Enough is enough.'

'But we cannot just throw her out.'

'Aren't there hospitals for them?'

'It would become known. Can't you get some cure for the dreams?'

'Tell you what. Take her back to that pansy of a sister-in-law of yours. She'll probably know something about dreams. Or maybe she'll even have a native cure. Wouldn't put it past her.'

Bridget dreamt of fights.

When she was brought back to her original house, Madam was horrified.

'This is death by pining,' she told her husband.

She would try to build her up. And she succeeded. A little. They sat her in the garden. They gave her their bird book – John Gould's beautiful production with the perfect drawings from his wife Elizabeth. Bridget shook the trees sometimes to get the birds out if there weren't enough of them at her feet. But there was a film over her eyes. She ate a little off small spoons, and then a little more. They brought her into George Street, sat her down to watch passing people. They would be back in five minutes. That was when Julia Cuffe passed by.

'I think I saw someone I know,' Bridget told Madam.

'Yes,' Madam said.

But eventually the dreams came back. Madam organised a rota of people to sit with her in the last week. Bridget relayed her dreams to these people, who then did their bests to forget them. Hearing such a deluge of grief could not be good for them. Bridget's last dream had all of her town on top of her sheets – all the people and all the streets. And eyes looking into eyes, looking into eyes that were looking at her. And larks and blue tits.

***

Two years to the day after the landing of the *Thomas Arbuthnot*, Honora Raftery set out baptismal clothes. To go with this good news she had sent a money order home – the beginnings of a fare for her brother. To think she might see him again. In the meantime, she would call the child for him, just in case.

Two years to the day after the landing of the *Thomas Arbuthnot*, Bridget Joyce was buried. One lorikeet sounded louder than the others as the priest said the prayers.

In Brisbane, Julia Cuffe shivered.

CHAPTER 21

'You would think one could forget them,' Charles said, in a rare moment of honesty about his work – he felt naked the moment he had said it. He was talking to the commissioner of Sydney about his impending crossing. The ship would be almost empty on the way back from Sydney, but had been signed up on its return journey to bring over the usual number – merchants, convicts, men and three women, a few Liverpool orphan boys, two civil servants, and wives and children of recently established ex-convicts, who at this very moment were trying to keep a lid on their excitements. It was still months away. The ship would probably have a few bright-eyed adventurous people, unburdened by the disturbances being suffered around them. He had noticed this new kind of passenger.

Charles and the commissioner were dining in the yellow sandstone house that gave a panoramic view of the harbour.

'It must be difficult, having dealt with the number you have in all the crossings. Perhaps you should have some time between journeys. A job here for a while?'

'No, not yet. I can forget mostly. It's just them. The faces of other people do come into my mind occasionally, but they seem to … Never mind.'

The commissioner could see that this most stalwart of men might have been excessively troubled by that cargo. He vowed to try to find some information for him, something that would put his mind at rest. He would have it for him the next time he returned. If he could remember. It was hard to remember everything when running a new colony: keeping an eye on all the possibilities, for the things that could go wrong, and things that could go right, juggling the desires and necessities of a people displaced, whether by choice or force. Still some by force – although he hoped that more choice would come into it soon. And of course those girls Strutt was talking about. They would have plenty of children that were needed if you were serious about a colony. He was glad he'd never seen them, easier then to put them out of his mind. Part of his job was to forget. Their pasts, their histories, were for another time and another place. And then there were the small things that could become big if not steered correctly. Only this morning he had to dampen down some hot emotions aroused by the family of a man who had died after a flogging. It had happened a year ago, but the relatives had only just arrived and got their hands on this information. There was a rumour that the man delivering the punishment exceeded all possible guidelines – if guidelines were even possible, it being hard to weigh pressure given to a whip. And it was possible that the man administering the punishment had borne a personal grudge against the prisoner, who, after all, had been sentenced to only ten lashes – surely not enough to kill him.

The commissioner remembered seeing the body. At first the injuries hadn't seemed too bad. But when the ribboned back was exposed, he was almost sick. And he remembered thinking at the time that it was lucky the man had no relatives here, the death could be reported some other way. And so it was. And here was Charles Strutt worrying about a shipload of girls, who were no doubt well settled by now.

Still, he would try to remember to get some news for him.

They finished their brandies in the drawing room, the drink burning off some of the present difficulties. Or so the commissioner thought. Charles looked out at the view and wondered if you could get too much of a good thing. Did excessive beauty make a person lethargic? Did benign weather stall the march forward? And surely being part of that march was the reason for being born. He shook his head. He wanted to shake his thoughts off, as a dog might shake off unwanted water after a swim. He picked up a recently published book.

'Enjoyable read. I had it on the ship. I found ...'

'Too much social conscience for me. Never get any work done that way,' the commissioner interrupted confidently.

'I suppose you're right,' Charles responded, untruthfully.

One more smaller brandy and the two men parted. Charles walked to his rooms, surprised at his fury. It was unlike him to be so aroused. He knew himself to be an even-tempered man, not given to excess, sufficiently practical to know the lesser of two evils, contemplative without being depressive, religious without being bigoted. His own Protestantism gave him no sense of superiority, unlike so many he knew. He thought of himself as a compact man. He was not overburdened by a strong libido – he knew this by comparison, having seen rampant desire make fools of many. And worse than fools, users and abusers. Men who could not be told that all in front of them was not theirs for the taking. He had seen these men marry, be cared for, and still have the need to prove their desirability, making a din of their lives, like babies in prams wailing for attention. And their wives continuing to love them despite the futility of such trustworthiness, wearing their stoicism like a shining badge of honour, hoping it might dazzle the men back to them. Charles's libido was more wistful. And then he reprimanded himself – perhaps he was jealous of those other men, perhaps aware that he had neglected to tend to that side of himself. Maybe there was still time. He would read some poetry next month. Best to turn in. He slept fitfully, waking several times in a net of dreams and dreads.

On the following morning he went to Pitt Street to conclude some personal business with George Winslow, a pleasant fellow county man, who had an enthusiasm for Charles to remove himself here permanently. A businessman, originally from County Clare, was visiting from Melbourne. He was accompanied by his daughter and was about to take his leave as Charles arrived. That was the measure of George Winslow – as broad a constituency as possible, so long as it led to profit.

'Do stay. You should meet Charles. He's off again next week, out on the – what's the name of the ship? – back to the seas.'

Introductions were made – Thomas Ryan and his daughter Margaret Bridget. Perhaps it was the hangover of last night's conversation or perhaps it was that Charles had remembered about the poetry when approaching the door, but the accidental brushing of the hand of Margaret Bridget sent an unfamiliar jolt through him, as if the glove had a flame in it. He blushed. He knew immediately what poetry he would like to read. Margaret – it would be better to use only one name – wished her father to continue the conversation that he had been having with Mr Winslow. Unfortunately, it had already been over before this stranger had come in. Luckily, her father and Mr Winslow were too insensitive to notice how flustered she had become. But not completely flustered.

The confusion was mixed with some sort of inexplicable determination.

The men began again a desultory conversation, and by way of Mr Winslow moving to the next business, he invited all of them to dinner on the night before Charles's departure. Dinner and a small dance in his drawing room. I should hope so, thought Margaret, wondering what on earth gave her the right to think that.

On the night of the dinner, Charles and Margaret, placed in opposite seats, appeared to listen attentively to what was being said to them by the guests at their respective sides who were unaware that they were not being accorded their full attention. They were listening instead to the amplified words of each other and, by doing so, learned what was necessary. Indeed, they could have been accused of veering their conversations in the direction required to mete out these bits of glowing information, of raising their voices so they could carry across the busy table. There was no doubt they would dance. The first was nervous and jagged, punctuated with stiff conversation. What if they were completely wrong about the feeling they had each suffered and enjoyed since their first meeting? By the second dance they had eased into a rhythm that could be seen in the mirror, both made momentarily speechless by the perfection of it. This will do nicely, thought Margaret. This will be the first time I have asked her to dance, thought Charles. And he knew he would always ask her in the same manner – hold his hand out, draw her to him, guide her to the floor, then pull her body slightly into him.

It was possible for Charles and Margaret to have a walk together before he boarded his ship. They strolled briefly down Queen Street. Her dress rustled, he held himself upright, and they conducted themselves as was proper. Here was someone Charles hoped might understand.

'You would think that one could forget them.'

'Oh, I hope not. That would be too much to forget.'

Thank God. And his future opened up before him.

'It's not that I remember each one individually, or indeed that I think of them every day. But when I don't think of them, I feel I have let them down.'

Margaret was not in the least jealous of this intractable bond. Remarkable, she thought to herself.

'And were they all chambermaids?'

'Well, they were all nothing. They had not begun to be what they might have been.'

'Oh yes, I forgot their ages.'

'And they had no choice once they came here, of course.'

Her dress continued to swish.

'I could have been nicer to them. I should have been,' Charles added.

'How?'

'Oh, maybe showed more interest in their getting haircuts ... things like that. Been less dismissive.'

'I'm sure you weren't. Dismissive I mean. You had to run a ship. I'm sure you have nothing to regret.'

'Yes, but regret doesn't follow logic.'

They walked on, keeping silence to that statement.

'And will they all have remained chambermaids?'

'Yes. They were all hungry and alone. So I'm afraid that will have determined their fates and defined what they will be. It does not matter what differences in intelligence or desire there was between them.'

'Poor things. And frightened too.'

'But their children may be able to be what they were supposed to be. Those who make it.'

'I hope so.'

It was an uncommon conversation to be having. Perhaps it was her nationality that made it possible.

'What age were you when you were brought here?' Charles asked.

'Fourteen.'

'So you will remember?'

'Yes. And I will have to see what may become of those memories.' She smiled. 'Maybe they will make me a good teacher, I could put them to use. But then I had my parents with me to hide bad things from me, spare me from the dark. I was exposed to nothing but good, so I can afford my memories.'

Charles sighed. 'Yes, normality can afford such a privilege.'

'I only once asked if I could go home,' Margaret said.

They came to the end of the street and turned back towards where Margaret's father's carriage was waiting.

'My father is interested in a hotel in Goulburn. Do you know where that is?'

'Yes,' said Charles, and sighed again.

He changed the conversation to more immediate matters. When they reached the carriage Charles informed her of his departure time and his expected arrival date of the return ship.

'I will write to this address?' he questioned, pointing at Mr Winslow's house.

'No, this one.' And Margaret handed him a slip of paper, already prepared and written on. He liked that. It gave him such hope. He leant and kissed her glove, not sure what was allowed. There was that shock again.

'Until then.'

Margaret's father hurried across the street and looked at Charles. It was a shrewd look and garnered as much information as the few seconds allowed. Charles waved as the horses drew away in a fine film of dust.

Charles stood on the street long after the carriage had rounded the corner. The glimpse of his future made him think of his past. What, for instance, had he done this past year? For the past few years? Had the sensibilities of his parents destined him for this? He remembered his father speaking to him one evening as he looked at the sky – the young Charles had followed his father's eye, expecting to be told about the stars. But his father said, 'Some people drink, I pray.'

Maybe I'll do both from now on, Charles thought, and walked with a featherweight heart in the direction of the ship.

In May 1854 Charles married Margaret Bridget Ryan born Ennis, County Clare, in Geelong Church of England church. And on that morning it was impossible not to briefly think of those other girls from Clare.

CHAPTER 22

In the beginning time had been slow for Honora, which was no harm. She needed it to be like that. She was seventeen when she arrived in Yass. She had to try to cure herself of the journey. She didn't want to remember any of it, particularly the leaving – the part before the journey started. Every moment of those weeks leading to that day was so long and full of unexpected thoughts. She did have an aunt who came to visit the day before she left. She had also left Florrie and Dan – Florrie in the workhouse, but with a possibility of leaving because Dan had been promised work building the wall around the landlord's house. That's what Florrie had told Honora. The others were in America. It would be best not to think of them either, because, as far as she knew, America was even further away from here than Ireland. Although there were some people who said it was nearer. There were questions that sometimes came to her but there was no one to ask. At least no one she could trust completely. Not yet.

In her first week she had asked if it was the same moon as at home. The question had plopped out of her mouth unexpectedly. The house manager had laughed out loud. Honora blushed. But he had not answered her. Maybe he didn't know himself. She couldn't ask that question again.

After the leaving was done, there was England. The strange smells of the port, all those other girls, some who knew one or two others, but most who knew no one. Then there was the warm bath. Then the journey itself. As each day passed, Honora could forget the bad more easily, elevating and elongating the better moments. School. The growing order. Holding hands dancing at night. The diminution of fear. The abatement of nightmares. The disappearance of the tic from her face. Soon, if she tried hard enough, she could filter out any memory that was harmful to her. What was the point in keeping it? And who could she tell? Perhaps while she was doing this she should also try to forget the death of her parents. She thought that forgetting them might diminish the constant pain at the stem of her throat. And maybe she could forget the deaths of her neighbours and her aunts and uncles. Already she had mixed up whether some of them had died or gone to America. It should be possible to forget. It was surely the best thing.

And it should be possible here because nothing was the same. The language was a little like the English she had learned at home, and a little more like what she had learned on the ship. But so much was not the same. The potatoes all seemed flavourless – the ones at home had not been like that, before they died that is. The first part of forgetting was to think of this new place as home. Yass as home. She said it to herself, felt the strangeness of it. But it would have to do.

She rose early in the morning. She got dressed and ready for the day, and made her way to the kitchen. She learned the ways fast. Once breakfast was over, it was important to know how many farm workers would be in later, if the shepherds would be coming, what was going on outside on the land and in the nearby mill. It was also important to fit in and around all the other staff – something Honora found easy to do. Easier than when on a moving ship. She lived with her thoughts and would talk later, when they wanted her to join in. She did not see much of her master now she was settled. She was still embarrassed, although he had told her not to mind. Sometime after her first few weeks he had walked through the kitchen. If he had not asked her how she was she would not have collapsed into tears. Her shoulders had fallen down into her chest as she had gulped for air and whimpered.

'Oh dear,' her master had said to no one in particular.

Cook dried her hands and came to her. She must have seated her, because when Honora came to she was sitting on a chair. She looked shyly about, but her master was gone. Then Cook left for some moments. She could hear mumbling outside. What if they told her she had to go? Was there any place to go? But Cook came and said that the master thought she should get ready, he was going to town and would take her to see one of the other girls. Cook fussed her out of the door into the yard. The horses smelled as they had on the road from Sydney.

Honora sat in the corner of the carriage, all her body tightened up. But her master talked in streams as if nothing was wrong, so gradually she loosened her muscles and felt better. They passed the people who were calling to collect the newly arrived post. Honora would have no business there. And then she thought, she could write to Florrie and Dan again. The last one might not have arrived. And even if they were away from the workhouse, that would not matter, Miss Lillis would bring them the letter, she was sure she would. Honora gulped. A hiccup was coming on. She swallowed. Maybe the thing to do was to swallow her memories if they were making her eyes wet. She could save money from her pay and send it to them so they could come here. Imagine that. She swallowed again.

'Here we are,' her master said.

They had stopped outside a red house. There were fourteen windows in the front. Honora counted them as her master made his way to the door. The black verandah iron gleamed in the sun, the wood creaked and whispered as it dried up in the heat. Underneath the verandah she could see the cool darkness. The master came back to the carriage after a quick chat at the door.

'Come this way,' he said, and led her round the back.

'I will be two hours,' he said, as they reached the back of the bank.

Honora and Teresa Furey saw each other and fell over themselves. Although they had not known each other well on the boat, they had talked in the camp on the way down here, not much, but that didn't matter now. Now they knew each other. The two masters smiled. They were both of the view, which was not always held out here, that kindness was a light load to carry, that one did not have to be as harsh as the earth, that there was joy to be metered out.

Four hours of talking were done in two, some of it whispered. The heat, the rivers without water, their kitchens, their bosses, their luck.

'We're lucky,' Honora said.

And if a God heard, he must have shaken his head in wonderment.

'I think so too,' said Teresa. 'Some of the others might not be so well done by.'

'And how do you hear?'

'There's an Annie in my kitchen and she brings news in every day. Funny, I'm mixing up some of the girls' names now. If I could see them I wouldn't.'

And they fell to talking about the journey, which was good Honora thought, and wondered if maybe forgetting was not a daft idea.

When they heard Honora's master come to the back door, their voices petered into one. They looked at him together, the relief that they had bathed in being the foremost expression on their faces.

'We can arrange this again in a month,' Honora's master said, before their eyes had a chance to fall into sadness.

We are lucky, they thought together, and smiled and hugged.

On the way home, Honora was filled with gratitude. It strengthened her spine. She could almost feel the steel growing. This time she chatted back.

And the following week she said a little more in the kitchen too. Put words in the pauses, looked up level to Cook's eyes once or twice.

'Talking's a tonic,' Cook said, to whoever was listening.

She too brought news each morning, but up until now Honora had not listened because it had meant nothing to her. Now, she thought, perhaps she would listen. Let this news be hers. If you could change country, you could change what was news to you.

On Sunday morning Cook sent Honora to the clothesline. All days were much the same but Sunday had a bustle about it. Honora looked out over the yellow fields. They were more rounded than those at home and flowed far away into the distance, occasionally covered with a patch of trees, white trunks with a tuft of leaves at the top. The large blue sky shone down on them, a thin stripe of cloud struggling by occasionally. It looked lost, out of place. The brightness made the morning silver.

Honora sneezed, a thing she did in the mornings here. She liked doing it outside because the echo came back to her.

Could anyone hear that noise over there beyond the trees? And if they could, what did they think it was? She could pick out a red roof in one of the dips, and wondered if a ship girl was there. They were dotted all over, Cook said. A white cockatoo with a yellow crest and yellow shining through its tail feathers, peered at her curiously, waiting to see if he would have to move. From faraway, cockatoos looked to have the face of mice – up close they had a startling headdress.

There were no ordinary birds here. Sometimes the lorikeets and parrots came into the yard in the evening, dazzling the place with their colour. Honora could not remember all the names, but wanted to, which was a start. To the right of the clothesline, far down in the valley, she could see the twisted patch of blue running out into the trees, the river where they had washed before their entrance into town. She could still feel every hour of that day. And then she saw it, a small sliver of familiar dew that had not dried up yet. She was mesmerised. Maybe if she could mix remembering with learning strange things, the two would even out into something new that didn't make her heart beat too fast. One of the sheets on the line was damp, the others already bone dry. She put the damp one to her face and smelled it.

Honora was six months or so into her life in Yass when talk began of the dance. There was a notice in the hotel window, which gave all the particulars and clearly stated there would be a moon.

'Why's the moon mentioned?' Honora asked.

'You need a moon for robbin' or dancin', it lights the way home.'

'Not for robbin'. You'd be seen if there was a moon, but dancin' yes.'

There would be clothes to be made, clothes to be cleaned,

shoes to be shone, ribbons to be spruced, cloaks to be brushed and bonnets to be made beautiful. And there would be food to make. Honora only gradually became aware that perhaps she might also be going. But she was still too unsure to become excited. In bed at night she wondered if she should ask Cook. She could say, 'Cook, will I be going with you?' or 'Cook, how many people from here go?' or 'Cook, who will be minding the house when the dance is on?'

But then Cook said, 'We'll have to do your bonnet too. You had one when you came, didn't you?'

'Yes,' said Honora, gratefully. And her heart gave a small bump.

'Tomorrow we'll have a look at your bonnet.'

In bed that night Honora wondered what might happen at the dance. Would it be like the ones in kitchens or barns at home? But she knew everyone there … What would happen if a stranger asked her to dance? What could she say to him? And he would be a stranger if he was not one of the men who had come into the kitchen. Would some of the other girls be at the dance? Would there be a place for them to talk?

The dance was held in the hotel. There was only one unpleasant moment, but it happened early in the night so it was possible to put it aside. The girl from the doctor's house said that Eliza Horgan wasn't coming because she had been hit.

'Who hit her?' the girl who hadn't been nervous coming into Yass said. Honora knew her name now, Molly Hogan.

'Her master,' the girl from the doctor's said.

'Her master!' Molly shrieked. 'Don't be silly. Why would a master hit you?'

They all became silent as they tried to add this piece of shocking possibility to the map of their futures.

'Her master? Are you sure?' Molly asked, resisting the intrusion of this troubling thought. And just then, they heard more noise outside and decided not to believe the girl from the doctor's. You could hear things that weren't true.

Horses and traps, men on bicycles, a few walkers, all heading towards the hotel. Voices lowered as they prepared themselves for stepping into the well of noise. Music, the sound of feet on floors, the talk. Although it was not the city, and there were not many here with refined tastes, it did itself proud in its dressing up. There was a gleam to the night because so many girls had come, those girls from Ireland. Young. Very young. Already this year there had been two weddings. There had only been one in the previous five years. You could never tell your luck. Honora had several dances, and in truth she could not particularly remember David as having been one of them. But she remembered the look of him on the way home, and stayed quiet in the carriage trying to hold on to the dance.

She did remember his name the next morning, the difference in it. David Taaffe. There was still some leftover noise from the night before hovering in the kitchen. Honora hid all her surprises in it and thought about some of the men she had danced with, and David. She had no picture of him, except that he had a moustache, black hair, grey eyes with a spot in one of them, freckles on the back of his hands. No picture at all.

When he called to ask Cook if Honora could come for a walk, Cook peered at her, as if sizing her up for the first time. She must also have been trying to read Honora's response – although how could she have a response to what she did not know.

'Yes,' she said, still peering at Honora to see if she

had done the right thing. Cook and David agreed a time.

At first Honora was too shy to speak. Even though all other things here were new, this was a different kind of new. He talked. And in time her talk came too, matching the rhythm of their feet on the dry mud roads.

'Dirt roads.'

'They look like mud to me.'

Honora sneaked looks at him. This man looked like her father, she was almost sure. But she hadn't seen her father for two years now, a little more, perhaps she was wrong. He didn't smell like her father. He didn't speak like her father.

Their walks became longer. Once he touched her hand. Honora froze. He withdrew. But she thought about the touch that night and grew used to the idea of it. The next time she touched his, as if by accident. His skin didn't feel like her father's, it was more papery. The next time he touched her hand she didn't pull away.

The time between walks decreased, and Honora came quicker to the back door when she heard David's footsteps.

The master thought it best to talk to Cook. They reassured each other.

It was on what was called a winter's evening that David said he needed to speak to Honora about a serious matter. He prefaced this serious matter by saying that protocol might demand that he speak to her master first, but he himself felt that he would like to speak first to her. After all, it had more to do with her than her master. And perhaps because she was alone in the world he felt she deserved different standards. This augured well. It seemed wrong that she should be alone in the world. He knew that Cook was very good to her, but maybe he could be with her, and then she would not be alone. Honora simply said yes, of course.

David then went to her master who felt that something in this was right. That was when he asked David about the possibility of Honora continuing to work, for a little while at least.

Cook prepared for the wedding as if it was a deeply personal matter. She wanted to have a new bonnet made for the bride, but Honora said that if Cook didn't mind, she would like to use her old one.

'If I don't mind? Of course I don't mind. But I might have one made for myself.'

Cook found out who of the girls from the ship could come. Annie spread the news. This was now the eighth wedding. Luck could come to this place.

Honora thought of Anne Sherry and wondered where she was and how she was. She was afraid to think of Bridget Joyce. And then she smiled as she thought of Julia Cuffe.

Honora's dress was white linen. Her bonnet was spruced yet again, and Cook had sewn a white ribbon around it. David looked serious in a black suit. Honora's voice, when saying her vows, seemed faint, as if the effort to make it carry beyond this place was too much. But she said them and people heard.

And then they had a wedding dance.

David closed the door on their room afterwards, and it was then that Honora knocked him off his heart with her look.

CHAPTER 23

Anne Sherry had looked back when she was at the gates of the barracks. She knew she was lucky because there were two of them going to the same house. This gave her a confidence she had not anticipated, and the nerve to look back. She waved. She thought it was to Honora Raftery, but couldn't be sure at this distance. When they arrived at the house there was another Irish woman there, the cook, who looked at the two of them for a long time, staring at them as if they might somehow have brought things with them on their faces. But they must have disappointed her, because after a moment or so she shrugged and said to Anne, 'Right, I'll show you where you'll be sleeping.' And when Rose made to come too, she said, 'No, not you. You're going to Pitt Street now, to his business. He has changed his mind, he needs only one here. But it will be told that he took the two of you for his home.'

Neither Anne nor Rose replied to this. There seemed to be nothing to say. Anne could feel her confidence ebb.

'But it's close, Pitt Street,' the woman said. 'If you ever have time you could walk there. Now, come with me.'

Anne followed her to her room. To her surprise there was a garden outside, well kept, bursting with all sorts of daring colour. Anne's mood changed again. She would like it here, she thought. She noticed the black boughs hanging from the branches.

'Oh, bats,' the woman said, as she saw the surprise on her face, 'I don't notice them now I'm so used to them. They hang here all the time, sleeping the day away. Lucky for them. And then they take off when the sun goes down, away for food. Wait till you see them taking off, it's a sight to behold.'

Anne surveyed her room quickly, it seemed fine and clean to her – she would take a closer look when she had time tonight. She laid her bonnet on the bed. The man would bring her trunk later and then Anne would be able to see what clothes she had. The cook brought her back to the kitchen where she gave Anne an apron. Rose was gone, spirited away by someone to Pitt Street. It was a blow, but one that would have to be borne.

'Now let me show you.'

The kitchen was bewildering. She would have to remember where things were, she would have to make this place her own, a place she could feel safe, stand in close and merge with the walls and hopefully not be seen. She had no choice. She rolled up her sleeves and got on with what was to be her life. If they left her here in the kitchen, she would be all right.

But they didn't leave her in the kitchen, at least not all the time. On her third day, she was sent to get water from the pipe in the street. Already she had got some from the buckets kept at the side of the house to catch the flow from the roof – that was easy, she knew that.

'We're still going to the pipe,' the cook said. 'Some of them further down get a water cart, but we're not on that. There's talk though that we're going to get water straight to the house soon. Out of the tap it will come, straight into the kitchen. Now what do you think of that?' and the cook laughed and laughed. 'Out of a tap and into the kitchen,' and she laughed some more and wiped her eyes.

'You know where the pipe is, just down there and to the left,' she said, as she swung her arm in a general direction.

Anne was afraid that she might not see it.

'You'll see others with cans.'

That should be manageable then. Anne walked past the men who were making the road. They made her nervous, but then she was always nervous these new days. Everything made her jump.

'She will not be able to serve at the table, not yet anyway, she will have to be kept here in the kitchen. You couldn't send her out to be jumping and dropping dishes,' Cook said to no one in particular.

So far, Anne was getting along fine with the cook. She could be cross sometimes for reasons Anne could not fathom. If only she could fathom the reasons then maybe she could avoid doing whatever it was that made her cross. But mostly she was even. One day Anne dared to ask, 'How did you get here?'

'By boat, how do you think, the same as every other soul in this place, except them who was here before us.'

And Anne thought about that – a country where every single person, that is every single person that looked the same colour as her, had come by boat. Imagine a place where everyone had been at sea for months to get there. It should be worth something after all that. Maybe she could make it worth it, if only she wasn't so nervous.

The cook knew Anne had probably meant a different question when she had asked how she got here. She would have to tell the girl to be careful about that. Not everyone liked being asked – it was enough to know that everyone had come by boat. But she would have to be careful how she warned her – the girl was as jumpy as a flea. And it would never do to make her cry. She hated crying girls. She would broach the subject carefully, sidle up to it, as if the thought had accidentally occurred to her.

'You know that there are people here who came for different reasons than you.'

'Oh yes. I know that,' Anne said emphatically.

Well that was good. 'But they don't all talk about it. Do you know that?'

Anne nodded her head. She did now.

'You can have a half-day tomorrow. Walk down to see that other one who was with you. Will you be able to go that far?'

Anne thought that she would. After her first few times getting water she allowed herself to look further up and down the street. In the beginning it had been essential to keep her eyes fixed firmly on the point of her journey, but now she could let them wander a little. She was still nervous about the men building the road, but less of them whistled at her now, and not for as long. The last time she thought that one of them might have said, 'Nice morning,' but she could have been wrong about that. The street at the end of hers disappeared into voluminous bushes, and the other end led to more houses. From the bottom she could hear carts and carriages and horses whinnying, louder sometimes than others, depending on the wind. Anne knew her house now. She did not make a mistake anymore, not like the first day with the water, when she had knocked on a door that was not her own, then stood outside, shaking first and then crying. A man had come.

'What's the name of the people in the house?' he asked.

'I don't know.'

'Well would you know the name of the cook?'

Anne did, but it wouldn't come to her.

'She's Irish.'

'Well, yes. That's not a great help. We'll try this one. You may just have stopped near the right one,' he said, waving at the houses that were all different, so how could she have made a mistake.

As soon as they came to the back door Anne recognised the kitchen and ran into it. The man doffed his hat to the cook.

'She was outside,' he said, 'lost.'

He did not mention the crying.

'Thanks,' the cook said, rubbing her hands on her apron. 'Sometimes I don't know what they send me.'

But when the man had gone, she stayed quiet and gave Anne easy jobs to do. The next day she told her about how the windows had been especially shipped out here from England, and that the ornament out the front had belonged to the master's father – they were seafarers, did their business on the water, that's why it was a boat and a sail on the glass in the window. So when Anne next went to get water, she had something to guide her back to the house. Now the cook came to the gate and directed Anne to Pitt Street.

'See where the buggy is going, go down that street, there's a dirt bit to go over, pass the tree covered in bats, more than out the back here, black with them. There will be a number on the house, go to the back and knock on the door. If you get lost, come back.'

Anne looked as if she needed to ask a question.

'Go on, spit it out.'

'When will I know if I'm lost?'

'Merciful hour. Pitt Street has a name on it, do you know where to look for the name?'

'Yes, I just didn't know if it had a name on it.'

'Go on.' And the cook hoped that Pitt Street did have a name on it.

It was a few months later, on another of these visits, by now well rehearsed, that Anne saw the hats in a shop window. She sometimes stopped at windows and looked briefly, but just for a moment, in case a man came up behind her. Oh what feathers on the hats, oh what feathers. And a thought came to her suddenly, out of nowhere, about how she could collect the feathers that dropped all over the garden and maybe make hats. Wouldn't that be an unusual thing. She stayed longer than normal at the window, not really looking into it, more thinking and wondering if she could indeed do something different and unusual. She felt that if she could, she would feel safer here. The window took on a new importance.

She lifted up all the lost feathers the next morning, discarding some, realising there would always be more, every morning, so she could pick and choose. She would use only the strong, unbroken ones. She collected dozens of them and hid them in her room. When she had a sufficient number, she began her first hat. She had to think of ways to sew it on to the remnants of cloth that she had spirited away, ways to stiffen the cloth, and ways to arrange the feathers, which was crucial – the lie of them, and not too many, and not colours that would clash. She had the beginning of a life now. And soon the cook came in the evenings to see how they were going, and Anne stayed up until the lamplighters lit the new lights outside. The cook found an old table for her room, and told her friends about where to get a hat for hat days.

'And she's not nervous now either. I can't understand it. How would making hats make you less nervous?'

Anne asked Cook if maybe she could post a hat to someone in Yass.

'Well, you could I suppose, if you had the address. Do you have the address?'

'No,' Anne said. 'I don't.'

CHAPTER 24

The one thing that Julia Cuffe was completely proud of was her lack of fear. She was partly proud of some other qualities, but so taken was she by her lack of fear that she deliberately cultivated it. When she had been growing up there hadn't been much time or need to notice things about herself, and then everyone started getting hungry and sick so all attention was placed on that. It was on the boat that she first became aware of this strength, not immediately, but after some weeks when girls would say that no they couldn't do that, but that Julia probably could. They taught her a thing or two, those girls. But some of them were much too scared for their own good. Julia had decided to take on anything. Might as well, look what had happened without her deciding. And now she was on the road to Brisbane. But she would not be afraid.

The authorities had her now. They had cut her hair and they would bring her to Brisbane where she would learn – well it didn't matter whether she did or not, she would live and do the dirty work needed at the start of any place. There is muck under every polished thing, all kinds of muck and slime. Julia could tackle muck and slime. And rum helped. Nothing much that rum couldn't brighten up.

Julia was put to work in Brisbane. There was no dribbling of dark here – it fell shockingly in a flash. She left her house when that happened. She met girls like herself who had come on boats before her. Not on her one. She heard there was a girl from her boat up here somewhere, but she wouldn't want to meet her now. She would have to grow her hair as fast as she could, people pointed and shouted, 'Short grass,' after her. It took some time for hair to grow when it had been totally shorn. Julia did not like having no hair. There were men too, roughened and toughened even beyond what can be noticed. If you had a soul here, it was hard to find a place to show it. People could be beaten and stamped into the very ground. And no one was watching. Every night four or five or eight of them would meet to drink rum outside one of their thrown together pits. The place was clean enough. At least the heat dried up the dirt. Dry dirt was easier than mud. The numbers changed each night – sometimes one woman, sometimes two, but always Julia. She made them laugh. They watched for her coming. Who would make them laugh if she wasn't here? Was there another among them who remembered how to make a body laugh?

But it was in this theatre one night – for that's what she was now, a one-woman walking theatre – that she realised it was herself she was mimicking, herself she was pulling apart and laughing at and drawing others to do so too. The more she could make these people laugh at her, the easier the night went. Clearly the rum this evening was not strong enough or Julia had moved up a notch and would soon need a full bottle to do the work of last year's half.

That was the moment – there was a choice to be made. The laughing died down. Julia had been given a choice before and didn't think much of it. Still, who could be afraid of a choice?

Julia met a man from Somerset, Samuel, he had stolen something, she never asked what. She would have thought that she neither loved him nor didn't love him, but that they would do each other for now because company made life easier. There were forests to be cut and a town to be built, and they knew how to do that. And Samuel didn't hit her, which was good. A lot of hitting went on, people lashing out at something that had been done to them, at God knows what that had been marked upon their souls. The field outside Samuel's slab hut merged into bush. Julia didn't look at the birds, what use would that do, but sometimes she caught the flash of a red or blue wing and would have liked to find some good in what was around her.

But Julia was careful not to take any calm for granted – she had learned that. And she was right. One day Samuel was felling trees when one of them hit him. They came to get her and she knew if she got there to him he would be all right. This was an ideal optimism to face the next few weeks and it served her well, although it drove others away, they couldn't bear it. She got him fixed up in the bed and set to waiting. She could do that. But now there was no money coming for food.

'No need to worry,' the men said, that was something they could do. Bring food. And rum if she wanted, but she didn't. Her days became ordered. She found a way to get Samuel to have some liquid. She sat beside his bed, watching, waiting. She learned a terrible patience. It was suspended all around her. She was grateful for the open window through which she could see a sliver of water in the creek at the bottom of the field. Sometimes she moved her chair to the middle of the bed, let Samuel's hand go, and stared at the water. It nurtured her patience. Sometimes she let his hand fall, to see if he would try to hold on to it before it hit the bed. She squinted her eyes when she looked at him. He was down some hole, some almighty hole, if only Julia knew how to get to him, how to pull him up.

The late evening that Samuel woke was just like the others. He did not flicker his eyelids, nor shift a finger, nor give any warning. If he had, she would have had something ready for him, tea, something. A biscuit if she could have found one. It would have been worthy of that. But there was no warning. Julia had been holding his hand and thought she felt something in it, an emotion almost. Then he opened his eyes and said, 'You came to see me. All this way. How nice.'

It was not a voice she had heard him use before. But he closed his eyes again and when the others heard her scream they ran to her.

'He talked, he talked,' she screamed.

'We know, we know,' they said.

What did they know?

'You don't believe me. He talked, he talked.'

They took her outside, where she fell into a trance. She sat all night. She would not move, nor go with the woman they got to take her away. And exactly as dawn came, as the sun climbed up swallowing the darkness in the sky, exactly as the early birds, unnoticed by Julia, shook their feathers and warbled out the first tentative notes of the day, exactly as the flowers moved in the earth in readiness for opening, Samuel died.

'Well, yes,' Julia said, when told. What on earth could she have expected? She did not know what to do now.

They buried him quickly in a field nearby that was growing into a graveyard. Julia wore her bonnet even though it wasn't black. No one knew much about Samuel, so there was not a lot to say. And what Julia knew could not be said. After the funeral she felt that if she didn't leave here she would be thrown out. Who would need a woman on her own here? She could not let herself sink so low as to be thrown out. She would have to go before that happened. There could be no further down to go than to wait to be shifted from this hovel. And without Samuel, that's what it was, a hovel. So that was love. At least she knew now. That was something. She looked out over the distance and wondered what the next months might hold. A benign voice told her that she needed to decide. It had to be her own voice, because no other had ever been benign.

One of Samuel's friends passed by to see if she needed anything.

'What would I need?'

The next time he called she was taking clothes from her trunk. It was still with her but was too big to move again.

'Where are you going?'

'I'm going to Ballarat,' she said, 'where the gold is.'

'But it's thousands of miles away.'

'Yes, well that should be no bother to us.'

Julia would find a carriage or something back to Sydney. It would be easier there to find her way to the gold.

CHAPTER 25

Friends of Samuel's came to see Julia off.

'Where will you live?'

'I'm going to try Dream Street.'

Oh, she was funny. They shifted about. 'As good a place as any,' one of them said.

But they were Samuel's friends, not hers. She had met girls here from Belfast, a lot of them seemed to be sent here, bolder, badder, more spirited, you could say. But they weren't Julia's friends either. Now she wondered if she had ever had friends. But she shook off the self-pity, it would not do to become crippled by moroseness. No, that would not do at all.

'Good luck,' they said.

And so she set off on an eternity of a journey, riding in coaches, working a day here and there. She was afforded safety because of the peculiarity of a woman travelling like this. Sometimes the road was interminable and she heard herself saying, soon, soon, soon. A small girl on the ship on a mattress near Julia had sometimes whispered that to herself, usually during a storm. Julia would lie there, raiding her head for nice thoughts and rocking with her mantra. What was her name? Where was she now? Stuck in some kitchen probably, not like Julia out on the road going somewhere. Julia's life was making a thread, not defined yet, but she could almost feel it going through her hands sometimes, as her body rattled with the coach along another dirt road.

When her bones got sore with the road, she stopped and found some work on a sheep farm for a time. The men left her alone, so struck were they by the nerve of her.

On her first day on her first farm she looked out.

'Is that grass?' she asked.

And they laughed at her. And she laughed at them.

'You call that grass!' she exclaimed.

The sheep blended into it, she had to blink to be sure she had seen them. She slept in a house with a tin roof. The weather was warm at night, so the accommodation suited her fine. The cracks in the door let in sufficient air. Julia was used to heat now, so used to it indeed that the occasional cold night came as a surprise to her. There were a few mangy trees near the back door, they sighed when even the slightest breeze blew up, wishing maybe they were better and more fulsome. Julia didn't know exactly where she was, or exactly what month it was, but she did know the days of the week, counting them from each Sunday. Time didn't matter much anyway. She woke with the sun and went to bed early, the belief being that lights in shacks might attract bushrangers, though in truth they were all tired as soon as the sun went down. Julia was cleaning outside the house when she saw an approaching figure in the distance. On and on he came, changing from a mere dot to something now resembling a man. And still he came, walking through the sun, on and on until he arrived. He had a fiddle with him, a thoroughly welcome calling card. The master and mistress were informed. And word of the dance began to filter through. It would be a crossing the line dance.

'A what?'

'So everyone can come. There's only one musician so the owners and us will all be at the one dance.'

The woolshed was cleaned but the floor was not scrubbed. The oil from the wool would make for a fine slippery dance surface. Then a chalk line was drawn down the middle, with one side for the owner, his wife, his family and their guests – of whom there would be many. The important word could be got far and farther. A dance should not be missed, it gave them the strength to continue. Ribbons and family lace were made ready. On the other side of the line was the floor space for the servants, the stockmen, the shearers and the roustabouts. There was to be no crossing of the line. Several lights were made for the shed, to be placed carefully away from harm's way. The tins were half filled with clay, topped with dripping and a long homemade wick was then inserted. The smell evaporated into the others.

Soon it was ready. The woolshed was a dance house, and they straightened their backs before they went to wash as best they could. Julia still had a good dress. It had stayed good, despite the road.

In the distance lights on carriages could be seen wobbling towards the shed, coming and going in the dark, twinkling like stars. There was much noise as the carriages arrived and men and women alighted. And so the dance began. The musician warmed up slowly to make the dancers put their feet through the roof, not stick them to the floor. Julia intended, and hoped, to enjoy herself, but would never have thought the occasion would point her straight ahead for her next few years.

It was while they were arranging a bush version of a quadrille that Julia made an unexpected dainty movement. The dancing that she had done on the ship came back to her feet but with an added lift. She must have learned something from those others. Oh, she said, and tried it again. And again.

Oh, they said.

And to think that she could do that despite the road and the roughness of the last year.

'Where did you say you were going?'

'To Ballarat.'

'And what will you do there?'

'Be a dancer.'

'Well, I can see that. Good luck.'

More luck was thrown after her as she left.

The journey proceeded as she had expected. She had a lift on a comfortable coach. They had provisions for the first two days, as the driver knew there was a scarcity of inns on this stretch. While they were cooking these on the first evening, diligently following the safety rules, the smells of fire and food running into each other, Julia allowed herself a certain amount of satisfaction. She had had a rocky start, had endured some hardship, had lowered herself to do what was necessary, had found ways out and up from that, had kept her own secrets, had loved even, and was now on her way to dance for gold. She was capable of managing the dangers. She slept deeply, being now used to the noises outside.

But in the morning Julia and the others were woken by an unfamiliar sound, a distant crackling, as if a giant was stepping on dry twigs. Julia crawled out from under the makeshift tent to see the faraway bushfire shooting balls of smoke into the horizon, as if the giant was blowing from a pipe. They were camped in a valley beside a river, surrounded by hills, and would have to climb out when the time was right. For a few hours they watched the progress of the fire as it leapt from patch to patch. The men debated its speed and direction. Julia stayed quiet while the voices of the men got louder as concern began to show itself. It was best not to interrupt the worry of men. Finally, in the afternoon, it was decided – by whom it was hard to tell – that it was time to move that way, not that way, and now, definitely now. The fires had begun to join up. They would have to move fast. They might have to discard belongings if the weight was delaying them. This was of little consequence to Julia, her belongings having dwindled almost to what would do a swagman. She had left her trunk behind in Brisbane in the shed by the river, perhaps someone would find it useful in some way. You never could tell. The fire continued to meet other fires – it looked as if the entire thing might gracefully become a complete circle and trap them in the valley. Julia looked at the river and wondered if they could hide there, but they were leaving it behind now. She wondered if she should voice this thought but decided against it. It had seemed too dangerous to light their own fire this morning so they were without tea, she would have liked tea.

As they moved up the hill and closer to the flames they stayed silent. The driver kept his eyes on the track. The passengers checked the progress of the fire behind them. They watched for sparks, and hoped that none would catch on to their coverings which they had wet with the last of the water, but which was drying rapidly. The smell of smoke grew even denser, the heat intensified. Animals ran this way and that over the road, searching for safety or maybe their own secret water into which to plunge. Trees spluttered red ash, spitting it out onto other trees and sparking another unlit tree into a burning life of its own. The smell brought fear with it, to the animals as well as to them, and worryingly now to their own horses, which panted and snorted and widened their eyes. But then, the fire suddenly turned, jumped as though in a triumphant display, and rushed off to another hill. They stopped, staring after it, seeing it, now that it was disappearing, for what it was: a beautiful ball of hot red glowing miracle. The passengers and the coach driver broke their silence and babbled uncontrollably. Julia stayed quiet and thought about all the luck that had been freely wished her since she had left Brisbane. The smell of burning followed them, and the next day stripes of rain passed over, dropping soot from the sky.

There were more days of travelling and two coach changes before Julia saw the miles of men heading to what might be wealth. There were plenty of inns now, with food for sale on the road and a rising air of excitement tempered with fearsome anticipation. The one other woman on the last coach worried excessively.

'There could be pirates,' she said.

'Bushrangers. Yes there could I suppose,' Julia replied.

'Or bushfires.'

'Yes,' Julia agreed.

'There could be floods.'

'Listen, if you're looking for one disaster after another you're going to the right place.'

What was the point of worrying? Whatever would be thrown at you would be thrown at you. The sun still beat down.

'We might be passing the place called Desolation Hill.'

'Well, I'll let you know if I see it coming up,' Julia said.

The other woman didn't smile, ever, not with all that expecting things to get worse.

'And there's a place called Poverty Point.'

'We must go looking for that, for sure,' Julia said.

'Any proper rain yet?' the driver asked.

'Not for months.'

Well that should settle the question of the floods, for the moment.

'Lovely evening now,' the driver added.

'Yes, it's cooled down nicely.'

They passed some emus, straining their necks to look disdainfully at them, before thinking better of the waste of time and wandering off into the distance. They passed a bunch of dashing vibrant parrots. 'You could use those for women's hats,' the men laughed.

You could too, thought Julia, always adding to her list of what could be done if the next thing failed. She wondered if anyone else had thought of that.

The following day turned out to be lovely. Grey clouds covered the entire sky, sent as consolation to the walkers. Drops of rain fell on them, one after the other. The walkers hoped the rain would never stop. They trudged right through the day until evening grew. The night sky cleared and filled up – there were never just a few stars in the sky here. They passed a deserted town. Rust is dry here, not wet, Julia thought.

The edge of the town began to fray. She had expected to see more houses up over the hill, but they ran out suddenly. These were huts that might have been houses, but the life was dried out of them now. And suddenly the pretence was over and they headed again into coal darkness.

'It's where they came first before they discovered there was better gold further on,' the driver told them, glancing back.

The lights on the coach shook and shivered and threw eerie shadows, just a little way, into the vast space. And finally they arrived. They would sleep in the coach until dawn. Tomorrow she would settle for however long.

In the morning Julia set about getting a roof for over her head. She was told of one place where a woman had come and wanted another to share. Julia surveyed the quarters – they seemed clean and there was a dark corner to help with the heat. How could she make tea? That's what mattered most at this moment.

'There are two husbands next door, friendly enough, but not any bother,' the woman said.

It seemed they were intent only on finding gold and getting out of here back to their wives as fast as possible. Julia lay down on the bed to stretch the miles out of her body. She woke to the smell of cooking.

'There's great noise in the evening, football, the Chinese against the rest. Here, take something to eat.'

Julia sat on a stool at the door to eat. When she was finished, she rubbed her plate with her finger and licked it.

'You don't have to do that here, there's plenty of food,' one of the husbands said as he passed her on the way into his house.

'What would you call that? A shack?' asked Julia, peering after him.

'Maybe, but it won't matter much when we hit gold,' the husband said, not for the first time.

This place looked promising, Julia thought, but she would keep herself to herself until she figured out what she was going to do. She walked out into the heat to survey the expanding street. Some women turned away from her, they were the ones who had come to join their husbands. They stayed well away from those who had not. There was word that Lola Montez was coming to dance. Julia listened to it and then knew her next move. Two days later the poster outside the hotel said that a professional dancer was being hired from Brisbane.

'You didn't tell us that's what you are.'

'Did I not?' said Julia. 'I must have forgotten.'

'You can dance anywhere,' the other woman said. 'They have a floor laid down at Kanangra Walls underneath the overhanging rock.'

'And where's that?' Julia asked, as if she cared.

One of the husbands, a womanly kind of a man, came in, pointed out the window, and asked them, 'Do you know what the name of that is?'

'It's a thistle,' they said together.

'Ah, but which kind?'

'Don't know. Tell us.'

'It's melancholy thistle, would you credit that, melancholy thistle.'

And who were they to argue, perhaps it was and perhaps it wasn't.

And so every night Julia danced, not too much hardship to that. She performed in the halls where men came to wind down from the misery of their disappointment, or came to mark a joy they had just seen, a possibility of great money that would see them and their families safe for as long as they lived and longer. A man came to draw her dancing. She collected more secrets and hid them safely. At nights or early mornings, the women sometimes sang their own song, to the flickering of their own candles. It told who they were and how they'd got there – it demanded understanding, it lamented what others might see in them, but with a slap of thigh it let the world know the things they knew and the intentions that only they could see. They wouldn't sing it for men – you had to be able to keep something for yourself. Sometimes Julia whistled and it never brought a storm on her.

And still she danced. Until, in time, she tired of this place too and decided to go back up to Queensland for the gold rush there.

'Have you got money now?' the woman who shared her room asked. It was only when a person was leaving that you could ask that question.

'Some,' Julia said. 'Some.'

They wished her luck as she took off. She passed the place where they were making the new Botanical Gardens, signalling an intention to stay. From the carriage she could see lines of coloured flowers bursting out into the heat, sucking it into them and getting brighter. After days and days of travelling, they stopped to refresh themselves in a place called Yass. That's the place she thought. She could have sworn she saw faces that she had seen before. But she thought it wise not to find out. The girls out here would not have lived her kind of life. I wonder what they're at. Honora, that was the name of one of them. Honora, yes.

'There are a lot of children about,' she said.

'Indeed there is,' the man coming back from getting gold said.

'Plenty of room, plenty to eat,' he added.

'It would stop you thinking too,' Julia said.

The man looked at her and then away again – a woman like her could be dangerous. She thought she would see Sydney again on her way – see if it had grown or if she liked it better now. See perhaps if she wouldn't want to come back there when she'd found some more gold. Or she might try to join a wandering theatre. Or she might try to be a fortune-teller. She could make up plenty of stories. She passed through Sydney on an October evening in 1858.

Julia went down to the harbour – no harm in having a look. It was as busy as she remembered. People walked past carrying picnic baskets. She wondered if she might see anyone she knew from the ship, it was a fleeting thought, surely most unlikely, but she couldn't help thinking of them on their first day. She wondered which of them would die first. This wasn't like her. Such thoughts didn't bother her often. A man very like that fellow Charles Strutt walked away from her at a distance.

'Hey Strutt, there's no danger at all.'

The man turned. He could have sworn that he heard a voice he knew from somewhere. But all he could see were well-dressed proper women, so it couldn't be the voice he thought he recognised. Julia turned her face north once again. She turned her face into living whatever might happen. They would all have to continue doing that.

CHAPTER 26

The business that was taking Charles Strutt to Sydney could be made to coincide with the Civic Ball. There was talk there would be ice there. Already they could get ice in Melbourne, for that was where the ships from Canada came in first, laden with their cargo, cut clean from Canadian lakes. Ice much superior to any from other parts of the world, and certainly would never be bettered by any other kind. It was not always possible to keep it frozen for the last journey to Sydney, but there was talk this time. The presence of ice enhanced the attractions of a ball, cooled the air and the drinks, and added to the splendour of the evening.

But even more important than this occasion, Charles was going to surprise his wife. News had come to him of a lecture on music to be given at the Lyceum Theatre, followed by a concert of Thomas Moore's songs on the evening of 5 October 1858. Margaret herself knew many of these songs and sometimes sang them at the piano in their drawing room. Charles considered himself fortunate and saw the procuring of the tickets as a token of his gratitude. It was not without difficulty that he had managed to get them. Because although they were available from Jeremiah Moore the stationer in George Street, Mr McMahon the perfumer, Tom O'Neill the confectioner, and Freehill the solicitor also on that street, as well as Daniel Donovan the tobacconist and Cleary the bootmaker in King Street, and now it appeared as well on Pitt Street at the Brougham Tavern, at the tailor Michael Riley's or at the bookseller William Dolman's, and too from Clinton in Hunter Street, Philip Walsh the grocer on Parramatta Road and J.G. O'Connor the printer out in Chippendale, it was nearly impossible to get tickets because of the rush on them. Everyone Irish of any note wanted to be there because the event was being hosted in aid of Archdeacon McEnroe's Donegal Relief Fund, a fund set up to bring evicted tenants to Sydney. Charles kept himself informed of matters such as these.

And as well as the Irish, the English who were not completely antipathetic and who sang Moore's songs in their own drawing rooms, wanted to be there too. As is the way with these things, momentum was created by momentum. It would be wonderful if he could manage to get some. Margaret would so appreciate it. But perhaps the ball would be sufficient. Of course the ball would be sufficient. Still, Margaret always read notices of theatre or concert visits. She read them as if they applied to someplace else, never with unreasonable longing. So, it was therefore even more important that he try every avenue possible. He wrote to his friend, George Winslow, and told him of their pending visit to Sydney and his desire to get tickets. Mr Winslow replied immediately, assuring him that of course he would do everything he could to oblige, always happy to be in a position to do a favour for his friends. It made life worthwhile, these small gestures of camaraderie. And soon a letter arrived to say that the tickets would be at George Winslow's house and did they need a place to stay?

They decided they would accept the kind offer. The journey to Sydney was of course long, but one got used to that. And when it came to the last few hours, one could look forward to a bath. Soon they saw the purple appearance of Sydney in the distance.

After they cleaned up at their host's house they went for a walk down by the Cadmans Cottage, where you could see silver twinkling on the water. The area was much cleaned up, Charles thought, and relaxed into his stroll. There were plenty of people out walking, taking the air. There were people who had no harbour on their streets and who, sometimes sick for it, came here to watch. They built pantheons of favourite viewing places. In particular they came in droves if they heard a ship was in, and there was one newly in this evening. The strollers watched as the boat disgorged dazed passengers, and some people waved at them. Only some of the passengers waved back, those who had already subconsciously understood the intricacies of exile and what new manners were required.

Many of the strollers were secretly trying to piece together what they had felt when their feet had first hit the ground, and perhaps checking if the dreams they had dared were still intact. Did they go home happier or sadder? It was a dangerous thing, this boat watching. And yet that sort of stride beside the harbour was also a strengthening moment – here they all were, a country full of people who had shared an extraordinary experience and carried it as if it was normal. They knew words that should only belong to seafarers, and brought them out occasionally, and shone them up, and threw them about on evenings like this. They timed their walk back so that Margaret would get to see the lamplighters at work, watching as they moved from lamp to lamp. She had been so looking forward to seeing the splendid gas lights in all the shops, and she was not disappointed. Later, they dined in the dining room where they had first met.

The table was laden with all the best food – the roast had been cooked not in the kitchen but in the local bakehouse, because there was much entertaining to be done in the next few days and the cook, an even-tempered woman from Wicklow, had decided that some tasks would have to be done away from their own kitchen. Food was served competently by one English and one Irish servant and all went smoothly, particularly so considering there was no Mrs Winslow present this evening, she having had a prior engagement that could not be altered.

In actual fact, Mrs and Mr Winslow had had a disagreement, a little more noisy than usual. It had begun when Mr Winslow had asked what on earth the hired help was doing at the end of the garden, staring out to sea.

'Leave her be, she might be lonely today.'

'Why particularly today?'

'Oh, you must know that there are days which have no explanation. Surely even you, who has come here to own an entire country, sometimes get lonely for your own place.'

'Well I cannot see that she has too much to be lonely about – when you're poor is it not a relief to leave that place, why on earth would one pine for it?

'The heart is not as easily organised as that.'

'But then I swear she looks through me sometimes, as if she's seeing beyond me, a blooming peasant girl. I find myself sometimes looking at my shadow in case there is someone else there.'

It was most unlike Mr Winslow to have thoughts like these, and even more unlike him to put them into words. He looked at his wife and creased his eyes, which he now did continuously every day, as if creasing his eyes might shut out some of the violence of the sun, she thought. Why, when he was asleep and his entire face was at rest there were white lines in the tanned skin.

'She may be resentful. I'm not saying that she knows she is, but she may hold us responsible for her loneliness.'

'Oh for God's sake, whose side are you on? It's not as if we were the cause of her hunger back home.'

Mrs Winslow thought it best not to look at her husband when she said, 'Well …'

And the argument had increased and the noise had risen and Mrs Winslow had ordered the coach. She was going to visit a nearby friend, she had never done that before – upped and gone to visit without prior warning – and Mr Winslow was trying not to worry.

'But she will be here tomorrow. Indeed her coach may be back before night.'

Margaret was glad of that, not only because she liked Mrs Winslow, but also because some of the conversation among the men could become disagreeable late in the evening. For instance there was the commissioner now and the man sitting next to him –

'Countries like those, what do you mean countries like those?'

'If you don't know what I mean …'

'No, what do you mean, do you mean countries where everyone does not want to be you? Maybe even countries where nobody wants to be you?'

The men laughed. Yes it could be funny, but Margaret was never sure when the conversation could take a turn, or why. A remark very similar to all the others could suddenly change the temperature in the room.

'Ah, Charles, we're discussing native populations, what to do about them. You know, in theory, we do not believe that

Aboriginal land can be legally possessed if it is occupied, but practice is another thing. Yes, an entirely different matter altogether,' the commissioner remarked. 'It is not always possible to get a definitive agreement on what constitutes *terra nullius.*'

'If they haven't put up fences, how could we know what they own?'

'But they don't believe in fences, have never seen the need.'

'Well, that's a pity for them. If they had known we were coming they might have.'

There was more laughter.

'But the theory still remains that we are not illegally taking land. We do not do that.'

'Ireland, William, Ireland.'

'Well, yes, but that's a different story. Ah, Margaret, how do you find the sauce?'

The men tried to rein in their conversation, but it had taken on a path of its own now.

'In the course of my studies of the recent period I am left with many questions, I am also left with appalling pictures, some of which take a lot of brandy to shift. Of course I know we don't have to think about these things here but ...'

Charles had heard this man speak before, this historian. He hoped the conversation could be changed. And just as he wished, the noise of a carriage pulling in to the side of the house could be heard above the clatter of dinner. Mr Winslow looked particularly relieved. Within minutes Mrs Winslow had breezed into the dining room.

'I am so sorry,' she said. 'I hope you can accept my apologies.'

She smiled at her husband and he smiled back. And she had all sorts of wonderful news. Caroline Chisholm was back in Sydney, doctor's orders, to get away from the inclement conditions in Kyneton. She had been very unwell when they arrived, had had to stay put in the hotel in York Street, too ill to move further. But now she was improving and Mrs Selby was organising some way to get the Chisholms some money, because of course they'd spent all theirs on everyone else. She is not eating well and said that she longed for some Irish food – it was the best she ever tasted, she said, all the way from Ireland when they were in India. Florence Nightingale is writing a book on nursing. Charles Dickens, you know that novelist, he has given money to Caroline, apparently he is very fond of her, Mrs Winslow had not known that before. And did you know that Thomas Moore was party to burning Byron's papers, that's the concert you are going to, is it not? Elizabeth Street is named after Governor Macquarie's wife – Mrs Winslow had thought until tonight that it was after the English queen – you never know what's out there to be learned. And she, Elizabeth Macquarie that is, was related to the Duke of Argyll, you know Argyll Street, also part of the Campbell Clan. The Duke you know was friendly with Harriet Wilson, and she turned to Margaret and whispered, 'You know the Harriet Wilson who was friendly with Lord Byron and the Duke of Wellington and the Prince of Wales ...' Margaret didn't know, but was very glad to have Mrs Winslow here whispering to her. And the men were not terribly interested so they pulled out their chairs and made to retire to another room.

Eventually Charles and Margaret retired to their bedroom. They were not aware of the fact that their window was open until they overheard the voices coming in to them on the salty wind. It was impossible to be sure to whom they belonged.

'The Irish Famine will always be one of those events that has a divisive effect, in that country as much as anywhere else. There cannot be a collective memory about it for that would presume everyone experienced it in the same way, which is certainly not true. Of course they will always have another country to blame, whereas our convicts won't.'

'Yes, it is always easier to have an outside place to blame.'

'And of course it is true that a lot of them did die.'

'More than a million they say.'

'And more than a million departed the country too.'

'Perhaps we could have avoided some of those.'

'And then, of course, there are Charles' girls.'

'They will be forgotten.'

'Well yes, if they are successful they certainly will, because they will blend in and will not be remarked upon.'

'I'm sure that most of them were sad to leave but glad to be gone.'

'And the ones he took to the country ... no place that for a nervous type of woman.'

The men laughed.

'But he does go on. He will not allow us to forget them.'

'Of course, he married one.'

'No, not one of them, just Irish.'

Charles made for the window and closed it loudly. The voices stopped – either because the closed window prevented them coming into the room, or because the men had realised they were overheard. Perhaps it would have been better to stay in a hotel, the Orient, near Argyll Street. Next time, certainly.

But the next day brought its own delicious to-ing and fro-ing, getting ready for the ball, and Mrs Winslow made a huge fuss over Margaret. They went into a room together and did something to their hair and then Margaret joined Charles in the bedroom to put on her dress. He pretended to be busy with his own apparel but he secretly watched the event of Margaret's clothing. He went down to the drawing room before she was completely ready so he could be there to watch her come down the stairs and be ready to put her arm on his. Mr Winslow commented that there was nothing like a ball to bring out the best in everyone.

'It's the thought of dancing,' he said. 'Did you know that Captain Cook made his crew dance a hornpipe before he gave them their ration of rum?'

Mr Winslow was like his wife in that he collected bits and pieces of obscure details. They both used them like nest linings to create a life that mattered here.

'And what about making their own ballroom out of ice!'

Margaret had heard about that. Two ships had met in the Antarctic and a piece of ice formed between them, which could be used for passage between the vessels. The sailors set to work so that they could celebrate the New Year. They carved an ice ballroom, ice seats for the captains, a table with steps down to it, a female figure near one ship, a male near another. And they had their dance. She pretended not to know the story, so that she could be told it again. Mrs Winslow liked Margaret.

The coach was brought to the side of the house and there was much ado to get the ladies into it without harming shoes or dress hems. Mrs Winslow was dressed in an Empire gown, while Margaret's was an ivory silk. Both wore gloves – Mrs Winslow's white, Margaret's a deep yellow – and their headdresses were elegant and sparkled in the evening light. They carried their decorated fans easily in their hands. The men looked handsome. They couldn't avoid doing so in their crushed hats, black dress suits with silk lapels, shining waistcoats and on Mr Winslow, a shining white tie. He also had a pocket watch and it was difficult to know whether one should remark on this or not. When seated in the carriage, Margaret thought this perhaps the loveliest part of the night, only themselves to appreciate before being overwhelmed by the festivities, and yet still the excitement of the future evening hanging in the air.

When they arrived, there was one whoosh of greeting and delight as people, perhaps not out often enough, set to enjoying themselves. The hall was decorated with shrubs and flowers hung from the walls. No detail had been ignored. The tables luxuriated in a fine display of food, everything you could possibly imagine, and there was champagne, wine, yellow and claret, as well as the usual sherry, port and brandy. And yes, there was ice, adding that final sparkle. The ladies floated to a room to freshen before the dancing. There was much talk about dresses, most of it joyous and benign.

'A *soie ondeleuse*? I ask you! Still, it's wonderful.'

When the music started there was a general rush to the floor. The programme had set out the dances for the evening: quadrilles, among them the Conlon, the newly arrived Lancers, the Caledonian, a mazurka, a great selection of waltzes and a medley polka. Most of the couples who took to the floor were more than proficient – at least one of them having at some time or another been to a dance master, so therefore capable of passing on the steps. Or indeed the men might have had occasion to dance with each other – perhaps on the ship out – if their own women had not been met yet. The single men eyed the single women with great appreciation, and the women were happy to glory in this, some of them engaging in the practice of fan talk to attract a man who might have caught their attention. And so the night wore on with remarkable vivaciousness. By the time the kitchen staff could be relieved for a few hours, the dance outside had already started, a competent caller with his nose to the window informing all of the exact steps, or as near as possible, that were being performed inside. And among the staff who joined in with great gusto – there being nothing like a dance to relieve tiredness – were a number of young Irish women. One was seen to stare at Charles Strutt, but before she could point him out she lost sight of him in the whirl of the dance.

It was almost five o'clock in the morning before the tired revellers returned home. A light breakfast was had and then all retired to a glorious, happy sleep. The next day involved a leisurely picnic, a small amount of prepared food being brought to a patch beside the harbour and laid out on a tablecloth. All looked at the water and carried on an easy conversation. The lecture and music would, tomorrow evening, round off a wonderful visit. Margaret had been delighted and amazed when Charles told her about the tickets. They repacked the picnic basket. Charles could have sworn he heard a familiar voice as they did this. No. It couldn't be.

The following evening torrential rain poured down, but the carriages were successfully brought as close to the Lyceum as possible, and when all were seated, Mr Denihey began his Master of Ceremonies role by introducing J.H. Plunkett Esq. MP, who was to deliver the lecture. People made themselves comfortable. In his opening remarks the lecturer gave a general appreciation of music – its delights as a spiritual recreation from incessant labour and a great source of renovation for the fatigued mind for those involved in more intellectual pursuits. He then did a European tour of music, landing on lessons for children, the promiscuous attendance of professors and amateurs alike at musical events in Germany, the human voice as instrument, and the architecture of music. He informed his audience that he was not one of those who condemned polkas, waltzes, quadrilles, mazurkas and light music, which came as much relief to those who had attended the recent ball. Mr Plunkett had an idea that people in the bush, far removed from society, would also benefit by playing some instrument. Why even the common shepherd would never feel lonely if he could play a flute under a gum tree. There was a slight drawing in of breath by those who had met the same shepherds and fancied this was a matter of opinion. He quoted Dr Burney, who in his history of music had remarked upon the disadvantages under which ancients laboured.

The Egyptian flute was only a cow's horn, with three or four holes in it, and their harp or lyre had only three strings; the Grecian lyre had only seven strings, and was very small, being held in one hand; the Jewish trumpets that made the walls of Jericho fall down, were only rams horns, their flute was the same as the Egyptians; they had no other instrumental music but by percussion, of which the greatest boast made was the psaltery, a small triangular harp or lyre with wire strings, and struck with as from needle or stick, their mebut was something like a bagpipe; the timbret was a tambourine, and the duletmar was a horizontal harp with wire strings. They had no written music; scarcely a vowel in their language and yet (according to Josephus) had two hundred thousand musicians playing at the dedication of the temple of Solomon.

Well, be that as it may. People were glad they had made themselves comfortable. After some time Mr Plunkett got to the point of the evening, Ancient Music of Ireland. And the night took on a new life of its own, particularly when, to the relief of some, the singing began, beautifully rendered by the men and women who had accompanied Mr Plunkett on stage, and who were doubtless now well and truly ready to give their vocal cords an airing. The singing of 'She is Far from the Land', created a particular silence of its own, followed by rapturous applause. As the voices soared, any discomfort felt at the length of the lecture was quickly forgiven on the grounds that it was the lecturer's first outing. The night concluded with a rendering of 'The Harp that Once through Tara's Halls', and when the reporter from the *Sydney Morning Herald* ran to check details with some of the concertgoers, he would have no problem finding plenty who knew all the words.

It was while they were departing the theatre that Charles came face to face with Anne Sherry, who was accompanied by an older woman. Anne became very flustered, which Charles put down to the surprise meeting. But at the door she drew him aside and hurriedly spoke, 'The woman with me is my mother.'

'But I thought your mother was dead?' said a surprised Charles.

'My mother had been sent out as a convict before me and I was not sure if she was still alive, but we have recently been reunited,' Anne said, formally.

She and her mother were wearing thoroughly interesting hats. Maybe Margaret would like one like that?

'But that is wonderful news.'

'Yes, except ...' and here Anne's eyes filled with tears,

'I told Honora Raftery that my mother was dead. It seemed the right thing to do, to fit in. But then when I saw what it really was to be certain that you had a dead mother, I felt ashamed. That's why I couldn't go to Yass.'

'Oh dear,' said Charles. 'But surely she would understand,' wondering, as he said it, if indeed she would.

'Perhaps you should write to explain,' he said, as gently as he could, considering that Margaret and the carriage were waiting for him and there would surely be such a jam in this rain.

'Maybe,' Anne Sherry said. And then added, 'But I don't know where she is, nor Julia Cuffe either.' She hurried back to her mother.

'I could try to find out,' Charles shouted after her disappearing navy coat.

CHAPTER 27

It was Margaret who brought it up with Charles, more than a year later, two days before they were to visit Sydney again.

'Maybe you should try to meet one of them or even two, you couldn't meet more than that. It might put your mind at rest,' she said.

Charles looked at her with surprise – she could be full of such practical ideas at times.

'Why not?' she questioned.

Indeed why not. That is what he would do, he thought. He would meet Anne Sherry first, although no doubt that would not be her name now. Still, it should be easy enough to locate her. He had the contacts.

So Charles set about finding her. Once married, and now twice married, he was lucky to find her after two name changes. A person could get completely lost like that. And so he came to stand at the door of a tidy house, some streets back from Pitt Street. He had decided not to inform Anne of his visit, he felt she might find a way not to see him if she had warning, she had run away after the concert. Maybe she had spoken to him on impulse with the shock of seeing him and then regretted it. Of course it might have been the rain. He remembered the rain. Or the man standing behind her. He knocked on the door. Anne opened it, a baby slung on her hip and followed by other children, who came out to look at him quietly. He did not like to count how many there were. She looked at him for a moment, then said, 'Come in, come in.' But Charles knew she was flustered by his presence. Probably it was unfair to call like this.

'No, no. I was passing,' he lied. 'I thought I would tell you that I will bring a letter to Honora Raftery if you wish to write to her. I can call again this time tomorrow?'

He suddenly felt foolish. But Anne Sherry smiled, a wide happy smile.

'That will be nice. Yes, that will be nice,' she said.

'So, I will see you tomorrow,' Charles said, hurrying back to his carriage, thinking his visit might bring up unwelcome memories.

But when he arrived the next day she brought him in to a good front room. She already had teacups laid out. She pointed at them but Charles said, 'No, no thank you. Really I have to get on.' He was aware this might be a difficult conversation, how could he not have thought so, how could he have thought he could turn up here as if she was still his business. Perhaps she found it an intrusion. They both sat down. Anne looked out the window at the trees dripping with an unusual shower.

'I make hats,' she said.

'Oh.'

'And I have children too. From my first husband as well.'

Charles tried to do subtractions but gave up.

'I don't say how many from each. They are children. People should mind children,' she said.

Charles felt uncomfortable.

'Oh no, it was too late for us,' Anne said, reading his mind, 'You did your best to get us here.'

And, now that he had been given it, Charles wondered if

he had been in need of some pardon or at least the sound of it.

'I don't talk about the past,' Anne said.

She pleated her dress over her knee and patted it down.

'Other people are welcome to do that, but not me. I wouldn't know what to say about it.'

She patted her dress some more.

'My husband is going to take me to the races some day. He says maybe even to Melbourne, because my hats have been seen there. It's not necessary to go, it's better that my hats have been there. But I might go. I might go.'

Charles swallowed. He could not seem to find anything to say. Anne Sherry had been a quiet girl he thought he remembered.

'I am very glad,' he said, 'about your hats – and your children of course,' he added.

'Would you like one?' Anne asked, 'A hat for your wife?' as if she had suddenly thought of a good way to end this conversation. 'Yes, I'll get a hat for your wife.'

'Thank you,' Charles said. 'My wife came from Ennis, in Ireland.'

'Really?' Anne said and paused. 'But that's the past too.'

She moved to the corner of the room and took a hat from what he could now see was a collection of feathered hats on a homemade tree. Charles stood up.

'This is so kind of you,' he said.

Anne bustled about, got paper, wrapped the hat. They moved to the door. She waited until Charles was out in the light before she said, 'About the letter ... I couldn't write it.' She looked past him to the tree outside. 'I did not know for sure that my mother was alive, the priest here helped me find her. She could have been dead. Now Julia, if you knew where Julia was, she would understand. But there would be too much explaining to do for Honora. I couldn't find a start to tell her. And without a start, well you never get anywhere. It's a pity. I hope Honora got on all right. I hope she was lucky.'

Charles wished he had news of Honora to relate.

'The people who took her seemed kind,' he said.

'Well, that would help,' Anne replied. 'As a beginning, that would help, the beginning can be frightening.'

'Yes,' Charles said, and coughed a little.

'There were others who went there too, a lot of us?'

'Yes,' Charles said, 'and maybe they will all still know each other.'

'Or maybe not,' Anne said. 'Children and husbands can keep you busy,' she smiled.

'And hats,' said Charles, and they laughed away the unease.

He walked to the gate, closed it, and turned to wave.

Anne had a frown on her face. She was tired from explaining her life. But she added with a tone of finality, to herself as much as to him, 'I try to live an ordered life. I try not to let sudden things happen. That's best, not to let sudden things happen.'

Charles lifted his hat to her and walked down the road. Anne put out her hand and touched the tree, then turned to go back in to her house. Charles would now find Honora Raftery.

The road to Yass was much improved. More and more miles had been reclaimed from the red earth and laid down as road. Charles had undertaken to do some business for Mr Winslow, it would add reason to his visit. Margaret would stay on the extra days in Sydney – Mrs Winslow was very pleased as she had lots for them to do. They waved him off and turned to their own business.

Other men heading in the direction of Yass accompanied

Charles on the coach. One man took out his Certificate of Freedom several times, read it and smiled. At last he read it aloud – 'This is to certify that fourteen years have elapsed since Sentence of Transportation for that term was passed upon,' and the man bowed, 'Yours Truly here … and now restored to all the Rights of a Free Subject under said circumstances.'

The others clapped. 'Under said circumstances indeed,' the man chuckled. 'Given at the Colonial Secretary's Office, Sydney. Would you credit that.' He stood up and bowed. The men clapped again. He was on his way to Ned Ryan's of Galong, he said, to work there for a while, to find his feet and decide what his next free move would be. A girl had gone to Ned Ryan's, Charles remembered.

'I know of him,' he told the man.

'Do you now.'

Charles attended to Mr Winslow's business at all the stops, including Goulburn, still a town he liked. When the horses finally stopped in Yass, he made his way to the new hotel and found a room for the night. As he did so, women looked at him and some shook their heads. He looked back but wasn't sure, he could not remember every face and they would have changed by now, grown up, got sun, looked into the eyes of babies. Later he made his way to the Catholic church, met the priest and found out details. There it was in black and white, so many weddings, and so many baptisms.

'And lots more in the other churches too,' the priest said. 'Yes, we are going well,' he added.

'Here is Honora Taffe's address, out that road,' he pointed. 'Second on the left, long hill up, you'll see the house, a tidy place, white.'

Yes, he would have thought it would be like that.

Charles had not told Honora he was coming. In the end it had worked out with Anne Sherry, he thought, different to what he might have expected, but as well as it could have done. Except of course for the letter, but that couldn't be helped. But unknown to Charles, Honora had been told that a man looking like Mr Strutt was seen going into the hotel. She had dusted her house just in case.

He got down from the carriage he had taken from the hotel and told the man he could wait. He galvanised himself. Yes, there had been difficult moments with Anne Sherry.

Honora stood back from the window and watched him coming to the door. She felt entitled. There were a lot of her memories tied up with his face. She went to the door to let him in.

'Hello, Mr Strutt,' she said.

'Hello, Honora,' he replied, smiling tentatively. 'I was on business nearby and thought I would call to see how you were.'

'Well this is how I am,' Honora said, and swept her hand in a circle. 'Come in.' They moved into a room in the front of the house and they sat.

'We'll have tea,' she said and lifted the pot, already made.

'My husband works in the mill,' she said, by way of opening. 'He came from Wales. Before me.'

Charles thought that perhaps he should mention what Wales might be like now. Or England even. He knew little of what Ireland was like now.

'But we don't go into the past,' she said, reading his mind the way Anne Sherry had done. 'I build new memories here,' she said, 'for my children. They're all at school, all my children like school,' she said. 'Except the baby, of course. He's asleep.'

'Oh, yes,' Charles said, and lifted his bag. He fumbled through it and brought out a book, which he handed to her. It was a dictionary.

'Thank you, I have one but this is better,' she said, feeling the cover. 'The children will like it too. My husband gets me books from the neighbours. They have a lot of books. We have one on birds. Did you ever hear of Bridget?'

Charles had found out about her death only last week when he was searching for Anne Sherry. He hesitated.

'I think she may have died, not long after we landed.'

Honora looked out. She listened for the birds, not a difficult thing to do, the sound was there all the time. If you stopped and paid attention you could pick up the most extraordinary sounds.

'I see,' she said, 'that might have been for the best.'

Charles had no answer to that. He drank some more tea and wondered why he was here, wondered what he was hoping Honora would say.

David Taffe drew up at the house, having finished work for this day. But when he saw the heads of the two of them, nodding to each other, he watched for a moment and decided to leave them to it. It would be good for Honora to have this conversation to herself and she would tell him later what was said and what she thought of it.

'We are fine you know,' Honora said, 'now that we're here. We have to be fine. And ...' She couldn't think of anything else to say.

There was the sound of a baby crying. Honora stood up.

'And tonight we go to Ned Ryan's. I am going too.'

'Ah, Ned Ryan's,' Charles said. 'I've heard of him.'

'Oh yes, everyone has heard of him,' Honora said,

including Charles in the new history of the place just for a moment. They moved to the door.

'That thing I said, about making new memories for my children, they wouldn't like mine, the early ones yes, they might, but not what happened after.'

'I understand,' Charles said.

'You know we don't talk like that among ourselves. There's no point. And anyway, no one would believe us.'

'It's all right,' Charles said, as if he was saying that he would not tell anyone.

The man pulled the carriage around, the horse snorted. They stood at the door of the carriage.

'My husband just made me a new clothesline,' Honora said, pointing out to the side of the house, and with that statement she claimed some contentment out of the debacle of her history.

Charles doffed his hat. He had not mentioned Anne Sherry, he wasn't sure whether he had forgotten or deliberately not done so.

Later, as a matter of courtesy, he called on the priest. Presumably he would not be going to Ned Ryan's.

'Come in, come in,' the priest said.

They went into a proper front parlour and sat down. A woman came in with a tray, which she placed on the table.

'Good evening, sir,' she said.

Charles looked at her and wondered desperately if he should recognise her.

'Good evening,' he said, as she hurried out of the room.

'One of yours, I think,' the priest said.

They passed an enjoyable evening, swapping stories they knew of this place. As Charles prepared to leave, the priest said, 'What is history anyway? The truth of history is a fable agreed upon, that's what Napoleon said.'

Charles made his way around the corner, down the small incline to the hotel. As he left town the following morning he thought he would not see any more of them. He passed a school. A stream of children was coming through its door.

CHAPTER 28

On a morning in 1860, the sun once again began its high climb in the sky in Sydney and Brisbane, Yass, Gundagai and thereabouts, Melbourne, Ballarat, Castlemaine, Adelaide and lots of other places – many of them just named or given new names. Women and men rose out of sleep, at that moment all equal to each other, until the joy or sadness or the in-between came over them with the full opening of their eyes.

Cissy Weir stretched her legs in bed. Still behind closed eyes she knew, by the weight of her body, that no child had woken in the night. She turned into her husband's back for another few minutes.

Celia McElroy, just down the road, decided to start a new list today. She did that regularly. It kept her life tripping along nicely.

Biddy Callaghan, in Gundagai, looked for the sixpence that she had put away. They gave it every year to Yarri, the man from the Wiradjuri people, who had rescued her and her baby from the Big Flood in 1852, as well as forty others. Her husband was thought to have drowned but she was never sure. She had a new husband now.

Rose Tighe, in Cootamundra, got things ready to sit her last baby outside for the first time. He had been the hardest to have, but smiled at her often as if to make up for it.

Teresa Furey thought she would clean her kitchen today as soon as she had it to herself. This need to clean came over her at this same time every year, she couldn't tell why. She started by washing last night's whiskey glasses.

Rose Larkin rolled herself out of bed. She felt that the baby might come today – there was a difference to the way it turned in her last night, maybe she should wash all the clothes in the bath outside. Maybe that would do it.

Ellen McGillicuddy cleared last night's playing cards from the small table and patted the heads of her children as they went out to school. She always had to remind herself to do it to all of them, not just the first. When she had looked at him on the second day of his life, she had said, 'Well that's that then. I'm from here now.'

Anne Sherry in Sydney started another hat.

Charles Strutt started another journey by sea.

Honora Taffe opened her trunk to clean it and took her bonnet out to air. She thought of herself as Raftery when she did this.

Julia Cuffe got on another coach.

It was Honora Raftery who realised what date it was. This time she wrote it down so she would remember next year. And the year after …

CHAPTER 29

It was Honora Raftery who died first. It was on an early autumn day. She would have liked that. She always said autumn was her favourite season, full of relief that another summer was over. Leaves blew in and around the streets of Yass that evening, scampered in the wind, rustled like paper and flew off to God knows where. Her coffin was brought to the chapel in Yass – she would be buried from where she had been married and had prayed. She was also well pleased that she had seen 1900. She told Cook that, who it turned out was only ten years older than Honora, give or take a year or two, it was hard to be sure. She was still going strong, living in her own house now with her second husband. The house was low, had a corrugated roof and was as close to a clump of trees as was safe. The trees cast a shadow in the afternoon, which fell near the house. Cook could sometimes be seen taking her chair outside and moving with the shadow. The best thing about the house was that it had a verandah at the front. Cook's second husband was handy – you could marry a man because he could build a verandah. Honora had told her that the new century would be much better than the last and that she was glad to wipe her feet of the old one, 'Not that I haven't been happy here, don't get me wrong, I'm not saying that at all.'

This reference to here surprised Cook because Honora never talked about here and there, not like some, whose conversation could mist over at the most unexpected of times.

'But I'll be gone before you,' Cook said, to this unexpected conversation.

'Not necessarily,' Honora said, as if she knew. She got up, moved over to the table and placed an envelope on it. 'You can open it when I die,' she said.

'Don't be silly,' Cook said, but lifted the letter and put it away, only opening it on the morning they brought her the news. She put away the part of the correspondence that applied to herself, it would take an evening to read and could wait. She brought the funeral instructions to Honora's son, David, who lived over at the north end of Yass. David worked in the bank and would become a politician for sure. He was surprised by the letter. Honora had left specific requests for her funeral, in particular, she had listed the names of six women. She was not sure if these were entirely correct now – in the case of two, the spelling might have lost a letter or two, in the case of one she knew she had married three times but believed the second and third husbands might have had the same name. About another she was not sure if she had ever married, so her name might be her own. She listed the husbands' names as best she could. In the case of the last two she said she was including them without much hope they could be contacted. It might be an impossible venture. She advised that no more than a night and a day be spent trying to locate these women, and she enclosed money for wires. And if her son wouldn't mind, could he pass on a small box that was inside her trunk in the bedroom if any of them turned up. If they didn't he could destroy the contents. The box was marked 'Girls'.

In the end David managed to locate only Anne Sherry and Cissy Weir, who came together by coach, having kept up a sporadic acquaintance over the years. Anne Sherry had been married three times but luckily had come back around to Sherry the third time, which made it possible to find her. And Anne knew where to find Cissy Weir. There were four local women who looked quizzically at them and were themselves looked at, before they all fell on each other with varying degrees of warmth and noise, depending on what kind of woman they had become. Inside the church the stained-glass windows glowed, throwing yellow, red and blue streaks of light across the seats. The floor was comfortably cold. The priest spoke of Honora's life. It appeared to begin at her marriage, flourish with her children, the six of them all here today, and glowed nicely with her grandchildren, twenty of them, also all here today. No deaths were mentioned, except for that of her husband a decade and a half ago. The two strange women and the four locals walked behind the coffin like ghosts from another place. When they reached the grave one of them could be heard saying, 'There you go.'

They buried Honora on the hill that rose above the town. From here you could see the dried-up ruin of her first house and the hill where she had stood after her first week here. You could not see the river. David invited people back to Honora's home, and it was sometime after much tea and some sherry, that he asked if the women would like to see Honora's trunk. He wasn't sure why he had done that, instead of getting them the box she had left them, but they seemed pleased, and he was glad.

'Look,' Anne Sherry said, rubbing her fingers over the name, still clearly written.

Cissy Weir opened the bedroom curtains. She and Anne Sherry stood at the head of the trunk, the same as the one they had at home. The others moved towards it, respectfully, as if it was a holy thing, then opened it slowly, letting the squeal of the rusted hinges settle into the room.

'Look at that,' they said, 'and this,' moving some things to the side and some on to the bed.

'Does anyone remember Julia Cuffe?'

'Yes,' they said together, and wondered silently what might have happened to her.

'Look at this,' Cissy said, fingering a bonnet, 'I put mine away too.'

And then Anne Sherry lifted the paper. It began 'Dear ...'

'I don't know who it's to. And I don't know if we should be reading this ...'

But she began.

There was a title: 'What I Remember. Why Not To Remember. Ways of Forgetting.'

'He who learns must suffer, and, even in our sleep, pain that cannot forget falls drop by drop upon the heart, and in our own despair, against our will, comes wisdom to us by the awful grace of God.' Aeschylus
But remember that I was happy too.
Mise Raifteirí an file, Lán dóchas is grá ...

So you are surprised. I did get my dictionary. But I had to wait twenty years to see the book of quotations that David brought from the Mechanic's Institute. The poem I know by heart. Like many things that are not much noticed here, the Institute was a great consolation to me and cheered my life greatly. I could not of course go into the lending room, but I could see into it when we went to dances there and David brought books home for me. Although you may find that quotation particularly hard, there were others that lightened my days and gave me new ways to look at what was around me. You see, I did like to remember but I knew it was bad for me and might have stopped me living in the present. Teresa Furey would not allow me to talk of before we came here. We talked about all other things – we were good for each other – and often I know I could not have lived so well without knowing that she was within a score of miles from me. We would talk about our wedding days, our children born and how we had managed. We were so afraid to hold a baby in our arms the first time, what might it do to us, all that longing ... But we became used to it. And we became used to new vegetables and fruit, making jam and talk of making ice – she was the first to know there was ice being made in Geelong, she was the first to know many things. Some people are like that – news comes to them on air. And because it does, people learn to tell them things because if you want things to be known, you must tell the news to gatherers. But I would have liked to have lived close to someone else too, someone who would have allowed me to talk about before. But perhaps no one would. Teresa says that there is no 'us'. She says that to see the 4000 of us as 'one', is nonsense. And yet it was she who told me 4000 – I had not known that number. I had to listen to her because she was louder and surer than me. But she was wrong there. I was told in Ryan's that they had a debate in the London Parliament about 'us'. It proves that we are one. And our names are all together in an office – I'm not sure if that's true, but I heard that in Ryan's too, it's always full of ticket of leavers and others. There are brick houses going up around there and there are plans to castellate and crenellate Ryan's house. As well as ice and vegetables, we talked about new materials and wool and how to get things added on to our houses. We talked about the Chinese going through and we talked sometimes about the Aborigines, who watched us and walked past us. But when I said that I didn't think they liked us, she said that was nonsense, why wouldn't they, and I said that maybe we had taken their land, and she laughed at me and said, 'Look at me, how much land have I taken?'

So I let it go. But I had my own thoughts. There's a man around here who watches me. He saw me before I saw him. He was here first. I know what he thinks of me. I want to say to him that I do not want to be in a house on his land, I have my own spot, even if I cannot get to it. But it doesn't matter to him if I think that, I'm still in a house on his earth. When he saw us coming he stared, then after staring long enough he thought that maybe he could share with us, but then he realised that we didn't want to share, we wanted to own. I've thought this out myself, because, after all, I've heard it before. I would have liked to talk to Teresa about that more. But she laughed at me a lot and I learned to move on to other things. She came with me to hear a talk about Jane Franklin, about how she travelled. I had a dream about Jane Franklin holding her bicycle close to her, as if this treasure might run away and disappear if she did not clasp it tight. The bicycle was all she needed. I would be like that about a bicycle. And was like that about other things too, as I learned to count my blessings. Teresa came to the talk and then said it was rubbish and what had she let herself get talked into by me. 'I've more to be doing,' she said, but then started about something else, as always, and never held the lecture against me. She came to the opening of the train station with me and we looked up the track and wondered would we ever be on it, going out there. 'That's the way to Sydney,' she said. She came to the town with me when the clock was installed at the post office. It was she who told me *that the first wire had been delivered to the Royal Hotel, to an upstairs room. She said that there had been a great fuss in the town and that she thought she knew what was in it, but wasn't sure, and then went on to something else before I could get her stopped and put back over it. I wanted to know how a wire came. When I mentioned it again she said she had never told me anything about what was in the wire, that it was a silly thing for me to say and so I had to believe that maybe I had imagined it.*

But I know what it is I have to forget. I do remember leaving Ireland. I remember being on the first boat. And I remember being cold at Plymouth. I remember some of the days on the ship, when all sense of dawn and dusk had been lost and water speeding under a ship was the only way of being. Sometimes it's a ship and sometimes a boat. And I remember one sunny dry day, after looking up into the ropes and sails, having the nerve to put my hands on the rail and look out at the sea. I remember coming to journey's end and knowing for sure that I would never do that again. And I remember the coves, following the coves into Sydney and the boat passing one, then another, sliding through them and another coming up and me thinking that they would go on forever and that the sea might open up again before us and that maybe we would never get off the boat. I remember the road coming here, parts of it, the ruts and the gullies and the scrub. Sometimes the hills were clumped together, but then when we crossed them we would suddenly see flat for miles. We could see so far. And I wondered when that would end. But then we would come to another hill, and that's when I learned to forget what had passed, and only look to what was coming up. I remember someone saying one morning that what she was looking at reminded her of Ireland and someone else scoffing, 'People can tell themselves anything. Look at the grass, it's yellow.' We all had to forget. 'And there are no hedges.'

I think perhaps that I remember what fields were like in Ireland. They were small. I remember a bird drinking from a puddle on a lane that had grass running down the middle of it. And I remember my father telling me that the birds outside making that racket in the autumn were discussing the best routes to Africa. And then the starlings would come to take the place of the small birds when they had left for Africa. Not much of a racket really, not when compared to every morning here. But I knew there was no point in telling my children. My daughters and Teresa's daughters sat together in class and knew nothing about their mothers. They might not have believed me. And I wanted my children to believe me.

The first day I saw a white tree I thought I would get used to that – forget it, if you will, for forgetting can be the same as becoming accustomed to – but I didn't. Instead, every morning when I saw one, I marvelled and wondered how it could be. How could there be such a thing as a white tree? And I saw animals that never failed to surprise me, no matter how often I saw them. And the birds that were unbelievable. There were other reasons too, not to remember. My brother, Dan, did come here. But he did not like this town. He left soon after he looked at our fields, and instead followed on to where there was gold. I never saw him again. He brought me a brooch belonging to our mother – Florrie had kept it. Florrie had died too, and that I knew I had to forget. I knew that if I forgot, she could still be alive. My brother did not want to remember anything. He said that remembering brought only desolation. We had seen the abyss *of hunger, the apocalypse of it. We had fallen into the open mouth of famine. Why would we want to remember? We couldn't cry with sadness, there wouldn't be enough tears. He was right about that too. You don't want to know about the intricacies of my hunger, the shame it brought on me, or if you do, I cannot understand why, because I don't need to know it anymore. I have forgotten about the workhouse and he's right, I never want to remember it. He was excited about gold, he said. He did write to me, a few times, the last time to say that he now had three children, three fine children is what he called them, that the gold had dried up and that he was leaving now to go droving for a time. His wife's name was Maisie, her father was from Wicklow and her mother's people were from Cork they thought. They had forgotten fast. After the droving he had a promise of a job managing a farm, belonging to none other than the son of our landlord from back home. Imagine. I don't know how all that worked out. Presumably he had to do extra forgetting.*

The reasons for not remembering are that you could spend your life running after moments, trying to catch them, and then not being sure if perhaps they were just dreams. No, Teresa Furey and my brother were right – it is a wise thing to forget. So that's what I did, sometimes more successfully than others. On my wedding day I felt a new beginning, not just like a normal new beginning, but the frightening one, the delicious one, the bright one, more an abandonment of my past, which I already had to fight for, now that I was coming out of the bad dreams. On that morning I loved the look of the land too, and I wondered if I had betrayed them all. There were some moments that were harder than others, births mainly, but then the baby would make so much noise and have to be attended to, leaving no time to be sad. And

having once liked the look of the land it was easier from
there on in. And so I looked to my future instead of to what
might have been my future. Tenses are important.

The letter was not signed; perhaps it hadn't been finished.
The women stood, unsure of what to say. They looked at
Teresa Furey, who was at a loss to know what to feel. She had
never expected to hear herself described.

'But who is it to?'

'What will we do with it?'

'I think we should destroy it,' Cissy said. 'If she didn't say
who it was for, then we need to destroy it.'

Teresa Furey thought it best she not express an opinion
on the matter.

'And also, it's not finished, there are no *Ways of Forgetting*.'

'Oh look, there's a box here for us,' she said.

Cissy poured out the contents on the bed. They would
look now and see what there was to remember.

'And an envelope for you, Anne.'

And others with names on them. They would read these
letters and see what sense they made. Teresa Furey lifted the
first letter and put it in her pocket for the moment, she would
read it again in peace and then maybe give it back to young
David, depending on what it said.

CHAPTER 30

2008, Dublin

Joy Kennedy got two more letters from Australia, and both intrigued her. One of them contained pamphlets, the other pieces of information, drops of history. It was not possible to put them away as if they were ordinary letters. After all, they did not carry an ordinary request, no more than her job was run of the mill. She would have to give them some consideration. But in the meantime she pushed them to the back of her mind. She had customers to see.

Joy's customers come into her workshop. Usually they rang first and asked tentative questions about lettering and such. There might be a little shake in their voices. Then they would broach price, and invariably the tremor gave way to embarrassment. They might try to cover this up by attempting a matter-of-fact tone, as if this was a normal kind of monetary questioning. How much is that coat, love? And does that take into account the ten per cent discount? But she knew the problem – it seems such a mean thing to be doing, putting a price on the name of your recently deceased loved one, deciding what to remember and what to forget. So Joy helped them along, guided by the tone of their voices. Over the years she'd become good at this, her ears able to pick up the unsaid, and perhaps unknown, wishes.

By the time the customers came in to see Joy to discuss the lettering, they had usually overcome their initial grief and so they approached the stone in her workshop at least with reverence, and often with love, as if the way they treated this marble must truly reflect their feeling for the deceased. They sometimes fondled it, trying to rub their good memories into it, looking as if they were blind and rooted to the spot by the whistle of past things. There were three due that day. They were coming to get her to scrape out the memorial for their dead. They could just as easily buy their own stone, or find it lying around Liscannor, and chip out their thoughts themselves. But they don't do this because there's not always agreement among those left about what should be said, and using her as a go-between was a way to cut down on argument and lying awake at night. Let's say there were four sons left – that's four synchronised tossing and turnings, four grown ups reversing into the theatre of their childhoods, taking up their positions, the ones that got them through safely until they could leave home. One wants what he thinks is perfectly apt – information and a bit of love. Another snorts, 'Sentimental balderdash. And on top of that you don't mean a word of it.' He has a different idea, a cool, clean, timeless comment. Finished. Clear. The third puts his hands over his ears, so he won't hear the now inevitable sounds that will soon burst out, sparking into the air like fireflies without the beauty. He tries to do this surreptitiously, but they see him, which makes them even madder, always did. 'Take yours hands away from your ears, you blooming sissy.' When the dull thump at the end of the batted insults makes itself known to him through his still covered ears, he jumps in with a compromise, although he hates it himself. The fourth is sick to the teeth of the lot of them, always jostling for supremacy, or smoothing down, as if life could be put on an ironing board and de-creased. He's the one who says that the stonemason will know best.

And he gets out the telephone book straight away, and rings Joy because she's a woman, and that will give those lunatics something to bang on about.

Nobody came to Joy by accident – they either stayed away from her because she was a woman, or they came to her for that same reason. Sometimes she wished she were a man, just for the straightforwardness of it. Different except the same, arguments happen if it's women left behind. Different, except the same, if it's a mix left behind. No argument if there's one.

So to today's three. Joy had them slotted in according to what suited them and her. She never saw more than three a day – acquainting herself with the relatives of three different deceased people was her daily limit. And she tried to have two days in the week when she saw no one, days in which she could chisel, smoke uninterrupted, and sing out of tune.

All three went well. And so did the difficult script she was finishing for one of last month's stones.

And those Australian letters hadn't come to her by accident either.

So Joy closed her shop and headed for home. Normally she cycled, wove boldly in and out of traffic, breaking the rules if need be. At Harold's Cross, some of the motorists looked out for her in their rear-vision mirrors so they could give her a wide berth. But she was not cycling today – she had been too miserable that morning after a bad dream to have the air flying around her throat. And walking was better for thinking. She would have to do something about those letters ... And here was her home.

Joy opened the door and Oscar came out from the back corridor. They usually made dinner separately, one either throwing scraps together or starting from the first onion, the other hovering in the loops of the conversation. It was

Oscar's turn today, but she didn't join him in the kitchen or hang around the table, instead she sat on the sofa and wondered. What was it about her work that she liked most? Was it the noise, the shapes, the dust, the customers, the people who worked on the half street with her? Or was it that she was tough enough to handle this business of memory. And for every single bit of it she had one teacher to thank.

At school when Joy was coming up to seventeen she got fed up with the decisiveness of her classmates. It was as if every day another traitor came in, all flushed, saying 'Miss, Miss, I know what I want to be.'

She sat at the back of the class and twisted bits of hair around her ear. The career guidance teacher sent for her. Joy had not been party to any discussions that may have taken place between her and other teachers before she obeyed the summons. She did not know if the teacher's tongue was in her cheek as she outlined all sorts of options and flattened her expression as Joy turned down the notion of all the jobs she could possibly bring to mind. A teacher. No way. The guidance person had put that in because it was *de rigueur* to consider it, she did not for a moment think that Joy had what it took. Next up was nurse. But it was clear to her that Joy had no interest whatsoever in tending ailments, far too flighty for that. It was even clearer to Joy. Secretary? 'Oh no, I couldn't work in an office,' she said, completely startled by now. 'Really?' The stalling at this suggestion may have been the point at which a noticeable barb entered the teacher's voice. There was silence while she regrouped. Joy wanted to be helpful. She did. She almost said she would like to be a poultry instructor, almost asked for the appropriate form, just to get out of the stifling room. She didn't know if there was still such a job, but she'd had an aunt who had been one before she died. She had travelled to farmers' wives, after they had day-old chickens posted to them, and she had advised them on feed, and what to do with sick chickens and how to diagnose diseases. But Joy thought it would be an insult to such a specific profession to feign interest in it. And presumably that job was long gone – there would be leaflets now and men in cars, or men ringing up, or maybe you just reared chickens yourself and hoped for the best.

The career guidance teacher had twenty-seven possibilities, and Joy couldn't bring herself to say yes to one. She did have a respect for the professions. Her reluctance to be flippant about them surely proved that.

The teacher told Joy to go away and at least think.

She must have reported back to the other teachers because the next day, when Joy was staring out the window again, the mathematics teacher sighed as she battled against the spectacular lack of interest being shown in her subject. She thumped the desk and declared, 'Joy Kennedy, the only thing you're any good at is hanging around waiting to fit under your own headstone.'

It was getting close to The Leaving Certificate.

Joy said, 'Thanks.' The mathematics teacher said, 'Don't be so smart.'

The following week Joy went to the career guidance teacher. She wanted her to be the first to know. She had not come into school and burbled about it, she hadn't wanted it to be sullied by puzzlement. The teacher thought for a moment and said, 'How did you get to be so modern?'

Joy then told the mathematics teacher, and even how she had contributed to the decision.

The teacher said, 'Well, I'm glad if I've been of some assistance in some way, because I have certainly failed to be able to teach you any trigonometry. And another thing, could you stop talking out of the side of your mouth like that, you'll tighten it and then you'll never be able to have a conversation that anyone will believe.'

So Joy had made up her mind. Her mother began to make enquiries about how a person could become a stonemason – part of this pleased her, the unusualness of it, but another part irked her slightly. Could her daughter not have been more normal? Less modern? And she would not be able to force her into conversation about her work when, or if, she did make it. She would have no common reference points, and feared that perhaps this was exactly why Joy was interested in such an odd job. She had always been a child more interested in what was not in front of her.

When it came time for Joy to leave home, she refused to think about what her mother might be thinking. She had already deserted her.

Joy entered the workshop of Bracken, O'Neill & Company and proceeded to learn her trade. She went to classes two mornings a week where the history of the work was explained, though in truth she preferred the work itself. She quickly became aware of the standoff between the new sandblasting and the old chiselling. She built loyalties in her work. At the quarry she learned the temperament of stone – some was so delicate that the slightest tap of a chisel along its nervous vein could split it in two, some was robust and seemed to say, come get me.

After three years with Bracken, O'Neill & Company, it seemed the right thing for Joy to branch out on her own. She acquired a workshop close to Mount Jerome Cemetery at Harold's Cross. She had a look at it, and then at Glasnevin, and formed the opinion that the type of person using

Mount Jerome would be more likely to choose her services. In Glasnevin there were too many people belonging to the unchanging part of Ireland. And she dismissed the idea of setting up near any of the newer or outlying graveyards – the suburbs would not have suited her, and she would not have suited them.

There was a block of busy little places beside her new premises. A bakery, a butcher and a florist, of course. And across the road was a café and pub. In no time at all, Joy had fitted in and found a companionable rhythm with the other businesses. It was nice, the baker said, having a woman about the place.

Joy lifted the Australian letters again as the smell from Oscar's cooking became more settled.

The bones of the story contained in the reading material – a considerable enough bunch of papers – had a way of drawing her in. She had been looking at them for weeks now. She had no idea what the information had to do with her, but she was still hooked. It made her heart catch sometimes before she went to sleep so that she dreamed dreams in several colours. Sometimes, too, what she learned of these girls brought her near to tears, being unable to forget them, no matter how she tried to see them merely as passengers from one place to another. At times she became aggravated because the story was too dreadful, it had nothing to do with her. Nothing whatsoever. And hadn't they fared well? Well, most of them. Surely we would have heard if they hadn't. She would write to Simon and tell him there were lots of Kennedys in Ireland. And out of it too.

But Joy kept the assorted pieces in one spot, piled on top of each other. If she looked at them in the evening, she was careful to tidy them neatly before she went to bed, to make sure the edges were lined up and there were no bits of photocopied pages sticking out, as if this act might retrospectively keep them safe for the night. She could tell when Oscar had been reading them – the pile would not be quite as she had left it. Sometimes Oscar read out paragraphs, sometimes Joy listened enthralled despite herself, and sometimes she said, 'Stop, I can't bear it.' And he would stop. But what he had read out loud might stay with her for days, and she would wonder about the consequences of choosing the job she had. And wonder what to do about those letters. You would have to think a lot before deciding to go to Australia, surely.

CHAPTER 31

But then a few pages arrived, and with them a short note from Simon.

Dear Joy,

In the process of my searches I found this. I've enclosed a photocopy of the original – it was from a child's copybook, which had been hand divided into weeks and days, like a diary would be. It has the name Julia Cuffe written on it. But clearly the writer gave up. Still, it's something. And I thought you'd like the reference to the gravestones. As you can see, a lot of it has faded and the spelling is not perfect. Looking forward to hearing from you. And please do excuse my persistence.

Sincerely,
Simon.

1 May 1856
I have no idea how I got talked into this – well actually I do. I met Lola Montez. Yes I did. Although of course if I told you that you wouldn't know if it was true or not. But it is. I met her, and now that I think of it, it wasn't as crazy as you might imagine. She wasn't like what they said she was – at least not with me. The news had come from Castlemaine that the council had stopped its meeting early so they could all go to see her, and everyone was excited, even those who were pretending they weren't. I dipped in and out of the

excitement – I've always found I like only a bit of it, I like to have my feet on the ground, even though people might not think so. I had been asked to do the warm-up dance, get the crowd in the mood, as if there was any need for that. I was a bit nervous – the men can turn on the warm-up if they feel like it. But nervous is like excitement, it does no good. I've learned that. So out I went and danced to the piano, mixing moves, keeping time, swirling to my own beat, losing myself as I always do. Best place to be lost. There was a lot of noise that night, more than normal, what with all those who were excited and those who were pretending not to be. But I'm good enough to dampen it down a bit, and I did too. They cheered me well when I'd finished, getting ready for the real cheers for Lola Montez. I never heard such noise, the banging of feet and crazy whooping. They let me stay behind the curtain so I heard her breathing as she stamped on the spiders and threw off the layers of her clothes. She made us believe the spiders were real. I'll remember that next time when I'm getting lost in a dance. I can still hear the roar that erupted when she finished, I might be able to remember it right. You can do that if you want to. You can think of a minute, hold your breath and let everything rush into your head. But you have to hold your breath. And then you have to sieve out what's not any use. At the back of the stage they had rigged up a corner for Lola to wash herself and dress for what would be happening after the dance. That's where I stood. I thought if I spoke to her I could bring the performance back to the woman in my house and the others who dropped in. I tried to practice what I'd say if I got close enough, although I find practising takes the sport out of things. In the end I didn't need it – she called out to me from behind the curtain.

'Are you the Irish girl?' she said.

'Yes,' I said, although I don't know what that means anymore. How can I be from Ireland if I'm not there. That Strutt was right.

'Me too,' she said. 'Before I went to India and Paris. Did you know that I dallied with Liszt – strange man that – and George Sand, and Alexandre Dumas? All that was before Ludwig of course. I waited in Switzerland for him for as long as I could.'

I knew who Liszt was, I picked it up somewhere, you pick up great things on the roads I've been on. Maybe someone will know who the others are. I will ask someone. Lola came out from behind the curtain. I'm not being smart calling her Lola – that's her name, or at least it is now.

'Keep a diary,' she said, 'because if you don't, they'll never know.'

They whisked her away then.

'Good night, Julia,' she shouted back to me. 'Keep a diary.'

So that's why I'm doing this. I saw Lola four nights after that and every night she told me to keep a diary. I asked one night, who for? She said I'd find someone. I said another night that nothing happened to me for a diary, I just stayed as safe as I could.

'You think nothing has happened you!' and she laughed out loud, a kind of tinkling sound that ran into an echo.

You hear birds doing it sometimes, once or twice, but then when you want to hear it again, they've gone.

'And don't marry,' she said. 'It's more trouble than it's worth.'

On the sixth night I came in, full of satisfaction, waiting to see what she'd say after the dance. But there was a huge melee in the hall. Lola had been involved in a terrible fracas with the man from the newspaper because of something he'd said about her dance. And now she had challenged him to a duel. So she was running late. And they wanted me to dance to the big crowd. I did my best, lost myself as well as I could, but they were shouting, 'Lola! Lola!' and it put me off a bit. They shouted for 'the spider', but I knew better than to try. When she did arrive she had no time to talk to me, and left the next day, off to Bendigo.

I made this diary a few weeks after she left. We'll see how I go.

July
I don't like writing much – it's too hard. I bet Lola didn't keep a diary herself. I heard she could have been on the same ship as that Gavan Duffy man.

1857
I left Ballarat. I went to the Melbourne Races. A man I met took me – he said he had two free tickets for women. The races were full of women with coloured feather hats. At home I bet they have children behind their skirts that they talk about all the time. I don't think I'm going to do that, why should I? You wouldn't believe this. I got a letter from Strutt. He said a relative of mine had contacted him. So that might be your mother or father maybe. So this will be for you then. I thought it funny getting a letter from Strutt, wonder how he knew where to send it. Fellows like him can do all sorts.

1858
I went back to Brisbane. You wouldn't believe it, but they're finally making a proper graveyard and some man found me

and asked me if I'd come out when they put up the headstones, one of them being for Samuel, a man I knew once. I think I will. It's a nice thing to have a stone.

I still don't like writing. It makes everything look peculiar when it's put down. It's only my life.

Joy read it again.

'Oh, I'll have to go now,' she said out loud.

CHAPTER 32

Joy Kennedy had heard people say, 'No one was more surprised than me ...' and she had said, 'Yeah,' she had never said, 'I know what you mean.' That would be a lie. She never believed them and wondered what effect they were trying to create. But here she was, getting a case filled, and a separate bag with aeroplane paraphernalia, getting ready to go to Australia for three weeks and, in truth, no one was more surprised than she was.

The travel agent knew a lot about the way she should go.

'You can't stop in both Bangkok and Singapore.'

'Oh, I see,' Joy said, believing him, disappointed that she was not allowed.

'Well you could if you wanted, but people don't usually.'

'Oh, well I will if I can.'

To think that her hesitation and her lack of knowing how to get to the bottom of the world had almost denied her this.

'Or you can stop in Singapore on the way there, and Bangkok on the way back. Or vice versa.'

But she wanted to see both on the way there, one after the other – two strange Asian places, before landing in the midst of her own language even further away. Clearly, the travel agent thought her contrary. Why couldn't she have the same package as everyone else?

'And you will need all the extra days you can manage, to get over the jetlag.'

'Oh, I see.'

'It's terrible, I believe.'

'Oh, so you haven't been.'

'No, not yet.'

That gave Joy a steadier footing – she was closer to getting there than he was. Unless he decided to go next week just to get one up on her. The crankiness was a manifestation of her concern about what she was about to do. Yes, no one was more surprised than she was. She had never intended to go to the other end of the world to face history.

'You'll need a hotel with a swimming pool. You'll need some exercise for sure after the flight.'

He would have the last word.

'Thank you,' she said, letting him.

He didn't know whether she could swim or not, some people can't.

The decision for Joy to go had been taken by Oscar and her the previous week – although she felt it was really Oscar who had decided.

'Why don't you go?' he said.

'Why don't you go?' she asked. 'I don't see why people should go to the end of the earth just because it's possible.'

'But it's you who needs to go. It's you they want for the memorial.'

'And still I don't know what they want.'

'And you'll get to see Sydney at last.'

'But I've never wanted to see Sydney.'

That seemed such an ungrateful thing to say. Not ungrateful to Oscar, no, to Sydney and all its flourishing, breathtaking beauty. She had seen it on television, and on the calendar that the committee had sent. Maybe it wouldn't be as beautiful as the pictures. Frankly, it couldn't be as beautiful as the pictures.

'And the harbour,' Oscar said.

Clearly, Oscar did want to go. He rushed Joy into getting the tickets, or so it felt. He said there was no point in waiting now the decision to go had been made. When she was at the door of the travel agent, with the tickets, one for each way, clasped in her hand – she felt they needed to be held tighter than would tickets to say Torremolinos or Prague – the travel agent said three weeks might not be enough, that maybe she should have thought of going for four. But she drew the line at that.

Over tea the next morning Joy talked about the tickets. The florist knew a story about a nest of storks, a vague story that had perhaps become mixed up with others, and the trouble was that he couldn't be definite enough about the source to check. He was good at checking – dictionaries, books of synonyms, going home after something came up during the day, getting a chair or a hop-up ladder to take books of fables from the top shelf, and getting utterly lost.

And here was the story about the storks. He had thought of it when Joy had first mentioned the memorial and Australia. The story was that the storks had their nest in Schwandorf in Bavaria, and lived happily there as far as the people who looked at them every day could see. And the townspeople who were going about their work, or out for an evening walk, did look at them, because it is hard to pass a stork's nest on the top of a deserted factory chimney and not look up. They lived their lives publicly. When they were asleep and flat on the nest, with their heads tucked in, they were quite private, people could only see the shape of them, and even then could not be sure if those shapes really were their storks. But when they stood up in all their tallness and their long necks, it was impossible not to see them and everything they did.

They were a kind of warning – you will always be seen. But they were also a rare unadorned beauty, a kind of majestic overlord, and this was even before the people remembered the business of them flying hither and thither with their baskets, dropping babies into houses for people to mind.

But one day it was noticed that they were not there. No one could quite put their finger on when they had last seen them. The man who tended the garden going down to the river could have sworn that it was Wednesday, the man who lived closer to the stack wasn't sure, a small girl knew they were wrong and that the storks couldn't have been seen since Monday. But the adults believed more in seeing than in not seeing, and so they set on Wednesday as the last day. One could not of course be absolutely sure, because they could have been asleep and sometimes it was hard to tell if that hump was them and it was possible to forget to look at a stork's nest. Unlikely. But possible. But whenever they had last been seen, and whatever doubts there were about it, they were not there now. Gone. But where? And why? The town felt unlucky. There were those who preferred not to think about the bad luck aspect of it, they'd had enough of that and more. But it was there, niggling, every day. The storks had deserted their town.

A man became a stork-man. He decided to keep the nest maintained, and not let it get hidden by moss. He would perhaps shake the sticks a bit, perhaps they would pick up the light, or perhaps when lightning dazzled the sky, running in and out of the trees, it might illuminate the nest so that the Schwandorf storks would see it no matter where they were, and it would make them want to come home. People knew what he was doing and were grateful, because even though in time they had to forget about the birds, they did know

223

that someone has to tend to memory, and keep both the dark and the light parts nurtured in some way, so that they're there when needed. Although they saw his caring, they did not know he also prayed. He sent copious prayers to God. He had a favourite place – the small round chapel past the graveyard, at the entrance to the castle. It wasn't open, unless by prior arrangement, but he took to walking that way every day, and he moved to the front of it, leaning against the metal gate, and prayed to St Johannes, for all he was worth. People didn't notice that this new walking habit of his had begun around about a month after the time of the disappearance of the storks, but then people are unreliable, and if they briefly saw the two events as being linked, they forgot immediately. But there he is now, not just a stork-man, but a prayer as well.

And who is to say which of the two things worked. Maybe they both did. One day two storks landed back in the nest, flew straight down the brown fast-flowing river, past the flowers on the bridge, past the fishermen on the bank, the cows and horses – none of which looked up – past the beautifully kept vegetable allotments and straight to the old, and thankfully well-kept, nest. Within days it was obvious to all, except the almost blind, that one of them was not of the original pair – the male or the female, it could not be agreed upon. The little girl said she was certain it was the female that was different, but who would believe her. No matter. They soon had a baby stork, right up there in front of everyone, and the three of them looked out of their nest, over the walking people's heads, as if they noticed but didn't care.

The little girl grew up and learned to be a sculptor, just so she could make one thing – three storks. She would protect the town from the bereft feeling of missing their birds, she would show the storks that they mattered, but most of all, she would get her chance to put right the day they had gone missing because she would include it at the foot of the statue.

She constructed a tall mirror-like structure and placed the storks in front of it so that as well as the three that were sculpted, they also reflected three more. She could have made mirrors looking into mirrors so they were infinitely reflected, but thought, no, once was enough. When this was done she didn't know what else she would like to make. Unfortunately, she was now known as a sculptor, and there was pressure on her to keep up this life of representation and metaphor. In the end, she too had to leave so that she could have an actual life somewhere else, unburdened by having to tell a town truths.

The florist tapped the newspaper clippings about the storks when the talk was big about Joy going. He had found them in a drawer thrown out from a neighbouring house that was being restored. They had called him in to talk flowers. Someone had been to Schwandorf, obviously. The story had touched him, this story for Joy. There wasn't actually any mention of the sculpture, but Joy didn't like to harp on about this. Later the florist did check and found that in that town there is a statue, but it is of three pigs. However, there is a stork's nest. He decided not to tell Joy about his further findings. He could see the sculpture of the storks in his mind's eye, so there didn't seem to be any point. And he was excited about the possibility of Joy going to Australia.

'See, that's what memorials are for,' he said.

'I suppose,' Joy replied. 'Thanks.'

CHAPTER 33

When it came to the morning of Joy's leaving, she and Oscar behaved as if she was travelling a short distance – Paris, Milan, New York even. There wasn't much else they could do, there's a limit to outwardly expressing what the inside is feeling. Tidy the bed as soon as hitting your feet on the floor. Make the bed properly as soon as you are standing. Going to Australia should not be treated like any old journey. Joy found her sunglasses in the drawer at the bottom of her summer things.

'You could buy a new pair at the airport,' Oscar said.

'No, I like these,' she said.

She wanted some of her own old things on such a long journey. Oscar made breakfast. Joy watched him doing it, as if she was already on her way to Australia and therefore different.

'Stop looking at me like that, you're making me nervous,' he said.

'Even now, it's a big journey,' Joy said.

In the shower she lined up the shampoos and face creams, changed the candles around. She felt the water running down her back. She made a few goodbye telephone calls, and felt better, felt gone.

Oscar drove to the airport and parked in Block C. Joy knew he would have a long walk back. But once she got into the departures area, she stopped thinking about these rooted things and felt airport protocol take over. Oscar wanted to wait until she had gone through the security gates. She said, 'That would be nice,' as if she didn't know him, as if he was a perfect stranger. He held her hand as they went to the bookshop. Joy bought English as well as Irish newspapers, although the headlines meant nothing to her, as if she was already in a strange place. She had become connected to the girls in history, girls whom she had not known a thing about a year ago.

She read the Irish newspaper on the way to London. When the plane landed she left it on the seat, its news now faded in importance. She read the English newspapers after she had checked in at Heathrow. These stories too were fading in importance. When all the stories were read, she watched the vast array of people of all nationalities moving about the airport, rushing, shuffling, all in their own place, where they had come from and where they were going to. It was a feast of difference. She could have watched all day. By the time her fourteen-, sixteen-hour flight – what's the difference? – was called, she was already tired.

There was a muteness once all the passengers were seated in the plane. The hours wrote themselves large and left little room for complacency. The passenger next to Joy, on her inside, to whom she was determined not to speak, at least for the first twelve hours, sighed loudly. An hour out, there was some sort of bustle, like birds might make if they were shaking feathers from their nest in the evening. There was a slight increase in the noise levels. Then food arrived, breaking up the hours. Her neighbour, like many others, took his tablet, put earplugs over his ears, smiled at her conspiratorially, and pulled a mask down over his eyes. She had no need to worry about him. He did not want to talk to her either.

227

Joy tried to sleep. But the hush, like that of a hospital ward, mesmerised her only halfway. Film over, people stretched their legs one inch, this way and that, and tried to plunge themselves into some way of passing the time, some semblance of personal rest. Many who had not taken tablets because they thought they might not need them, now searched for them in their bags and went to get water. And then hush. Occasionally a passenger plodded up and down the aisle in stockinged feet, and back, and back, their legs, she supposed, itching with the ludicrousness of it all. Her eyes opened and closed. She would think now, without distraction, about those who had gone before her. That would be something to do.

To her amazement there were six hours gone. She watched the aeroplane make progress on her television map. She could not believe they had already passed over Turkey, Iran, India. Her eyes closed again. There was one more hour gone. Oh God. She would get horse tablets for coming back. Joy became fascinated by the screen in front of her and returned to it, too often. They were on their way to Bangkok. Altitude, 390,000 feet. Distance to destination, skip. Tailwind, eleven miles per hour. Useless that one. Sometimes it was up to seventy and the plane gobbled hours, speed, five hundred and seventy-eight miles per hour, air temperature outside, minus fifty-three. She toyed with the map pictures, went close up and far away, let her fingers touch Palembamg, Ujungpangdang, Banjarmasam, Jakarta, Surabaya, Bandung away ahead. It made her take the flight seriously. Would she be able to leave the screen for a while? And her eyes must have closed again, without her knowing, because next time she looked there were more hours gone. She had tried forcing herself not to check, but failed. She felt sunrise happening outside, felt them flying into it.

The last hours had minor diversions built into them. The first two of these hours had stirrings in them – more than the sound of the solitary sock walkers. The second two had tentative peering out the bottom of the blinds. Then breakfast? Dinner? The last two hours had moving, washing, awakening. And sun. Not the same sun as in Ireland.

Joy was ridiculously grateful to be getting off in Bangkok. She did not think she could have gone another inch, mile, hour, minute. But others were going to do that, were coming off to have one hour's break. They looked different from her, not yet released. Some of them were still staggering from the effects of their tablets. One man looked high on sleepless turmoil, his face pale, eyes sunken and bewildered. She felt guilty to be walking in a straight line, outside into the fresh air. The travel agent had even organised a bus to pick her up – her and six others, or so he said. Now she would find out. The man at the desk directed her to the correct bay. But when the door opened and she stepped outside, she changed her mind. She had inadvertently gulped a mouthful of boiling air. She stepped back in, giving herself a moment to assimilate to the density of the heat before trying again. No, it was boiling air. It hissed, as a distant whistling kettle might. She went back in again and found her way to the bay, via the inside route. They would wait fifteen minutes. Only fifteen minutes. All that time in the sky, all those miles, and only fifteen minutes separated the timetable of the Thai bus driver and the Dublin travel agent.

The smokers now sauntered slowly to the ashtray. It would be unwise to rush, to unnecessarily expend energy. They did not speak much, still dazed from the flight and involved in the privacy of their smoking. Some of them had another cigarette. The bus driver revved the bus. There was an amount of switching and moving and clapping. The heat began to exasperate some of the passengers, but they tried to remain polite. And then they were on their way, speeding towards hotels. Joy was expelled into a hallway, whispering with palm plants. A marble sleeping Buddha, with lipstick on, reclined at the foot of the stairs, inviting the weary to climb up.

Joy telephoned Oscar from her room. There didn't seem to be very much to say, just a check on the sound of their voices, consolation enough. She found the outdoor swimming pool at the top floor. She was too tired, but felt obliged to use it. How could she look the travel agent in the eye if she bumped into him accidentally in a month's time, and bump into him she would, particularly if she did not use the pool. As she kicked her legs out she thought how well he knew. Knots ran up and down her veins like mercury, cramps undid themselves, curls straightened. She kicked some more. The sun and the heat were white. She felt as if she should be able to look at them. She turned on her back, kicked gently, and fell asleep. Her body doubled up, and she gulped mouthfuls of water as she sank. Kicking her way back to the surface, she emptied her mouth of chlorine, and thought of the travel agent.

It was time for sleep. She lay on the bed in the darkened room and it stole into every sinew of her, humming luxuriously up her body until it had reached her head, her eyes, her mouth. She tasted it before she moved into another consciousness.

A few hours later, Joy ventured outside the hotel, strolled down two-foot-wide footpaths. Every few doors had a thin table for two outside, set for eating. Men on bicycles, their compact stalls hung with dried, flattened tiny fowl, pigeons maybe, pegged to the thin rack that was neatly attached to the front of their bicycles, rang their bells, whistled, and smiled. She smiled back. They smiled again. Everyone smiled. She managed to walk and take in the sights, even though sleep kept stealing behind her eyes. Eventually she had to give up, but was glad for even this glimpse of a street she had never known, and would never see again.

In the morning she swam, kicking and breathing like a normal person. She had *foo yung* and other assorted dishes for breakfast. She had another walk down the street, and then waited outside in the warming air where the bus would pick her up. The porter was reverently placing offerings in the hotel Buddha's glass jars. The bus pulled in, and pulled out headed for the airport. She could still see the porter cleaning the rims of the jars.

This time Joy booked on to the plane as if it was a bus. A mere hop. She thought she would count the number of people on the plane, see if there were as many as on those ships, it would give her something to do for ten minutes, maybe fifteen. She was an educated screen watcher by now, could congratulate herself on how good the tailwinds were. She was glad to see Singapore, although people had advised her that she'd be sorry to have taken the two stops. But she had needed two descents from the sky to help her with distance. Singapore puzzled her. Her hotel had no sleeping nor receiving Buddhas. From the twentieth-floor window, it looked like New York without the menace.

'Hard to beat a good totalitarian state,' Oscar said, when she telephoned him.

'But it's not totalitarian,' she said.

'Not now,' Oscar said.

And Joy didn't know what to say to that.

She was warm, clean, aired, smiled at, but confused. She had a pool here too, but sat mostly in the foyer watching a glass internal lift go up and down, stopping at all floors. She watched people getting in and out and marvelled to herself about the festooned lights at the top and the bottom. When it was at the far floors and she craned her neck to look, it could have been the dissect of a Swiss roll cake. A man came and joined her. He wanted to talk, just a little, she let him, just a little. She was not ready yet to be drawn from her lift watching. She excused herself, swam, slept and got herself ready for the last leg of the journey. She felt prepared now.

Joy stood to attention for as long as possible during the circling and the banking into Sydney, which was clearly even more beautiful than all the calendars put together. She was met at the airport by Simon, who did not want to talk about her amazement at what she'd just seen from the air. He got her and her bags to his car. She bumped into trolleys and people. They were delighted that she'd come, he said, 'You don't come to see us often enough,' he said, as if Joy might indeed be his relative and had just proven herself remiss again in familial geographic duty. He had a plan worked out for her, but in the meantime he would bring her to the lodgings he had found for her, a friend's empty house. She would be able to sleep her journey off in peace and he would collect her in the morning.

CHAPTER 34

It seemed a peculiar thing to Simon, to have to explain his interest in these girls. He had found out about his own possible link a number of years ago, and although it was hard to verify, he was fairly sure. It was only an outsider who would have expected an explanation. Here, in Australia, many people were quietly picking up bits and pieces of history, always with wonderment. But delight often became frustrated because the gems were always attached to somewhere else. You couldn't polish a thing off and know it. Its beginning was always from far away. As well as that, accidental history was so unsettling. What if the grandfather of the man who had organised the theatre tour of 1906 had not been caught? Caught at what? Doesn't matter. Caught. What if the other grandfathers had all made it home safely to the cottage second and third from the end of the lane? What if the women had bucked at the boat and refused to come? What if it had been the French who had started the first penal colony in south-west Australia, as they had indeed intended? You wouldn't be here at all. Or you'd be quarter Corsican. But then you wouldn't be you.

And what of the people who were here forever, whose history this really was, who would always know more of here than you, who could never be caught up with? How could your few hundred years matter? Would you not have to add it on? Would they let you? And what did that make you? Could this stream of yours, this history you were trying to tie up, die out completely, become eventually an interesting exotica in the whole?

At what point does the wonderment vanish? The faint-hearted changed the conversation, but did not question why others still dug. They, too, had been there. They had simply seen something in the gap of their history that made them turn away, for the sake of week-to-week, year-to-year, survival.

Simon collected Joy the next morning. He was cheerful and delighted to have her here, though she was by now furious with jetlag and wondering if she had made a mistake by doing the two stopovers. Or would it have been worse if she hadn't? She was consumed by the length of time she had been in the air, and now understood the logic of ships. Simon brought her to the Records Office on Globe Street – he thought she would enjoy it, and she hoped only that she wouldn't fall asleep. A young man hurried from behind his desk and beamed with enthusiasm. He loved it when people came to him. He could spread out his knowledge of his subject, throw it out to them like a Turkish salesman with the best carpet in the bazaar, or a fiddler with the best tune. He loved to tell them that when he was sorting the papers, trying to separate these particular girls from all the others, he had discovered that his great-great-grandmother was one of them. He was amazed. His hair was so red, his freckles so prominent, dotted in such a precise line across his face, it was almost laughable. Surely not that amazed?

'Well, I knew I had Irish in me.'

'Never,' Joy smiled.

'But not one of those girls. Although if you take the number of them and the scarcity of single white men here at the time, and the number of children they had with the number of husbands they had, they're at the top of a lot of us.'

'The number of husbands?' Joy said, making a question out of it.

'They weren't afraid to marry again.'

He thought they married much older men to perhaps replace their fathers – only a theory, mind you – and had children with them. And when they died, married again and had more children. And maybe even a third time. He led her to the papers.

'Half of them married older Protestant Englishmen. I suppose they were mostly available. Or maybe it's because they had no one to tell them not to. I don't know.'

'Half of them?' Joy said.

'Oh no, I mean a lot. I wouldn't have the exact numbers. It's hard to be sure with all the name changes.'

He handed her the boxes, pulled a chair out for her and walked to the door where he stood as if to attention to what he had found and what Joy might find in the papers.

It was these papers that fed articles, books and essays – upright detached essays, examining everything from court appearances to the prevalence of spontaneous symphysio-tomies at birth, the babies having grown stronger than the weak pelvises of the girl starved at a crucial bone-making time of her life. There were good stories too – stories of success, outward success at least. Children becoming educated, maybe to be what their mothers had wanted to be but couldn't. The young man came back.

'Of course, we'll never know what they actually felt, what was in their hearts.' And he thumped his heart dramatically, as if there was no one else in the room with him. 'No, we can't measure that.'

Simon and Joy returned to the heat outside and went to

visit Hyde Park Barracks. Joy got the occasional glimpse of what she thought might have been extraordinary sights – surely that couldn't have been the top of the bridge she had just seen. Standing on the quay, walking towards the Opera House on the right, the Harbour Bridge on the left, she found it almost impossible to believe she was there. At that moment the vista flaring around her rattled every one of her senses. What genius had made an already beautiful place even more so? How could anyone distract themselves long enough to add an adornment to this harbour? Mentioning it seemed pointless. Simon hurried her along as if knowing that the surfeit of beauty might distract her. He wanted her to see the plan for the memorial and to show her what it might be possible for her to do. They detoured through the Botanic Gardens.

'Jesus, what are they?' Joy shouted. She pointed in alarm at black shapes hanging dead from the trees.

'Oh, them,' Simon said, 'they're just bats. They're asleep.'

'Right,' Joy said.

By the time they arrived at the Barracks, she was already starting to burn.

They walked in through the door and what she felt most was relief at being able to escape the draining heat. She knew, surely, that this could not be the right feeling to be having. Simon tried to hurry her along to the room – 'their room' – but she said no, that she wished to read this, pointing to a display board in the permanent exhibition. Standing in the one spot would give her a moment to regain balance. And this is what she read. Once she had started she couldn't stop.

Seven-thousand-and-twenty lashes equalled about one-hundred-and-eighty floggings.

Before 1830, mostly Barracks men were flogged on site.

After 1830, the Barracks became the site for floggings of other government convicts. The new regulation lash designed by Superintendent Slade flogged about a thousand men here in 1833. Life became even harsher in the 1840s – tougher men and harder masters.

I was strapped spread-eagled on the triangle, my mates standing in front of me.

If a man shouted out through pain he was looked upon as a sandstone or crawler. While the flogger was fixing me up he said to me quietly, 'Is there any hangings to it?'

Meaning had I anything to give him to lay the lash lightly.

'Yes,' I answered.

'All right,' he said and then buckled to his work.

The falls of the cat were enough to take my breath away and to draw my blood freely. In the cell I got one of my mates to wash my back drying it with a rough towel, removing clotted blood and applying cloths soaked in water.

A band of from ten to twenty were daily at one period marched into this yard to be flogged.

Joy moved slowly a few inches from the board, shocked by the words and pictures. The cruelty was made worse by the banality of the language. It would have been better to walk past.

Upstairs, the girls' room seemed peaceful in contrast to the savagery of the descriptions on the stand. The white hammocks, in place now instead of beds, a foot or so apart, conjured up the gentle swinging of resting bodies. She had to remind herself of the fear and apprehension that would have been felt. Perhaps that was why the stand was placed where it was – so that the visitor would come to this room and regard it as a comparative sanctuary, not see young frightened girls hiding their sanitary rags under the floorboards, walking downstairs to stand like exhibits at a fair while prospective employers looked them over. Then walking back up again if they had been hired to collect their meagre belongings, and if not to fall on the suspended bed and wonder whether they would have been luckier today with that man who nearly chose them, or was there a kinder life to be given to them tomorrow? When Joy could bear the room no longer, she left.

This time she rushed past the flogging board and out into the scorching heat. Simon came after her.

'And now let me show you the proposed memorial drawings,' he said, either oblivious to her distress or determined to ignore it. The writing proclaimed that many of these women, here named, were refugees from The Great Irish Famine. No they weren't, Joy thought. That suggests that they were taking refuge, shelter. They were virtual prisoners, girl slaves, she thought.

'Peculiar word that, "great", for a famine,' she said, through jaws that were tightening.

The proposed memorial was tasteful. A part of the handsome stone wall was to be cut out and moved back, as if it was a stage curtain. In the drawing it seemed to stand respectfully to allow the insertion of a glass-like material. Names were to be etched into this glass – heartbreaking in their familiarity only because of where they were written and why. Joy would not have noticed them in her own graveyard. On the other side of the glass, a different set of names was to be carved out. Each set of names would run out to its outer line and then fade.

'Obviously, some of them would have changed their names into English for the boat.'

'Nothing like a name change to make you feel good,' Simon joked.

Joy began to recite names from the souvenir booklet and to look for them on the glass.

'What are you doing?' Simon asked, alarmed.

'I'm learning one name from each county off by heart.'

Slattery, Margaret, Dungarvan, County Waterford.
Moloney, Anne, Golden, County Tipperary
Dempsey, Celia, Kingstown, County Dublin
McDonnell, Rose, Killaid, County Armagh
Larkin, Sarah, Dora, County Offaly
McArdle, Issabella, Camlough, County Down
Callaghan, Biddy, Glaslough, County Monaghan
Tighe, Rose, Oldcastle, County Meath
Geoghegan, Mary, Athlone, County Westmeath
Keilly, Honora, Kanturk, County Cork
Bassett, Charlotte, Killmilling, County Wicklow
Murray, Bridget, Ardagh, County Longford
Burt, Sarah, Glen Nevis, County Antrim
Keefe, Alice, Ballilone, County Laois
Sharkey, Eliza, Omagh, County Tyrone
Hurley, Margaret, Gort, County Galway
Blundell, Maria, Naas, County Kildare
Briers, Ann, Isle and Burt, County Derry
McGrath, Bridget, Tullow, County Carlow
Roughan, Mary Ann, Scarrif, County Clare
Thornton, Mary, Ardee, County Louth
Patterson, Frances, Killishandra, County Cavan
Rafferty, Joy, Castlerea, County Roscommon
McGillicuddy, Ellen, Dingle, County Kerry
Brophy, Anastasia M., Johnstown, County Kilkenny

Shannon, Ellen, Ballingarry, County Limerick
Burke, Catherine, Ballinsloe, County Sligo
Haggerty, Mary, Ballina, County Mayo
Hogan, Rose, Mogul, County Leitrim
Carbary, Jane, Ballyshannon, County Donegal
McElroy, Mary Ann, Lisnaskea, County Fermanagh
Connolly, Elizabeth, Greig, County Wexford

The short end of a table, bereft of food settings, symbolising the hunger in Ireland, would protrude on to the street. The long end, complete with plate and spoon, would stretch inside the wall.

'Well, yes,' Joy said, and turned to walk towards Circular Quay. She had remembered the direction, which pleased her.

'What do you think?' Simon asked, keeping up with her. He knew she would be sorry in a few minutes for undertaking this speed.

'It depends on what memorials are for. Are they to let us know? To make us accept? Or are they to make us weep?'

'All three, I suppose.'

'I'm not sure.'

'That's a peculiar uncertainty for someone in your job.'

That could have meant anything.

'Doesn't anyone here ever get angry?' she said, more angrily than she had intended.

Sydney didn't look so gorgeous now. But Simon steered her to the Opera House, whose unanswerable beauty could stop an army in its tracks and keep poets busy forever. In the toilets she found a cold tap at ground level, under which she soaked her swollen, sore feet. The sharp pain caused by the water hitting the nerves in her toes brought tears to her eyes.

And then they made their way to the ferry – they would

go home via the water. They bought the tickets by means of a simple transaction. For some reason Joy had expected it to be complicated. She examined the ticket, Single/Return tickets valid day of issue only. State Transit. Sydney Ferries. Ordinary enough for such an extraordinary journey. She wondered if she would be able to keep it. They walked down the wooden creaking jetty to a green and yellow boat, stepped onto it, over the plank, and found a seat outside – one that had miraculously a slight breeze blowing around it. A large liner was being nudged out to sea, and there were crowds staring from the dockside, waving it off. Who wouldn't? It would have seemed curmudgeonly not to raise a hand.

'Just for you,' Simon said.

Joy smiled at him.

'Yes,' she said.

But then as she talked about the ship, he seemed to tire of this wonder. He was still discommoded by her reaction at the Barracks.

Their own small boat then reversed from its spot and ploughed its way past the Opera House and under the bridge. Further out she could see other ships crawling their way into their massive journeys, swallowing up the middle distance.

Looking up at the underbelly of the bridge, the air of unreality came back to her, but she lifted her face to the breeze and let it ripple over her. She would close her eyes for a moment.

'Did you see the lilly pilly on the monument drawings?' Simon asked.

On the morning of the Gundagai journey, Joy came to Simon's house where he was packing the car. She tried to help but didn't know what was needed. His wife, Irene, English born, was coming with them. They had accoutrements for travel and knew where they were. Joy moved around the kitchen and hallway, out of their way, wishing she had stayed longer in bed, wishing they had told her about the production required. This was nothing like she had ever seen. But, eventually, they were ready and she sank into the back seat of their large Holden, suddenly missing her bicycle, home, and Oscar. She would have to concentrate on the scenery.

'So are you related, do you think?' Irene asked.

In truth Joy hadn't thought about it much, and either Simon had decided to leave pursuing the possibility or he was waiting for her to take the initiative – surely she would know more about how to go about it than he would. She felt cornered.

'I must get some details, Simon, and see if I can come up with anything,' she said.

'That would be good,' he said, looking at her in the rear-vision mirror. 'But no rush.'

The negotiation out of the city took about an hour. They crossed the Bridge, and Joy peered down through any gap she could find to the water below. She would never want to take a place, or a wonder, like this for granted. They then edged their way through suburbs of red-tiled houses, punctuated by patches of unexpected, nondescript high-rise offices. Then back to red roofs, mixing now with green, both corrugated and tiled. The outer suburbs boasted long, wide gardens. There seemed to be no people around, but then maybe she was looking in the wrong places. She opened the back window to see if she could catch sounds. There was an air of melancholy, the only noise that of the car tyres. And then, suddenly, they were out of the suburbs and in an entirely new country. The atmosphere in the car changed, almost as it does on planes when the seatbelt sign is switched off. That's that done then.

At Goulburn, Simon angle parked the car in line with all

the others and they made their way to get coffee in the hotel. They settled themselves and ordered. Joy got up and looked at the photographs of the city at various stages of its building. Hard labour. You could hear the sound of convicts building the roads. They wouldn't have reached this far when the girls were passing through. There were photographs too of days when the city was showing off to itself, hat days. And who among them penned such vicious remarks about girls? She did not know, nor could she imagine. She went to the toilet. While fixing her hair and checking that she still looked like herself despite all the travel, the woman at the sink beside her asked, 'Are you here on holidays?'

'Yes, we're on the way to Gundagai,' she said.

'I see. Great place for the Irish.' She whispered the last word. 'Lots of them settled there.'

'Really,' Joy said, not knowing what was expected of her. 'And Yass too,' she added.

'Don't know if there were many of them there, but you could be right,' the woman said.

After the coffee they set forth again.

The girls would have pulled out of this town too – although this road would not have been here for them. They would have travelled down there below the road, had their accident there, camped there, stopped for repairs there, laughed there, wept there. They rounded a bend and saw a blue river – she could imagine the girls washing themselves there, blowing dust from their dresses and flouncing up their hats on their way into town.

'I know what you mean,' Simon said, though Joy had said nothing.

Irene said nothing too, just stared at the river.

The first stop was at the church where so many had

been married, baptised and observed their children's lives and finally, where they were buried. It looked like any Irish chapel – at least the simple ones – its only peculiarity being that the bottom quarters of the stained-glass windows opened out.

'It's unusual to see stained-glass windows that open out,' Joy said.

'Heat, I presume,' Simon said.

'I suppose, yes,' Joy said, wiping her neck again.

The second stop was at a church where a lesser number had recorded their lives.

The gravestones were sun-bleached, making them appear neglected. Modern, well-tended headstones spoke for the newly arrived. Joy rubbed some of the dust off a Shannon grave. She could see herself working out here – scrubbing, mending, chiselling. She could pick out the names, tumbling over each other, into a single testament. She wondered aloud if any of them had kept a diary. And then thought to herself that perhaps they had decided their lives would frighten people – particularly the children – and were best left put away. They might, too, have lost the language to tell the story. Somewhere on the sea, it might have left them. The graveyard was high up and looked out over silver sunburned hills that rolled into one another. An occasional tree stood out as if boasting. Some snow-white clouds were bundled up like mountains in the corner of the sky. They carried no promise of rain. They couldn't. There was no rain in them.

They stayed quiet as they left the town – it seemed the least they could do. They were on their way to the hotel in Gundagai where they would stay the night. The silence went with the thinning light, which was casually throwing shadows and colours this way and that.

With the evening coming in rapidly, Irene and Simon took pictures of Joy. She would keep them forever. Standing beside the Holden, looking completely startled. Standing at the statue of the Dog on the Tucker Box, its neck stretched in a howl to the heavens, looking puzzled. There was one of her looking happy enough on the street that pours directly into another series of streets that roll like flour mounds into the distance. There is a shadow in her hair in that one. And there is one of her under the verandah, looking startled again, but smiling, her foot out in front of her as if she doesn't know where to put it. In none of these does she look like she felt.

The three of them sat in the hotel and had dinner and deep-red wine. Sitting on the verandah afterwards they watched the night come in over the hills. You could wrap this darkness around you, ring the hills with it and call it home. You could make believe that beyond those valleys was the unknown. There must have always been the unknown. The crickets were still out in force, singing away, much louder than in the city. It was impossible to imagine you could not see what was making this swashbuckle of noise. The last of the birds were fussing about, getting their place for the night into shape, just as Joy, Simon and Irene had done before dinner in their rooms. A brilliant moon began to make its way up the sky. They watched stars dropping at will, and out here, under this endless sky, they thought too much of this cascade to say anything at all. They turned their backs on it and went inside to the warmth of more wine and people living a Friday night. When Joy had taken two sips, the need for sleep consumed her again, and she had to stumble upstairs where she fell onto the bed, feeling strangely fulfilled.

At breakfast, Joy counted the postcards she had bought the day before and took them outside. With her head down, she forgot where she was, even though she was in the open air, at a wooden dried-up table, sitting outside under a tree in the warmth – unlikely to be home. Then she lifted her eyes and saw the blue sky. Again. Today it had not even one godforsaken cloud. She could hear the crackle of the gum trees, shedding their covers. Or so she thought. No doubt it was something else. But she didn't ask, too often she had been ridiculously wrong in this foreign landscape. Irene joined her, looked down the street and said something about yellow wattle. She could make sporadic remarks like that on the beauty of things around her, casual, observed. But it sounded as if she didn't feel anything, as if she had just passed her eyes over whatever it was, but had not stopped them moving on to something else. Irene was adrift between two hemispheres, and although she was mostly happy, it was easy to see that she was occasionally overcome with longing, the sound of it could sometimes be heard in her voice. And then Simon put the paraphernalia back into the car. Joy helped this time. They retraced their journey and were contemplative as they travelled the road.

All that was left now was for Joy to come up with possible ways in which she could help. Would she offer to be a part of the stonework? – that was what she did really. But then again should she offer to do some of the lettering on the surface, after all that's also what she did? She was in two minds about the whole thing, confused about her place here, when this letter, if you could call it that, was found in the belongings of one recently deceased David Taaffe, Member of State Parliament. It looked as if the letter had been in his family for a very long time. It began 'Dear ...' and a name had been added: Honora Raftery. Joy was glad she was there for the brouhaha. It certainly took the attention away from her.

The historians got into the swing of it. What did the letter really mean, they questioned. Of course the facts of it were easy to find out, and find out now they would. But what was the tenor of this letter? That's a hard thing for historians to decide. And can we agree on tenor so many years later? Does language not change? Was there a danger that we would make a mistake in our ascribing of certain emotions to this woman? And of course it wasn't technically a letter, because it was addressed to no one, and could this mean therefore that she had deliberately left it to one and all? It's a pity David was dead, perhaps he would have known more. Clearly he knew enough to hold on to it. You could see, too, a row brewing as to who could understand best, who could interpret the emotions and who owned them.

'What do they mean who owned them?' Joy asked Simon.

'No, not them, I think they mean who owns the letter and the things with it.'

'Ah.'

'I think,' Simon said.

On the night before Joy left, she listened to the crickets for as long as she could – she wanted to store the sound of them. When she fell asleep she had a restless night, her dreams being impatient for the morning and the marathon journey home ahead of her. Irene picked her up, she had insisted.

'It's good you're going back to Oscar,' she said. 'There's no point in being lonely if you don't have to be.'

Joy persuaded her not to come into the airport building. She wanted some time between the leaving of her and the leaving of the place.

When the plane banked over the harbour, she felt that the city was on her tongue, going into her throat, as she swallowed her farewell.

CHAPTER 35

Joy's homecoming was a delight. Her return stopover in Singapore had been interesting – it was a marker against which she could check all the things she now knew that she hadn't known weeks ago. She was surprised that her impatience to get home disappeared. The flight from Singapore to London dragged interminably, but she tried to practice stoicism. In London she was crazy with sleep, her eyelids unbearably weighty. Having checked in at the Aer Lingus desk, she curled up on a chair and fell into a half consciousness, thinking, so these are the people who fall dead asleep at airports, people who have traversed the globe. But you wouldn't know that to look at them, unless you noticed the depth of their disappearance into the chair. She could see webs of colour behind her lids, floating gossamer soothing her taut eyes. She let herself sink further into the chair. One of the other passengers woke her when it was time to board, and she staggered slightly as she walked towards the plane.

The plane moved in over Ireland – a small island at the best and the worst of times.

When Joy saw Oscar she was suddenly shy and didn't know why. These unexpected things happen when you decide to live your life with a stranger: moments of disbelief – surely this cannot be? Moments of puzzlement – what do I do now? And moments of extreme bashfulness. Presumably this strangeness was also because Joy felt that she was a different person now than when she had left a mere few weeks ago. She was going to have to live with those girls, they were inside her now.

They conversed their way across the city, Oscar giving her news of friends and thoughts he'd had while she was away, her giving him bits of pictures out of chronology. The chat would have to spread out over weeks. Even the dry talk, of which there wasn't much, was charged with interest as they contemplated each other. And then they reached home.

Two days later Joy went back to work.

'Well, what did they do?'

'They lived, for one thing, and they had children, a lot of children.'

'And is the fellow related to you?'

'Well, we never really established whether he is or not. It didn't seem to matter that much.'

'What! After all that?'

And soon the butcher and the baker did not want to hear another word about Australia, which was a pity because Joy hadn't finished with it yet, hadn't taken out all the surprises. The florist, who stayed interested the longest, wanted to know if she thought a memorial here would be a good idea, but she said that she wasn't sure, she thought the story was there, not here. All that was left of them here was their names. Many of them surely had sisters left behind whose hearts broke afresh every morning. Opened every single morning with the first light, and broke all over again, even though they might have mended a little during sleep. But in time, those sisters too would have realised that they needed the mornings to live. They would, however, have named all their first-born daughters for them.

'And also, I don't know what memorials are for now. Why pick one thing and not another?' Joy said.

'That's an odd thought for someone in your job.'

But maybe it was because of her job that she thought names were all that mattered. But not the name itself, what was done with it, how the person had carried it.

In time Joy talked of these things less. She wanted to be where she was, the modern world, and she wanted to stay there.

Oscar and she were trying to ignore the incessant din that was making its way towards Christmas, and although they wanted to close their door, there were people to be seen. They went to visit her parents and had a sober, cared-for, evening. Joy's aunt was there, her face puckered, her mind off searching for something to complain about, some disaster to remember, some grievance not dusted for a while. Joy and her mother raised their eyebrows together behind her back and the history of that made them happy. Oscar was happy too, nothing other than his presence being expected from him. And then there was Oscar's parents' party. And then their own. None of us have children, Joy thought.

'So, Joy, are you going back to Australia to do the memorial thing?'

She told them that she didn't know, couldn't decide, but that she was glad she had gone. 'It's very far,' she told them.

On Tuesday they had their drinks. They were all there, even the quarry men. Joy warmed the place as best she could before they arrived and made hot punch – she did not believe in mulling wine, she would not do that to wine.

On Friday, Christmas Eve, Oscar checked the last post. There was a letter from Australia.

Joy began to make a map of bird migration. She found a picture of Coronelli's globe, and although New Zealand isn't there and Australia is marked *inconnue*, and Ireland is not the shape of Ireland, it's fine to mark the movement of birds. They can fly over and under Saturn and rest on flying horses. The swifts, being perfectly designed for life on the wing, can sleep as they fly. Marine invertebrates are carried by ocean currents, crustaceans migrate to reproduce in seawater, insects and frogs move too. But it is the flight of birds that interests her most. It is their fine art that moves her. They go from where they breed to where they winter. They may travel over the open seas or close to the coasts – even the most private of them become gregarious on these journeys and flock together, often making a comfortable V shape to help them in their travels. They have learned where the sun and the stars are. They move when their pituitary glands feel the darkening evenings. They go to where the food is, a lot like us. Some of them have altruistic tendencies and some don't – also like us. And there are regional variations in some birdsong. They get their accents and put them in their mouths, so no matter where they are we should know from where they came.

Acknowledgements

This novel, which started with a personal 'hungry grass' moment in Gundagai in 1973, is based on the true story of the Irish Famine Orphan Girls, who were shipped to Australia between 1848 and 1850. Although the facts of their shipping are accurate the characters are fictional. A number of works were essential to the research:

Barefoot and Pregnant? Irish Famine Orphans in Australia, Trevor McClaughlin, The Genealogical Society of Victoria, Melbourne, 1991, second edition, 2001.

A Decent Set of Girls, Richard Reid and Cheryl Mongan, Yass Heritage Project, 1996.

The diary of Charles Strutt, La Trobe Library, Melbourne.

The Famine Girls, a radio documentary by Siobhan McHugh, RTE and ABC, 2001.

I would like to thank my friends who have had to put up with the vagaries associated with a work like this. Particular thanks to Pat Murphy, Helen Carey of Mockingbird Arts, Gina Moxley, Patsy Murphy, Sean O'Reilly, Anne Haverty, Michael Cronin and Barra O Seaghdha. Thanks also to Rebecca Draisey-Collishaw and Deirdre O'Neill, the staff at *The Jeanie Johnston* ship on the Liffey and Mary Clemmey of Mary Clemmey Literary Agency, London. Most thanks have to go to Fintan Vallely, Warren, Trevor and all their care. Thanks are also due to Louth County Council, Monaghan County Council, Somhairle Mac Conghail and the Arts Council of Ireland.

In Australia my appreciation goes to The Writers' House in Varuna, all at the Hyde Park Barracks Museum for their help, Cheryl and Edgar Mongan for times wandering in Yass, Gundagai and thereabouts, Jeff Kildea for, among many things, bringing me to hear the lecture by Tony Earls on Thomas Moore at The Aisling Society, and Tom Power for inviting me to give the 2010 Memorial Address at Hyde Park Barracks. Thanks to Meg and Terry, Liz and Lorraine, Rebecca and Trevor, Siobhan, and my nephew Andrew Roe. I am grateful to Perry McIntyre for encouragement.

The late, beloved Diana and Sol Encel have always been a constant for me in Sydney.

In Melbourne my thanks go to Frances Devlin-Glass, Mike Richards, Jenny Little, Greg Rochlin, but in particular to Marianne Wallace-Crabbe.

It has been a pleasure to work with Julia Beaven, Laura Andary and all at Wakefield Press.

Plein Airs and Graces
The life and times of George Collingridge
Adrian Mitchell

Plein Airs and Graces examines the extraordinary life of George Collingridge de Tourcey, a landscape painter of the late nineteenth century, just ahead of the Australian impressionists. When he emigrated from France to Australia he grew passionate about the possibilities of his new country, and worked tirelessly to contribute to it – not least for his *Discovery of Australia* (1895), in which on the evidence of ancient maps he argued controversially for Portuguese and Hispanic pre-discovery of Australia.

Includes 28 full-colour illustrations.

Shortlisted for the 2013 Prime Minister's Literary Awards
in the Non-fiction category

'As well as a well written biography and art journal, this is an excellent history book ...' – HEATHER STONE, Bonzer

'His book is beautifully illustrated with full colour plates of the artist's magnificent paintings of early Sydney. This is a volume to treasure.'
– MARY ANN ELLIOTT, The Chronicle, Toowoomba

'Very readable ... belongs in any art lover's collection ... Fascinating stuff ... a wonderful job of bringing this most interesting man to life.' – LISA HILL, ANZLitLovers

'... a must-read biography for all fans of Australian art ... Plein Airs and Graces is a straightforward and historical biography which is also a colourful companion for every Australian art enthusiast.'
– STEPHEN DAVENPORT, Indaily

ISBN 978 1 74305 095 8

For more information visit www.wakefieldpress.com.au

Servants Depots

Marie Steiner

In 1855 the colony of South Australia experienced 'excessive female immigration', with large numbers of single females arriving from the British Isles to work as servants. When an economic downturn led to a shortage of domestic help positions, the Colonial Government established servants depots around the country to house them.

Servants Depots is a fascinating account of a little-known period in South Australian history. The book details the day-to-day running of these depots, and reveals much about the attitudes toward women in colonial South Australia.

ISBN 978 1 86254 805 3

For more information visit www.wakefieldpress.com.au

Time's Long Ruin

A novel

Stephen Orr

Nine-year-old Henry Page is a club-footed, deep-thinking loner, spending his summer holidays reading, roaming the melting streets of his suburb, playing with his best friend Janice and her younger brother and sister. Then one day Janice asks Henry to spend the day at the beach with them. He declines, a decision that will stay with him forever.

Time's Long Ruin is based loosely on the disappearance of the Beaumont children from Glenelg beach on Australia Day, 1966. It is a novel about friendship, love and loss; a story about those left behind, and how they carry on: the searching, the disappointments, the plans and dreams that are only ever put on hold.

WINNER, Unpublished manuscript award,
Adelaide Festival awards for literature

South Australian winner, 2012 National Year of Reading awards

'*In* Time's Long Ruin *Orr has conjured up the suburban claustrophobia of the ifties and added streaks of these darker pigments ... Adelaide's very distinctive version of Winton's* Cloudstreet, Malouf's Edmondstone Street *and White's* Sarsaparilla; *but the quality and vividness of Orr's evocation ... ensures he can hold his head high in such illustrious company ... a compelling page-turner.*'

– RICHARD WALSH

'*... eloquent, unusual, bold but responsible retelling of a veritable urban nightmare that still haunts the Australian imagination.*'

– PETER PIERCE, *Sydney Morning Herald*

ISBN 978 1 86254 830 5

For more information visit www.wakefieldpress.com.au

Dissonance

A novel

Stephen Orr

Dissonance begins with piano practice. Fifteen-year-old Erwin Hergert is forced to tackle scales and studies for six hours a day by his mother, Madge, who is determined to produce Australia's first great pianist. To help Erwin focus, Madge has exiled her husband, Johann, to the back shed. Jo is diagnosed with cancer and Madge allows him back inside – only for long enough to die.

Madge takes Erwin to Hamburg to continue his studies. Erwin prospers in Germany with his new teacher until he meets a neighbour, sixteen-year-old Luise, and finds there's more to life than music. Meanwhile, Germany is moving towards war.

Dissonance is a re-imagining of the 'Frankfurt years' of Rose and Percy Grainger. This is a novel about love in one of its most extreme and destructive forms, and how people attempt to survive the threat of possession.

> '*Compelling … an engrossing novel. Orr is a vivid storyteller.*'
> – STELLA CLARKE, Weekend Australian

> '*Dissonance is a rich, layered and absorbing novel.*'
> – SUZANNE EGGINS, Canberra Times

> '*A compelling fiction of a young man propelled towards musical renown by his ambitious, manipulative, ever-attentive mother.*'
> – ANTHONY LYNCH, Australian Book Review

ISBN 978 1 86254 945 6

For more information visit www.wakefieldpress.com.au